T0354682

# UNCHARTED TERRITORY

## Gerry McDowell

# UNCHARTED TERRITORY

Copyright © 2022 Gerry McDowell.

All rights reserved. No part of this book may be used or reproduced by any means, graphic, electronic, or mechanical, including photocopying, recording, taping or by any information storage retrieval system without the written permission of the author except in the case of brief quotations embodied in critical articles and reviews.

iUniverse books may be ordered through booksellers or by contacting:

iUniverse
1663 Liberty Drive
Bloomington, IN 47403
www.iuniverse.com
844-349-9409

Because of the dynamic nature of the Internet, any web addresses or links contained in this book may have changed since publication and may no longer be valid. The views expressed in this work are solely those of the author and do not necessarily reflect the views of the publisher, and the publisher hereby disclaims any responsibility for them.

Any people depicted in stock imagery provided by Getty Images are models, and such images are being used for illustrative purposes only.
Certain stock imagery © Getty Images.

ISBN: 978-1-6632-3310-3 (sc)
ISBN: 978-1-6632-3311-0 (e)

Print information available on the last page.

iUniverse rev. date: 12/03/2021

# CHAPTER 1

## 1

John Cramer was in hog heaven. He had just made the deal of a lifetime. As he cruised down I-40, headed back home to Benson, North Carolina, he was thinking of all the things he was going to do with all the money he had under the back seat of his new truck. If he could just make it back home, without being stopped by the "Man," he would be all right. Under the back seat of his new truck, in a little compartment, he had two and a half million dollars. The money was all his. He had acted on his own behalf and had made the people believe that he was there representing their usual buyers. It was a piece of cake. No one had even suspected that he was using his own money. Now he could disappear for a couple of years, and give his superiors time to forget about him.

John was a courier for the largest drug-running operation on the East Coast. He had been doing this, off and on, for the last seven years. His bosses were a group of the most well-known doctors and lawyers in the Johnston and Harnett county area. They were politically strong and had the right people in law-enforcement on their payroll. He felt that if he could keep them in the dark until he made it home, and got the rest of his money, he would be able to get away scot-free.

Over the years, he had been saving money just waiting for an opportunity like this to show itself. He never skimmed money off the top of any of his runs, and he was well paid for the cross-country trips he made four times a year. One hundred thousand dollars per trip. All he had to do was drive to Nevada, go to a certain parking deck, leave his car, and pick up another one, and drive back home. He never saw or touched the drugs. He knew the routine. Put one million dollars in the trunk of one car, and swap it for a car that has been specially fitted to carry the drugs. Once you got home, you'd take the car to a certain car dealership for a tune-up, and walk away with a suitcase full of money. It was all very simple.

This time, however, John had taken a slight detour. He'd told some people he knew in Des Moines, Iowa that he could deliver a car full of uncut cocaine, directly to their door, for two and a half million dollars. They jumped on the chance. Now the deal was done, and he had enough money to be his own boss for the rest of his life. He had bought a Ford Expedition for the trip home from the drop, hoping no one would recognize him once he got back to Benson. The vision of his bright future had taken his mind off of his driving. He would live to regret that.

# 2

Josephine Fishbourne was tired. She had lived a long life. She was 81 years old, 5'4" tall, and around 110 pounds. Despite her age, she had long, wavy black hair with a two-inch gray streak running from her left temple down to the tips. Her beautiful hair always drew comments, until her admirers saw her advanced age. Her eyes were another stopper. They were a piercing coal-black, with a white ring around each pupil. Her eyes would make your skin crawl. For most of her life, she had been known as a healer. But most folks just called her a witch.

She was born somewhere in the backwaters of Louisiana. Even as a little girl her powers were phenomenal. Her mother and grandmother were known throughout southern Louisiana as the people to see if you had "problems". They were said to be able to lift spells placed on you by someone wishing you harm, and they were able as well to put spells on people that had wronged you. They were said to be able to cure anything, from cold sores to cancer. Many people were said to be alive today, thanks to Jo's family.

Hoping to escape the stigma of witch-woman, Jo had left home at the age of fifteen to start a new life. What she found was a lot of prejudice and hatred at every turn. Her strange eyes didn't help matters much. She struggled for eight years trying to live a normal life. It was an uphill battle every day. On many occasions, she thought about going back home. But when she'd think about being stuck in the same life as her mother and grandmother, she would struggle harder. She didn't like the idea of being treated like a leper until she was needed to help get someone out of a bind. She would rather struggle every day than live a life like that. She fell in love at the age of twenty-three and learned what real abuse was. Her new husband, Bob, believed in total control. Control of his own life and control of everyone he came in contact with. He treated her more like a possession than a wife. She'd made up her mind not to let him know about her extraordinary powers, but as the marriage progressed, she found that the only way to stop him from beating on her was to put him to sleep almost as soon as supper was over. He thought he was sleeping so much because he had to work so hard on his job. He mentioned his odd sleeping habits to one of his co-workers one day during lunch and got a shock. His co-worker just laughed and said, "She's probably got a spell on you, you know how those witches are. You just say the wrong thing and they put a spell on you, you know, to break you of the habit."

After punching the guy in the mouth, Bob asked him what he meant, and demanded an apology. His co-worker knew all about Jo and her family. He told Bob that when he was a little boy, he had broken his leg, his grandfather had taken him to see Jo's mother. According to him, the woman had told him to close his eyes, when he woke up three days later; he was at home in his bed. When he woke up he realized that he was starving and when he started to get up he found that his leg was completely healed. There were no bruises or scars; it was as if his leg had never been broken. That was how he got to know Jo and her kinfolk.

Bob was furious. He left work early, went home, and immediately knocked her unconscious. When she woke up, she was tied to her bed; he had stuffed a washcloth in her mouth so she couldn't speak. He started asking her questions, knowing fool well that she couldn't talk with the washcloth stuffed in her mouth. He wanted to know why she didn't tell him what she was. He wanted to know why she had let him struggle all the months they had been married. He said that they could be rich by now if she had just used her power to help him become successful. Then he began to torture her, verbally and physically. He tortured her, off and on, for six days. He tried to make her promise to make his life a success. But knowing the type of man he was, she knew he could be mean, but she had no idea that he was capable of the things he had done to her over the last six days. She didn't want to be under his influence anymore. She decided that she would rather be dead than to be controlled by someone like him. She berated herself for staying with him the few months they had been married after she found out he was so abusive. And now she realized that her decision to stay was going to cost her, her life.

And when she thought that she was about to die, she withdrew inwardly. And there she saw the true scope of her power. That was when she met her personal demon. She was waiting for her to realize that she, the demon, was there for Jo and Jo alone. Though she couldn't tell Jo what to do, she let her know that she could stop the pain, if Jo would just give her permission. Jo didn't hesitate, she told the demon to stop the pain.

Bob was about to deliver another blow with the leather strap he was using when someone grabbed his wrist. He looked around and saw that a woman had hold of him. That *really* pissed him off.

"You'd better turn me loose woman, or you're next!" He yelled. He tried to snatch his arm out of her grasp, and threw a solid roundhouse, connecting with the woman's jaw. To his surprise, she just smiled, and with the one hand that she was holding his arm with, she lifted him off the floor, and just held him there. Bob began to curse and threaten the woman, he had no idea that his life was hanging in the balance. When the woman didn't respond to his threats, Bob began kicking her anywhere he could, on her legs, in her crotch, anywhere he could get in a good kick. But the kicking had no effect.

Then the woman held up her right hand, showed it to Bob, and smiled again. As Bob watched, the hand began to change. The fingers started growing. They grew longer, and the fingernails began to curve into a claw. Bob finally realized the situation he was in. He had no idea that his wife was strong enough to have control of something this powerful. Although he had never seen anything like this woman, he knew that she had to be a demon and that she was here because Jo wanted her here. He started screaming to Jo that he was sorry for hitting her. He promised that he would never hit her again if she would just forgive him. As he watched, the woman began to use the claw on him. First, she ripped his shirt into rags, and then she started ripping the flesh from his chest. She would dig just under his skin, and then peel the skin off. She was peeling him like a banana. Bob cried and screamed, trying to get Jo to make the woman stop. The last thing he saw was the claw coming toward his eyes. But that wasn't the last thing he felt. The demon made sure that he didn't pass out for a very long time. Bob was fully aware when the demon reached into his chest cavity and ripped out his heart.

When the demon first grabbed Bob, Jo was ecstatic, but as it started peeling him she got scared. And before it was half done with Bob, she was screaming for it to stop. But the demon turned a deaf ear. It looked like it was having a good time. Finally, the demon finished with Bob and threw him in the corner, and then it turned to Jo. To Jo's surprise, the woman gently removed her gag.

"Please don't hurt me!" Screamed Jo, as the washcloth was removed from her mouth.

"I have no wish to harm you," it said, as it untied her hands and feet. "I am Sephra; I have been with you from the day you were born. You left home before your mother could tell you about me. I exist to serve and protect you. Your every desire that is in my power I will give to you. What is your desire?"

"I didn't want him dead," Jo cried, looking in the corner where Bob looked like a heap of bloody rags. "Can you bring him back?"

"No, that is not within my power," Sephra said.

"How am I going to explain this?" She cried. "I didn't want you to kill him! I just wanted you to make him stop beating on me! Now what am I going to do? Because I know I couldn't explain this mess to the authorities, and I don't want to spend the rest of my life in prison! I've got to get out of here! I think maybe I should move! Yes! I'll move to another state!"

"Where-ever you go, I'll be there with you," said the demon.

"No, I will never call on you again!" Jo cried.

"Oh, but you will," said Sephra. Then she vanished.

Jo quietly left Louisiana that night. She moved to southern Florida and laid low for a few months. She never did hear anything about Bob being found. She just assumed that the demon took care of the body. But actually, nobody really liked Bob. And when he failed to show up for work, everybody, including his boss, said good riddance. What really happened is that the house was struck by lightning during a thunderstorm a couple of days after Jo skipped town. The house burned to the ground. Since no one had seen Jo or Bob for over a week, everyone thought they were out of town. The bones they found in the house were thought to be one of the homeless that roamed the area. There was no investigation.

After a few months, Jo decided to risk going back out into society. She found that she had to rely on her mysterious powers just to survive. She helped the truly needy for nothing. And by word of mouth, she stayed pretty busy. She became the one to have on your side, be you in politics or dealing in drugs. If you wanted to be successful in any field, you got Josephine Fishbourne on your side. She was a lot more popular than her family because she had ventured out into a world full of dirty politicians, and drug lords. Jo didn't try to judge the people that she represented; she just did the job she was hired to do. The rivals of the people she backed would either get too sick to keep up the fight or just die. It depended on the situation, but she was always successful. She made sure that the people with money paid through the nose. And by the age of thirty-five, she was wealthy enough to live any way she chose. She lived well up to a year ago.

That's when she was enlisted to help a struggling crew-leader in North Carolina that was trying to do things the right way. He treated his workers like human beings, and he needed help to get the other crew-leaders off his back. When the workers from other camps had taken all they could stand from their crew-leaders, they would come to him and beg for help to get back home. And being a man of good heart, he would always do what he could. That made all the other crew-leaders very angry. He started finding trucks with flat tires, and he had a few engines ruined because someone had put sugar in the gas tanks.

While telling a friend about his problems during a phone conversation, he learned about Jo. His friend lived in Miami and knew about Jo through an acquaintance. That was how Jo came to be in Benson, North Carolina. What she thought would be easy and quickly handled, turned out to be quite a job. One of the other crew-leaders had a very strong Voodoo man from the West Indies. He and Jo had been battling back and forth for almost a year. But tonight she had struck the fatal blow. She had stood and watched, through arcane means, her opponent die in intense pain. She had decided to take off the kid gloves and get this thing over with. It really didn't bother her when she heard the curse he put on her as he died. He screamed the curse at her through lips that were almost gone. His skin was decaying as if he was aging twenty years a second.

He screamed, "You will not see another sunrise! This I swear! You may have won this round, but I will see you in hell, soon!" Then he died. She was aware that there was such a thing as a death curse, but she figured that she had drained so much power out of the voodoo man that his words were powerless. So she dismissed them.

Jo decided to take a little walk, to try to wind down. There was a creek about a mile from the camp, down the interstate. And the sound of running water always seemed to have a calming effect on her. As she was walking along, she was thinking about how hard it was for her to dispose of the little man from the "Islands". She'd had to use methods that she didn't approve of. That was what bothered her about this job. She had been tempted to call on her personal demon several times. Like the time she woke up blind, or the time she couldn't walk for three days. But she was afraid of turning the demon loose again. So she finally decided to use some of the things her mother and grandmother would have used. And it had worked. She had seen the aging spell work only once when she was a little girl. She had forgotten how painful it was. In a way, she was going to miss the little creep.

She was almost to the bridge when she looked up and saw a truck bearing down on her. Although she was well off the road, walking on the paved shoulder, the truck was coming straight for her. She didn't have a chance to jump out of the way. She now realized that she should have taken the curse seriously. The little creep had more power than she'd given him credit. He was reaching out from the grave to get his revenge.

# 3

Cruising along at 72 miles per hour, John was startled awake from his vision; by a collision with what he first thought was a deer. As he looked in the rear-view mirror, he thought he could see the deer, lying at the edge of the road. He was going to pull over to the shoulder, and back up, to remove the deer from the road, when he realized that he was already driving on the shoulder. Now he realized that the noise he thought was just road noise was in fact the noise of the warning strips along the concrete shoulder. He stopped, and backed up until he could see the deer, (traffic was light since it was four in the morning), and got out to move the deer off the road.

IT WASN'T A DEER!!!

John rushed to the prone figure lying in the roadway where she had been thrown after the impact, and hastily pulled the body off the road, and rolled it over. The victim was an incredibly old woman. Her eyes were rolled up into her head. When John shook her, her eyes rolled down and locked onto his. The moment she looked at him, he felt icy fingers run up and down his spine.

"You drove off the road to hit me," she moaned, with a Creole accent.

"No, I didn't see you!" John cried.

"For this, your life is mine," she said weakly.

"Please, don't try to talk, I'm going to get you to a hospital," sobbed John. "I really didn't see you; I've been driving for three days straight. I'm sorry I hit you."

"I put a curse on you now as I lay here dying, I release my personal demon to deal with you as she sees fit," she gasped, spraying blood from between her clenched teeth.

"Lady, you are in a lot of pain, and you're starting to talk real crazy, I'm going to take you to the hospital," John said.

The old lady coughed, shuddered, and died. Then from out of nowhere, there was a woman standing over John. She had a radiance about her that lit up the area surrounding John and the old woman. He had never seen so much beauty bestowed on one woman before in his life. She looked down at the woman in John's arms. Tears began to form at the corner of her eyes. She looked up from the old woman and stared at John for a moment.

"You now belong to me, mortal," she snarled. Then she slapped John with the back of her left hand, knocking him about ten feet off the shoulder of the road into a ditch. He must have momentarily lost consciousness because when he looked up, the woman was standing with the old woman in her arms. He heard her tell the old woman that it was time to go home. Then she and the old woman vanished.

The first thing that crossed John's mind was that all the evidence of the accident had just vanished. He looked both ways, up and down the interstate. He didn't see the two women anywhere. He wondered where they had gone. He just couldn't believe that they had just disappeared. The next thing that hit him was the pain. It felt like his jaw had been broken into little pieces. Holding his jaw, he climbed out of the ditch and went to check out how badly his new truck had been damaged. The old woman had been so fragile and small, that she hadn't even put a dent in the grille of the truck. It was as if the accident hadn't even happened.

He climbed into his truck and turned on the interior light. He looked in the rear-view mirror to check his face to see how much damage was done to his jaw. Though it was black and blue, he was sure that it wasn't broken. He regretted hitting the old woman, and he had a lot of remorse over her death. He wished there was something he could do to change the events of the early morning accident. He had never taken a life before. He never wanted to again.

He started the truck and eased out into the travel lane of the interstate. He wondered what the strange woman meant when she said that he belonged to her now. She was extremely beautiful, but she hit like Mike Tyson. He had never been hit that hard before in his life. The supernatural was something that he never paid much attention to. He thought it was all just a lot of hoopla. But after tonight he was going to have to re-think his opinion of the occult. In the back of his mind, he wished that he had been drinking. That way he could say that it was all a hallucination. But his aching jaw was living testament that all of it had happened. So he decided that he would deal with it when and if she showed up again.

When he reached home, he didn't stop at the front of his house as he normally would, but he drove on around to the back door. He had made up his mind that he would be seen by as few people as possible. His neighbors, most of them old, would still be in bed at this ungodly hour. He could only hope that none of them were early risers.

Keeping as quiet as he could, he went in the back door and headed for his stash. He had no intention of staying at home any longer than it took to gather a few clothes, and get his money. The accident with the old woman had not made him forget that he was going to be hunted down like a fox when his associates found out what he had done. He didn't turn on any lights because he didn't know how much time he had before he was found out. He slid the sofa in the living room away from the wall and lifted up the heating vent cover that was located there. He pulled out a white trash-bag that he had stuffed down in the duct. This bag of money was just one of many that he had stashed all over the house. As he rose up from behind the sofa, he saw a sheriff's patrol car coasting down the street. As the car got abreast of his house a bright spotlight pierced the darkness. John ducked down to keep from being seen. The light swept the front of his house as the car cruised on by. He wasn't really surprised that his associates had found out so soon. He wondered which one of the top men had sicced their dogs on him. In twenty minutes he had gathered all his loot and got a couple of changes of clothes. He eased out the back door and got in his truck. He was about to start the truck when something jumped on the hood. He looked up, wide-eyed, and saw to his relief one of his neighbor's cats. It was the large tomcat from next door. The cat sat down on the hood and started washing with its tongue. John didn't want to blow his horn to scare the cat off the hood, so he climbed out of the truck and tried to pick the cat up to put him on the ground. As he reached for him, the cat took a swipe at him and dived off the truck.

"And stay off," whispered John.

John got back in the truck, started it up, and then froze. He had the feeling that someone was watching him. He felt the hairs on the back of his neck began to stand on end. He slowly scanned the back of his house, and then he studied the surrounding houses and saw no one. As he looked out the passenger's side window, the feeling of being watched intensified. As he turned to put the truck in gear, he jumped, because someone was standing right beside the truck looking in the driver's side window. Before he could get a good look at whoever it was the person vanished. John broke out in a cold sweat; he tightened his grip on the steering wheel.

"Shit! Shit! Shit!" He said. Although he didn't get a good look at the person, he knew who or what it was standing there. It had to have been the woman from the interstate. He knew that he had to get rid of that problem before he could begin his new life. He remembered hearing people talk about a root-worker that lived in Dunn. He made up his mind to contact him as soon as he could. But first, he had to try to survive the rest of the night. He knew he had to get away from his house and everyone that knew him.

He had at one time worked for one of the local farmers who had a house and small pond hidden way back in some woods. He decided that he would hide there until he felt it was safe to venture out. He drove on around his house with his lights off. He made sure not to touch the brakes. He eased on out to the street and made a left turn. He didn't stop at the stop sign at the end of the block; he just rolled right on out into the intersection and made a left. When he had almost made it to the end of the next block, he saw the headlights of a car come out at the end of his block. He was at one of the local parking lots that the people that worked in Raleigh parked to carpool. He whipped into the parking lot, and shifted the truck into neutral and coasted to a stop. He was more than halfway through the parking lot, so he felt that maybe he was safe. He watched as the police car went by. It slowed at the intersection but the light was green, so the officer drove on through. John waited about five minutes before he could get up the nerve to try it again.

This time as he pulled out of the parking lot he turned his lights on. He had decided to drive on out of town just like everyone else. He drove straight down Church Street, to the Burger King, made a right, went one block, took a left on 50, crossed I-95, and took a right on 242. After driving for about eight miles he started to relax. He knew if he ever made it to the woods he would be all right.

As he neared the woods, he looked for the small path that led back to the little house. He slowed down so he wouldn't miss it. Finally, he saw the path and made the turn. The path had grown up a little since he'd last seen it. But that fits into his plans perfectly. He drove down the path slowly hoping the weeds would stand back up behind him. To his satisfaction, the weeds stood back up as if no one had been down the path in weeks.

The old house was in terrible condition. It had partially collapsed. The roof had fallen in on the front porch. John took the time to spread his cash throughout the Expedition. He put bags of cash in every cubbyhole he could find. Once he was satisfied that no one could find all of his money in one search, grabbing his penlight he went to check out the house. Although the house was falling down in some areas, some rooms were still intact. The room that was in the best condition had an old mattress positioned in the middle of the floor. The rest of the floor was littered with beer cans, fast food wrappers, used condoms, and old clothing. John figured that with a little work he could make the place almost livable.

He found an old broom standing in the corner of one of the other rooms, and started sweeping up the trash. As he was cleaning out the food wrappers, he realized that he hadn't brought any food or water with him. He decided to get the room as clean as he could before he started worrying about anything else. Then he remembered that the farmer that owned this land always kept cases of canned food in the room between two of his bulk barns. The food was there for the workers that couldn't afford to eat out of a restaurant every day. John felt that if he left some money and a note, maybe the guy wouldn't call the sheriff's department before he could disappear.

It took quite a while to get the place fairly decent. It was well after nine in the morning when he finished. Just as he was finishing his cleanup, he heard the roar of a motor. He ducked down at the window to keep from being seen. Much to his relief, it was one of the farmhands that he knew quite well. The driver's name was, Slim, the name fit him well. He was over six feet tall and was as thin as a reed. He was so thin that it looked like he might have to hold onto something when he sneezed, just to keep from blowing himself away. As Slim drove up to the front of the house, John stepped out of the back-door and walked around the side of the house to talk to him. When Slim saw who it was he broke out in a big grin.

"Well I'll be," said Slim. "John-boy how you doin'?"

"Just find Slim," said John. "How have you been doing?"

"Still kickin', still kickin'."

"Look Slim, I've got a problem and I need your help," said John.

"Whut-chu need son?" Asked Slim.

"I'm in a shitload of trouble, and I need a place to hide out for a few days. And I need you to keep the fact that I'm here real quiet," said John. "Can you do that for me, buddy?"

Slim said, "Show nuff, you know you can trust me man."

"Listen, I need something to eat and drink, just enough to last me a couple of days, okay?" Said John.

"You got it, just give me a couple of hours to get things together, and I'll be back," said Slim.

"All right, buddy, I'll be waiting," said John.

After Slim turned the truck around and started driving off, he waved and said he'd be back in a little while. John returned around the back of the house to finish getting the place fit for sleeping. Wondering all the while, why Slim had come way back in here, on the day he began using it for a hideaway. When he finished cleaning, he went out and sat on the bank of the little pond that was behind the house. As he sat there he thought about the rapid changes that his life was going through. One week ago he was an average guy trying to make it through the workweek. And now he had enough money to retire on. If he had not had the accident this morning, everything would be just peachy. He felt that he could handle his associates, but he was really worried about that beautiful woman, or thing that had threatened him this morning.

Even as he was thinking about the woman, the small hairs on the back of his neck started to rise. He jumped up and spun around because he felt that she was right behind him. To his relief, she wasn't standing right behind him, but she was standing inside the house, staring out of one of the broken windows. As they stood there looking at each other, John heard Slim making his way back with the food and water. When John broke eye contact with the woman as Slim came around the last curve in the path, he was pushed, or thrown about twenty feet out into the pond. As he was airborne, he searched all along the bank to see who had pushed him. He saw no one anywhere near where he was standing, but the woman was still standing in the window, smiling.

As he hit the water, he thought about Slim. He was afraid that the woman might attack him and maybe even kill him. He immediately began screaming for Slim to go back. He started swimming toward the bank as fast as he could. When he reached the bank, he looked up at the window to see if the woman was still there. She was just turning from the window heading toward the front of the house. He heard the door of the truck slam shut, and he took off at a dead run around the house, trying to beat the woman to the front of the house.

As he rounded the side of the house, he saw Slim walking around the truck, headed for the side of the house with that big, stupid grin on his face as usual. When John hollered for him to get outta here, the grin dropped off his face, and he dropped down as if someone was about to start shooting at him. As he dropped down, the bag he was carrying burst, and cans of potted meat, pork-n-beans, vienna sausage, and cokes flew everywhere.

"What, what, what?" Shouted Slim.

"Where did she go?" Ask John.

"She who?" Asked Slim.

"You didn't see anyone come out of the house when you pulled up?"

"Hell no!" Shouted Slim. "You ain't loosin' it, is you son?" Asked Slim.

"No, it's just that I thought I saw someone in the house," said John as calmly as he could manage.

"Who the hell is after you son?" Asked Slim. "You hain't fucked up the deal you got goin' with them damn doctors have you?"

"What are you talking about man?" John asked. Slim just laughed and shook his head, and said, "Nuttin' son." Slim began gathering up the can goods as John walked over to the house to look around. When John got back inside the house, he didn't see anyone. He checked every room including the room that the roof had fallen into. The house was empty. As he turned around to go back outside where Slim was, he jumped back and hollered, because Slim was standing right behind him.

"Don't do that," breathed John clutching his chest.

"What did you do, go for a swim?" Slim asked.

"I slipped and fell in," said John.

"Well I've got to go back to work, I went to the store and bought this stuff for you, you owe me seventeen fifty," he said.

"Okay," said John reaching for his wallet. "I don't have any change, but I want you to take this and keep the change." John thought Slim's eyes were going to pop out of his head when he saw the one-hundred-dollar bill he was offering him.

"No, I think I'll wait until I see you again, because the way you're actin', you're gonna need all the money you can get your hands on for a while," Slim said.

John said, "No, I insist, you've put your job on the line doing this for me this morning, and this is a way I can show you that I appreciate what you've done."

"Well, if you insist," Slim said slowly taking the money. "You ain't done somethin' stupid have you son?"

"Of course not Slim, you know me."

Slim put the money in his pocket as he turned to leave. As he walked out the back door he turned and said, "If you need anythin', anythin' at tall, you know how to reach me. Here at work, or at home. I don't care how late it is, if you need me, you just give me a call. Okay?"

"Sure Slim, and you know the same goes for me," said John, feeling a pinch in his chest. Good friends are hard to find, and it really touched John to know that even though he hadn't seen Slim for a long time, the friendship had survived. He didn't have the heart to tell him that he had forgotten his number.

After Slim left, he decided to get out of the wet clothes he was wearing. He hung the wet clothing on nails and doors throughout the house.

Having retrieved another set of clothes from the truck, he got dressed quickly and went back out on the back-porch to think awhile, while eating a can of Pork-n-Beans and sipping on a coke. He found that he had problems concentrating, and realized that he hadn't had any sleep for a few days. He decided to go inside and try to take a nap. He went inside and gave the mattress another good shake. After the dust settled, he stretched out and went out like a light.

# 4

The demon, Sephra, had never had it so good. She became aware of her existence the moment Jo drew her first breath at birth. And from that day forward she had existed somewhere in the back of Jo's mind. She had been fully aware of the things going on in Jo's life from the start. Unlike Jo, she didn't have to grow up and learn from daily experiences. She was the same now as she was then. Though she was the instrument Jo used to ply her trade; Jo had only called on her once to materialize. That was when she had been called upon to deal with Jo's husband. That was the only taste she'd had of the mortal world. And she liked it. She had been fascinated with the wide-open spaces that mortals took for granted.

Looking through Jo's eyes, and seeing all the things she had to endure just to survive, had taught her to despise men in all shapes and sizes. And now through a strange turn of events, she had the freedom to act and do anything she desired. Normally when the master of a demon died, the demon would instantly cease to exist. But Jo had given Sephra the chance to deal with the man that had run her down, "any way she saw fit". That gave Sephra a chance to draw his suffering out as long as she wished. She had decided to make it last as long as she could, because the moment the man died, Sephra would cease to exist too. So she decided to torture and punish this man for all eternity if it was anyway possible.

Night had fallen, and Sephra stood over the man as he slept the sleep of the dead. The mortal had not had any sleep for quite a while, and he was making up for it. Although the sleeping arrangements were crude, the human was sleeping like a baby. This angered Sephra because the man was sleeping like nothing had happened. It was almost as if the fact that he had killed someone the night before had slipped his mind. Sephra decided it was time to remind him of the facts. She smiled as the mattress began to rise off the floor.

# 5

John woke with a start. He was dreaming about the old woman he had killed the night before. He was drenched in sweat, and scared. He didn't know why he felt so frightened right now, but he knew if he heard any sudden noise he would probably piss his pants. So he just lay there trying to calm himself, when he noticed that night had fallen. He stared at the patterns that the moonlight made on the ceiling, and wondered how late it was.

As he went to turn over to get up, the ceiling fell in on him. He threw up his arms and legs to keep the ceiling from breaking him up so bad, and it landed on his outstretched arms and knees, and as he was wondering why it wasn't as heavy as it should have been, the mattress hit him in the back and sprang back, flipped over, and landed on the ceiling in front of him.

"Wait a minute," he thought. "How did the mattress get out from under me?" Then he noticed that he couldn't feel the floor behind his back. He slowly turned his head to look back behind him when he got a big shock. The floor was behind him about eight feet down. He looked around frantically trying to find something to hang onto. He felt as if he was going to fall. Then he remembered the moonlight shining on the ceiling. There was no way that the moonlight could shine on the ceiling unless it was a reflection off the pond. But would it have been that bright? John didn't think so. Crawling very slowly to keep from falling up/down, John made it to the window. Before he even reached the window, he could see the moon right where it should be. So he realized that the ceiling hadn't fallen in on him, he had fallen to the floor. He realized that he had to have been sleeping on the ceiling. He didn't know how that could be.

Trembling he made his way outside, by climbing through the window, and sat down on the ground. He grabbed two hands full of grass to keep himself from falling into the sky. He was very disoriented, he still wasn't sure which way was up or down. He sat there for about an hour trying to get his equilibrium back. When he finally got control over his senses, he slowly got up and walked over to the window of the room he'd been in. The mattress was where it had fallen after it had bounced off his back. He could see the marks where he had crawled to the window. He was beginning to worry about his sanity again when he heard a chuckle behind him. He whirled around and screamed. The woman from the interstate was standing about two feet behind him.

Acting instinctively, he lunged for the woman; he wanted to strangle her for frightening the shit out of him. But when he reached her, she stuck like a snake. She grabbed him around the neck, picked him up, and slammed him up against the house.

"You have just begun paying the debt that you owe, human," said the woman. When she said, "human", she said it like it tasted rotten in her mouth. She smiled and vanished. John fell down off the wall where she was holding him and fainted.

# 6

Cam Suffour placed the bowl of water on the small table in front of him. For six hours he had been trying to contact his go-between to the spirit world. He had never had this much trouble making contact before, and he felt that he knew what the problem was. Some idiot somewhere had left an entity unbound, and that entity was disturbing the ether. When he would close his eyes to concentrate, to make contact with his friendly spirit, he could see that the void between this world and the spirit world was in turmoil. The void usually was a place where you could get totally relaxed, and prepare for your encounter with the spirit world. But today it was just the opposite. The void was like the ocean in the grips of a hurricane.

The waves of energy were clashing together unlike anything he had ever encountered before. He didn't know if someone had called on an entity that was too powerful for them to control, or if it was something occurring that had never happened before. In his gut, he felt that somebody was in a world of trouble.

He bent down over the bowl of water and tried to make contact again. And just like the last time, his probe into the ether was ripped away. He had been at this kind of work for nearly forty years. And this was the first time he had found his abilities useless. He got up, and emptied his bowl, wiped it out, and put it away. He knew how the ether reacted when someone was working with a spirit, but it was never this hard to break through. Someone had given an entity permission to roam freely. And that entity was using a lot of power. It took a lot of power, just to maintain a link with a spirit, even if you just wanted information. But to let one run free and use power anyway it wanted to, spelled disaster. He could only hope that whoever was doing this would finish quickly, so he could get back to the business at hand. He had clients waiting for results, and he could do nothing until the ether cleared.

He had been trying to break through since five o'clock this evening and hadn't had any supper. So he decided to cook something to eat before he went to bed. He could only hope that things would be back to normal in the morning. If things weren't right by then, he would take stronger measures. He felt that he could have forced his way tonight, but that might take longer than he was willing to go at this late hour. So he cooked and ate supper and decided to prepare himself for a hard day tomorrow. He showered and went to bed. Sleep was slow coming, but when he went to sleep, he had a nightmare, about a very beautiful woman tearing him limb from limb.

Cam wasn't *actually* a root-worker, but with the 900 numbers, and the Psychic Friends Network, people with true ability tried to stay out of the public eye. He kept the usual props around, herbs, spices, and the little jars with weird looking things in them, just for his customers to see. Nowadays no one took psychics seriously. You say, "Psychic," and everyone will smile, and shake their heads, but you say, "root-worker," and everyone will look around as if they are expecting something to happen. People will say that they don't believe in any of that stuff, but they say it softly.

Cam was one of three true psychics in about a three hundred-mile radius. Oh, there were plenty of people claiming to be workers of the metaphysical, but in truth, they are just charlatans. Of the three, Cam was the most powerful. He had the uncanny ability to actually know who you are, and what you need, just seconds after you walk into his home. Of course, you never knew it. That was why people that would come in talking about a friend in need would leave feeling that Cam knew they were talking about themselves, and would have the answer they were seeking.

So Cam slept, feeling that he was in for the fight of his life. And as he slept, John was just waking up from his swoon.

# 7

As John regained consciousness, he continued to lie there on the ground, looking up at the moon, and the stars. For a moment, he had forgotten about the woman, his associates, and the old lady that he had killed. He remained there enjoying the view. Then it hit him like a ton of bricks. He jumped up in a crouch, looking around like a wild man, expecting to be attacked again by the demon.

Much to his relief, there was no one there. John knew now that the demon could attack him at will, any time she chose. And there was absolutely nothing he could do about it.

Walking slowly around the house, he made his way to the truck. He had decided to spend the rest of the night locked in the truck. He didn't think locked doors would stop her, but he felt that was the only way he was going to get any more sleep tonight. He put the keys in the ignition, just in case he had to make a quick getaway, and stretched out as best he could in the front seat of the Expedition. He felt like he was aching all over. His jaw was sore, from the slap she had given him out on the interstate, his neck was sore, from almost being hanged, and held up beside the house, and his chest was sore, from being knocked into the pond. His knees were sore from falling eight feet to the floor. He wondered where she would hurt him next. But he was more than willing to wait a lifetime to find out. He made up his mind that the next time she showed up, he was going to try to talk to her. He didn't know what he could offer her, but he was going to try. Because he felt that the end result would be his death, and he definitely didn't want that to happen.

After trying to go to sleep for an hour, he finally dozed off. He immediately began to dream. In the dream, he was sitting in a boat, out on the pond behind the house. The woman was in the boat with him. She held in her hand his heart.

She said, "This heart belongs to me now, and I can do anything I wish with it." She began squeezing the heart. As she squeezed the heart in the dream, John, in his sleep, clutched his chest and moaned, in the agony of a heart attack. In the dream, the woman stopped squeezing the heart, and in the truck, John stopped struggling and continued to sleep. In the dream, John asked the woman what he could do to make up for the death of the old woman.

"All you can do now is suffer, and I am going to see to it that your suffering is long," said the woman.

"Please, there must be something I can do, short of my death, that can prove to you that I wish to atone," pleaded John. "Just tell me, and I'll go to the ends of the earth to repay the debt for killing her. It was an accident."

"It was no accident," spat Sephra. "You were the instrument used to fulfill a curse put on my master by an evil Voodoo man, as my master got the best of him. It was no accident."

John was hoping that he didn't anger her anymore, because when she got angry, she would start to squeeze his heart again, and he didn't know how many times he could stand that before he really had a heart attack. John decided to try another tactic.

"Then let me be your servant," John begged. "I'll serve you faithfully."

As John was saying that, the woman jumped up in the boat, and threw his heart at him.

"I would never have a man do anything for me but die," she yelled! "And if you wish to live a little longer, you will never say a thing like that to me again!" And she vanished in a splash of color. As she vanished, so did the boat. As John began to sink into the water, he woke up with a yell and quickly sat up bumping his head on the ceiling of the truck. Now he knew the next place on him that was going to be sore, his head.

John sat there in the truck and tried to figure out what he was going to do to save his behind. If the dream was any indication, it was going to be very hard to bargain with the woman. He just couldn't figure out how someone that beautiful could be so cold-hearted. He didn't know how long she would keep toying with him, because he felt that if she had wanted him dead, he would already *be* dead. John decided that he would change locations, and hope that he could have something worked out before she found him again. He started up the truck, and by moonlight, made his way back out to the highway. He planned to be at the rootworker's house, first thing in the morning.

# 8

Cooter Cobb had more money in his pocket than he'd ever had at one time in his life. When he received the call this morning from Dr. Siddig, he had no idea what was going on. According to the Doctor, old John-boy had fucked up big time. The Doctor hadn't told him what John had done, but he could tell that the Doctor was really pissed off. The Doctor was so angry that Cooter could hardly understand what he was saying. To make a long story short, Dr. Siddig gave Cooter fifty thousand dollars to find John and bring him back to him. He told Cooter that there would be another fifty thousand for him when the job was done. Cooter didn't know what John had done, but he was sure glad that he had done it. He could have a ball with one hundred thousand dollars in his pockets. He knew a little cutie that would love to help him spend it. He might even drive up to Atlantic City for a long weekend of gambling. As he pulled up to John's house, his mind was on all the fun he was going to be having in a few days.

Just as John had done, he drove on around to the back of the house. As he climbed out of his pickup, he scanned the area to make sure no one was watching him. He walked up to the back door and knocked. He didn't know if John was at home or not, but he doubted it. He waited a few seconds and knocked again. He finally tried the door. It was unlocked. Moving cautiously, he eased into the back room of John's house. As he looked through the house, he noticed that things didn't look quite right. Pieces of furniture had been moved haphazardly throughout the house. A heating vent here, a picture lying on the floor underneath a hole in the wall, floorboards ripped up, leaving holes in the floor in out of the way places.

He had a feeling that the way John left the house that he had no plans to return. He could see that it was going to be a while before he could go to Atlantic City. He sat down at the kitchen table to try to figure out where John might have gone. He reached over and got a beer out of the fridge.

Before he could pop the top, there came a knock at the back-door. He got up and answered the door just like he was a welcomed guest. One of John's neighbors was standing there looking suspicious.

"Howdy," said the old man, "is John in there?"

Thinking fast Cooter said, "No he's not, and I'm beginning to worry about him. I've been trying to get up with him all day. You haven't seen him have you?"

"Nope, not since yistiddy mornin' afore day," said the old man.

"About what time did you see him?" Asked Cooter.

"Oh, I reckon it was sommers around four-thirty or five o'clock," said the neighbor. "And he was actin' real 'spicious. It don't make no sense to me, for a man to act like that at his own house. And while he was in the house, a p'trol car came by and shined a light at the house. I even woke up the old lady to tell her about it. And that won't the only one to come by neither. I told the old lady that I hain't seen that many cops in one day on this street since we've been livin' here. He hain't done broke the law, has he?"

"No," said Cooter. "We just want to make sure that he's all right. If you see him, you tell him to call Cooter, okay?"

"I will if I see him," said the old man. Then he turned and walked away. As Cooter was about to turn to go back inside, he noticed the wide tire tracks in the backyard. He rushed outside to catch the old man and asked him what John was driving. The old man told him that he was driving one of them damn four-wheel-drive trucks that the kids like to drive nowadays. Now Cooter could see why nobody could find John, he had changed vehicles.

Cooter checked the house over again, without finding any clues. As he left the house, he turned and locked the door. What he thought was going to be an easy job, was turning out to be not so easy. He realized that he was actually going to have to work to find John. And he was determined to find him. He was not going to lose all that money, just because John thought he could be a smart-ass. John would find that Cooter Cobb could be smart too.

# CHAPTER 2

## 1

D r. Johnod Siddig slowly hung up the phone. He had just gotten off the phone with one of his associates, having a heated discussion about John Cramer. He couldn't understand how John could've done him this way.

When he approached John about being a courier for him, he felt that John could be trusted. John had taken care of all the yard work for him, and a few of his friends, for years before he talked to him about becoming their transport man. John had never shown that he was getting restless, or greedy. He always felt that John knew that if he needed some extra cash, or for that matter anything, that he could come to him. Now he was out there with a carload of drugs, (he had no idea that John had already sold the drugs). And if he got caught with it, he had no doubt that John would tell the police that he was only the wheelman, and send them straight to him. He wasn't worried about the local police, but if a state trooper stopped him, all would be lost. As he sat there worrying, the phone rang. He snatched it up quickly, hoping that it was John calling to say that he was sorry for what he had done, and was ready to bring the drugs back where they belonged, but it was only Cooter Cobb.

"Hello? Dr. Siddig?" Asked the voice on the other end.

"Yes, this is the Doctor. Who am I speaking with?"

"It's me, Cooter," said the caller.

"Mr. Cobb, I hope you are calling me with good news," said Siddig.

"Well, I know he ain't at home, cause I just left there," said Cooter. "I talked to one of his neighbors, and he said that John came home early day before yesterday around four-thirty or five o'clock in the morning. He said that he was driving what looked like a four-wheel-drive pickup. I believe that he may have changed vehicles unless it belonged to one of his friends."

"Mr. Cobb, go down to the police station and tell Chief Hamilton what you've just told me. Tell him, uh, ask him to run a check and see if John has registered a new truck with DMV. If he has, get all the information you can. And call me back later," said Siddig.

As he hung up the phone, he didn't know whether to be happy or angry. If John had another car, that meant that the car and the drugs were hidden somewhere. He knew that John couldn't sell the drugs to anyone around here without word getting back to him. He liked John quite a bit. He hoped that he wouldn't have to order his death. But if he kept this up, he may not have a choice.

# 2

As John slowly came awake, he was instantly aware of all the bruised parts of his body. At the moment, the most painful parts were his knees. It wasn't every day that you fell to your knees from the ceiling. Knees weren't made to handle an eight-foot fall to a hard wooden floor. He could only pray to God that the worse was over.

During the night he had driven from the farmer's property to the rootworker's house. He had taken the long way around, just in case someone spotted him. He had driven around to the back of the house as quietly as he could. Then he had gotten as comfortable as he could and dozed off to sleep. Now he glanced at his watch. It was just a little past six-thirty. He didn't want to wake up the strange man that lived here. He didn't want to put him in a bad mood this morning, because he really needed his help. If it turned out that he couldn't help him, he didn't know what he would do. He began rehearsing what he was going to tell him. He didn't want to make the man think that he was nuts. John wished that he at least knew the man's name.

While John was trying to come up with the right words to say, Cam had spotted the truck hidden in his back yard. He knew exactly what the owner of the truck wanted. He showered and shaved, and then prepared breakfast for two. After he got the meal cooked, he went out to the truck to offer the gentleman some breakfast.

When he got to the truck he saw that the man was staring straight out the front of the truck. From the look in his eyes, Cam could tell that he wasn't seeing what he was looking at. His eyes had a faraway look in them, a sure sign of someone in deep thought. Tapping lightly on the window brought an unexpected reaction from the man. He jerked his head around and looked at Cam as if he had suddenly grown horns. With a little yelp, John grabbed the steering wheel and steeled himself for the worse. Cam stepped back from the truck and held up both of his hands in a gesture of surrender. After a few seconds, John began to relax a little. At first, he thought it was the woman that had been beating on him. When he saw the old man standing there with his hands raised, he couldn't help but smile. The rush of relief that he felt was almost sexual.

Rolling down the window, he said, "I guess I'm a little jumpy. I've had a couple of bad days. I hope you don't mind that I slept in your back yard last night."

With a shake of his head, Cam said, "Of course not. I imagine I was your last resort. Most people don't come to me unless they've tried every other option first. Come on inside. I've fixed us a good meal, and we can get to know one another. By the way, what am I to call you?"

"John Cramer," John said, offering his hand.

Cam shook his hand and said, "I'm Cam Suffour, at your service." Together they made their way back to the house. Cam led John to the bathroom so he could wash up. When John returned, Cam had fixed two helpings of eggs, grits, sausage, bacon, and buttered toast. John's mouth began to water as he came out of the bathroom. Cam saw the way he was looking at the food, so he decided to let him eat his fill before he started asking questions. After two helpings, John eased back from the table looking ashamed for the way he had gulped down the meal. Cam led John to the den and offered him a comfortable chair. He waited until John began to relax, then he said, "So, tell me what your problem is."

For the next thirty minutes, John told his tale of woe. As John told his story, Cam began to understand why he'd been having so much trouble getting through to his friendly spirit. John had no idea how much trouble he was in. There was something very powerful out there, and John was the focal point. As John finished his story, Cam wondered if he should show John the door. He had no doubt that if he decided to help John; he would be laying his life on the line for someone that probably deserved everything he was getting. John was really surprised that he had told Cam so much about his personal life. He had never told anyone about him being a drug courier. But when he started talking, he just couldn't seem to stop. He wanted to. But for some reason, his mouth got into gear, and wouldn't stop talking. As he sat there wondering if he had said too much, Cam said, "I think I will try to help you. I can't give you any guarantees, mind you, but I know that if I don't help you, you'll be dead in a few days. I don't particularly like the idea that you are mixed up in the local drug trade, but I can't just sit back and let you be killed by a vengeful demon. I would not have gone looking for you, but since you came to me for help, I won't turn you away."

With a sigh of relief, John sat back in the plush recliner he was sitting in. He was beginning to feel that he had made the right decision coming to this man for help. For the first time in two days, he was able to relax just a little. Now he felt that he might have a fighting chance against that beautiful woman that was so intent on killing him.

# 3

Through mere chance, Cooter Cobb ran into Fanny Mae at the local Piggly Wiggly. Fanny Mae was the wife of Slim. She was one of those black women that are euphemistically called "redbone" because her skin-tone is so light you can't tell if she's white or black. It seemed that those two had been together forever. She was one of those people that once you get her talking, it takes a major effort to get away from her. On a whim, he asked her when was the last time she'd seen John?

"I hain't seen him in a long time," she said, "but Slim told me last night that he talked to him just yesterday. He told me that John seemed to be in some kind of trouble, but he wouldn't talk about it. Do you know if he's in any kind of trouble?"

"No," Cooter said, "I haven't seen him in a long time either." As he was finishing his sentence, Fanny Mae started talking about something else. Cooter knew that if he didn't get away now he would be stuck there all day. So he told her that he had to go. Fanny just kept talking, so Cooter just turned and walked away. That didn't even faze Fanny; she followed him all the way to his truck. She even added in the fact the John was staying in the old house in the woods. Cooter was so pleased with himself. He had found out what he wanted to know without even trying. He knew all about the little house by the pond hidden in the woods. He'd taken a few young ladies out that way many times. That would be his next stop. If John were still there, Cooter would take him to the Doctor and collect the rest of his money. Cooter knew that John wasn't smart enough to stay hidden for long. Any chance of getting away disappeared the moment Cooter Cobb was put on his trail.

As Cooter drove away from the store, Fanny Mae realized that she might have said too much. Slim told her not to tell anybody, and here she had gone and told everything. Slim was going to really be pissed with her. She decided not to tell him about this little conversation with Cooter Cobb. As she got in her car, she hoped that she wouldn't start running her mouth tonight at supper. She always knew her mouth would get somebody in trouble one of these days. She hoped that Cooter wasn't the one looking for John. She was torn between trying to warn John and just keeping her mouth shut for once. In the end, she decided to keep quiet. This was one time that she felt that she should just shut up already.

Cooter began to smile to himself when he finally reached the path that led to the house in the woods. The weeds that were growing up in the path had been mashed down, a sure sign that a vehicle had been through there recently. He turned down the path and slowly made his way to the house. As he made the last turn, he saw a young woman sitting on what was left of the front porch. He drove up to the house and got out.

"Well, hello darling," said Cooter.

The young lady just dipped her head at him. Cooter had never seen this gal before, but he made up his mind that this wouldn't be the last time he saw her.

"Where have you been hiding, young lady?" Asked Cooter. "Do you live around here?" The woman shook her head "no". Cooter was beginning to think that the girl must be dumb or something. He didn't say it out loud, because he didn't want to mess up his chance to get with her later. She had to be the most beautiful thing he had ever seen in his life. She had enough beauty in her that she could give away half of it and still be the prettiest thing around.

"Do you know a fellow named John, darling?" Asked Cooter.

"I sure do," she said.

"Can you tell me where I can find him?" He asked.

"Yes," she said.

After waiting a while, Cooter said, "Well? Are you going to tell me?"

"He's mine," she said.

"What?"

"He's mine. And I won't let you have him," she said.

Cooter said, "Darling, you can have him. All I want to do is talk to him."

"Liar!" She spat.

That startled Cooter. She actually looked like she was getting angry. He decided that the girl must be slightly on the stupid side. If he had to, he'd put her on his knee and give her a little spanking. He felt that he would enjoy that. He decided to try again. He said, "Look darling, you shouldn't go around calling people liars, it's not nice. Now, you tell me where he is before I put you over my knee. You don't want to make me angry."

The young lady got up and walked over to Cooter. With a smile that could curdle milk, she said, "Go ahead, get angry, and try to put me over your knee. I would really like for you to try that one."

Cooter thought the young lady was coming on to him, so he reached out to stroke her hair. Her reaction came out of nowhere. It was a simple punch. If a man had thrown it, Cooter would have managed to block it and throw a counter punch. But since he wasn't expecting it, it caught him square in the right eye. When he came to himself he was sprawled on the ground in front of his truck. He knew that she couldn't have hit him as hard as it felt, because she was just a girl. His eye felt like he had been hit with a bowling ball. It was already swelling shut. He looked up at the beautiful girl, and said, "What did you do that for?"

"If you ever touch me again, I will kill you," she said.

For a moment Cooter actually believed her. He got up slowly and held out his hands in surrender. "Now hold on, little lady," he said. "I was just going to touch your hair. You shouldn't hit grown men like that. What if I had hit you back? I could have hurt you. Now! Tell me where he is, damn it!"

"You can't possibly be this stupid," she said. "If you ever cross my path again, I won't hesitate to take you out of your misery." Then she turned and walked away. As she walked around the back of the truck, Cooter started running after her.

"You wait a minute, you stupid cunt, I ain't through with you yet!" He shouted. As he reached the rear of his truck, he slid to a stop. He stood there looking around. He was alone. It was almost like the girl hadn't been there at all. After walking around the truck a few times, Cooter stopped at the rear-view mirror to see how bad his eye looked. The eye was swollen completely shut. Cursing, he climbed into his truck. He decided that the next time he saw that bitch; he was going to teach her some manners.

# 4

John sat quietly watching the old man work his magic. Cam sat staring into his bowl of water. Every now and then, the water in the bowl would ripple as if someone had dropped a small pebble into the center. Suddenly John noticed that Cam had stopped breathing. He didn't know how long Cam had been holding his breath, but he caught himself holding his breath also. As he sat there looking at Cam as he worked, he wondered if his life would ever get back to normal again. If he could go back to just being a handyman, he would do it in a hot minute.

Although at the moment he was independently wealthy, he would trade it all if he could bring the old lady back to life. Things had been happening so fast, that everything hadn't had a chance to sink in. All he had gone through to acquire his wealth didn't bother him. But the accidental death of the old woman had not been on his agenda. He knew deep in his heart that he wasn't a murderer. He had never harmed anyone intentionally. He was always happy if he could just get along with the people that he met day to day. Now he was guilty of vehicular homicide.

He knew that he would have to pay for the death of the old woman. And he knew that the price would be high.

With a gasp, Cam looked up from the bowl. It took a few moments for his eyes to re-adjust to the dim light in the room. He looked over at John and shook his head.

"You, my friend, are in a world of trouble," he said. "Most of the time, people that have been wronged will call up a demon to do their dirty work. In situations like that, the demon doesn't care who it terrorizes. It would turn on the caller if it got the opportunity. That's why very few people bother with demons, it can turn out to be a two-edged sword. You see, it makes demons very angry to be ordered around by mere mortals, and if the caller is not strong enough or lets down his guard for just a moment, the demon will strike like lightning. Once you lose control, it is almost impossible to regain it. You would be surprised at how many people you hear about on the news that are found dead in their homes are victims of demons that they themselves called. They usually classify the death as spontaneous combustion or some silly thing like that. It's not something anyone should try without a lot of training. But you don't have that kind of demon on your tail."

"That's a relief," said John.

"Wait a minute," said Cam. "Let me tell you about the other kind of demon before you start counting your blessings."

"I don't feel like I have any blessings to count so far," said John. "That little lady has been giving me a pretty good whipping."

"John, to coin a phrase, you ain't seen nothing yet," said Cam. "So far you have been lucky, very lucky."

"What was the other type of demon you spoke of," asked John.

Cam got up and walked over to one of the windows. He slid back the drapes and stared out at his well-managed yard. He drew a deep breath and said, "Some people are born with extraordinary powers. Where it took me years of study and practice, some people have power at birth. Apparently, the old woman you ran down was one of those people. According to my go-between in the spirit world, your demon has been with this woman since birth. And if I understood my friendly spirit correctly, the demon should have vanished when the old woman died. But that didn't happen. Could you tell me what she said to you before she died?"

"She said something about turning me over to her personal demon," said John. "To do with me as she pleased. Apparently, she thought I ran over her on purpose. But that's just not so, I really didn't see her!"

"Calm down," said Cam softly, "you don't have to convince me. I believe you when you say it was an accident. What we must do is try to convince the demon that it was an accident. We may have a hard time convincing her. Because if she decides to kill you now, there's very little we can do about it. But I don't think she will want to do that too quickly, because the moment you die, she will instantly wink out of existence. That will happen because its host is dead. That may buy us enough time to figure you a way out of this mess."

John felt his spirits begin to rise. "Do you mean to say that if she kills me, she will die too?" He asked.

"According to my information, yes," answered Cam.

"Well I don't have anything to worry about then," exclaimed John.

"You have never been more wrong," cautioned Cam. "It all depends on how much she hates you for killing her host. If you are lucky, she may want to see more of this world before she kills you."

John thought for a few minutes, then he remembered what the demon said about men. He turned to Cam and said, "She told me that the only thing a man could do for her was to die. I don't think she cares much for men, not just me, but all men. You remember that she threw my heart at me when I offered to be her servant in that dream. I thought she was going to kill me right then. But she just disappeared again, I guess I was lucky."

"You're right," said Cam. "She could have killed you then and there. I think that means that she is aware of the circumstances. I think that she may let you live awhile. That is if you don't make her too angry the next time she shows up. And please don't let her know that you are aware of the situation. That information alone would probably make her kill you right away."

"I won't say a word," John promised.

# 5

Sephra leaned against John's truck. She thought it was quite funny that the stupid mortal thought he could lose her. She had made up her mind that she would toy with him a little longer. She found that she got a lot of joy out of seeing the fear in his eyes when she was tormenting him. She knew that she should go ahead and kill him and get it over with, but she was having too much fun. She walked around the truck, opened up the driver's side door, and climbed in. She decided to wait for him to come out of the house before she tortured him again.

"I think I'll go outside and have a cigarette," said John.

"You can smoke it in here if you like," said Cam.

"No, I think I need some fresh air," said John. "I won't be out there long. I just need some time to think. I always think better on my feet. You don't think she'll find me here, do you?"

"I imagine she has always known where you were," said Cam. "Let me make something clear to you. When the old lady turned you over to the demon, she marked you. You can run as far away from her as you like. But she can find you in an instant. So don't think that by being here you are safe. There is nowhere for you to hide."

John almost changed his mind about going outside. But he'd always been a stubborn man. He was not going to hide for the rest of his life. No matter how short that time might be.

As John strolled around the yard smoking his cigarette, he suddenly had the feeling that his money was in jeopardy. He walked up to the back of his Expedition and opened the rear hatch. As he leaned into the back of the truck, he noticed that someone was sitting in the front seat. He was about to start raising hell with the person when she turned and said, "Hi John, did you miss me?"

John jumped back from the Expedition and turned to run. As he completed his turn, he ran into the woman. It was like running into a brick wall. John bounced back and landed on his back in the rear of the Expedition. He had so much momentum that he ended up against the back seat. When his head stopped spinning, he locked his eyes on the woman. She was standing behind the truck smiling at him as usual. Neither one said anything. They just looked at one another.

Finally, John asked, "What now?"

Sephra said, "Now you die."

John quickly climbed over the rear seat, and then scrambled into the driver's seat. As he fumbled for his keys, the woman opened the passenger side door and climbed in. Before she could get settled, John was out of the truck and halfway to the back-door of the house. He was yelling for Cam at the top of his voice. Suddenly he was stopped dead in his tracks. He couldn't move. He tried to turn his head so that he could check to see if she was coming, but the only things he could move were his eyes and his lungs. He wondered why Cam hadn't appeared at the back door to see what he was screaming about. From the corner of his eye, he saw the woman walking slowly around him. When she got in front of him, she began talking to him.

"Did you think that you could hide from me? Don't you realize that you are mine now? If you were to drop dead right now, I would follow you to hell just to get my revenge. You owe me a life, and I am going to collect. Do you doubt me, John? Do you think that you are going to get away with murder? Do you? You little piece of shit!"

At first when she started talking she was almost whispering, but the more she talked, the louder she got. Before she finished, she was screaming. Her face was a portrait of rage. Just as she was about to attack, she stopped as if someone had slapped her.

"No!!" She screamed. She jerked around and looked at the house. "How?" She shouted. And then she looked back at John. "This is going to make your suffering far, far greater. You will know what real suffering is before I let you die. Count on it!"

Just as she vanished, Cam burst out of the back door. In his hand, he had a small pouch. He ran with the pouch held out in front of him. John could tell by the look on his face that he was furious. He ran up to John and handed him the pouch. He looked around the yard. Then he said, "Keep this with you always. Hang it around your neck if you like, but never be without it until we get this thing worked out. Come inside and tell me what transpired out here." As he turned to go back to the house, John grabbed his arm.

"Where were you man?" He shouted. "I was yelling for you to come and help me. She could have killed me. Why did you take so long to come out of the house?"

Cam put one hand on John's shoulder and said, "I didn't hear you John. She put up a wall of silence, and she almost put me to sleep. She was so subtle with the use of her power that I almost didn't notice it. If she hadn't put up the wall of silence, I may not have noticed that something was wrong. Listen, do you hear the birds, and the insects, the wind in the leaves? You see, the thing about country living is that there is always the sound of nature in the background. If you were to bring someone that lives in a city out here, they would say that it is too quiet out here. But if you live in the country, you know that there is always the background noise of mother earth, living, and breathing. But I promise you that she will never catch me off guard again. Let's go inside."

He turned and headed for the house. John followed him in silence. He had foolishly thought that Cam would be too powerful for the demon, but now he realized that Cam was just an old man, a powerful old man, but still an old man. At that moment John decided that he had better not put all of his eggs in one basket. He started trying to come up with plan B.

# 6

Sephra was angry with herself. She had almost let John's cowardice make her kill him on the spot. And too, she had underestimated the old man. When he had broken her hold on him, it had felt like he was ripping her skin off. The old fool has no idea how much power he possesses. She had probed him before she went to work on him. She didn't know if he was ignorant of his powers, or if it was his way of catching his enemies off guard. If that were the case, he might turn out to be more of a problem than she expected. She couldn't let John trick her into killing him before she was ready. She knew that killing him would be the end of her, but she hated men so much that sometimes she just couldn't control herself. She just wanted to rip them apart over and over again. Now she figured she would sit back and listen to those poor old stupid fools make their plans to destroy her. Mortals could be quite humorous sometimes. As she extended her probe toward the house her head almost blew apart. This was the second time the old man had hurt her. She wasn't used to being the one being hurt.

The old man had put up a ward around his property. She probed lightly upon the ward. It was something new to her. And for the first time in her existence, she had encountered a mortal as powerful as her former master. She had to figure out a way to get John away from the old man because she was beginning to doubt if she could get the best of the old man. So she decided that she would wait. She couldn't take the chance of being banished before she could kill John. Killing him was her destiny.

John and Cam stopped in the kitchen. That was as far as their legs would take them after the ordeal with the demon. Over a cup of coffee, they talked about it. John could tell that Cam was obviously upset.

So he asked, "Have you ever had anything like that happen to you before?"

Cam shook his head and said, "Never. I have talked with all sorts of otherworldly spirits, but I never had to deal with their power. My go-between always paved the way for me. So there was never a need for a show of force."

Suddenly Cam put the heels of his hands against his temples. John thought that he had a headache. He was about to ask if he could get him something for it when he got a glimpse of his eyes. It looked like he was about to have a fit. He decided to wait it out. He was sure that Cam would tell him what was going on after he regained control of his head.

Cam, on the other hand, was trying to hold his head together. He never knew that his wards remained connected to him after he deployed them. But now he knew. He could feel the demon's probe in his head. He knew that she had tried to eavesdrop on their conversation. As a matter of fact, he found that he knew more about the demon now than he could have found out in years of searching. When she sent out her probe, she had been wide open. Cam looked over at John. John looked very frightened. So Cam decided to ease his mind a little.

So he said, "John, I think we just hit the jackpot. She just tried to send a probe in here to see what we were planning to do about her. She didn't know that I had put up wards around the house. So she was unprepared for the resistance she encountered, and her mind was completely open and unguarded. The woman you hit with your truck was a very powerful individual, and quite unique.

Her name was Josephine Fishbourne. She was born with extraordinary powers, powers that she never wanted to use. She ran away from home when she was in her teens. Her mother never got the chance to teach her her full potential. She only learned of her demon when her husband was trying to kill her. That was when she found out how much power she had. But the demon went too far. It killed her husband before her eyes. She tried to make it stop, but the demon wouldn't listen. It ripped him apart like a rag doll. Josephine promised herself that she would never call on her demon again. She kept her word until you ran her down on the interstate. She wasn't an evil person. Bad things always had a way of finding her. She was the type that did what she had to do to survive. She had just won a battle with a very strong adversary. It seems that he had put a curse on her as he died. You were the instrument used to carry out the curse."

"Me", cried John! "I didn't even know the guy. Why would he use me?"

"Calm down," said Cam softly. "You just happened to be in the wrong place at the right time. If you had been at home, it would have been someone else. So don't take it personally. Getting angry now will only make matters worse."

"Worse? How much worse could it get. The woman is out there trying to kill me for God's sake!" Shouted John.

"It could be a lot worse," said Cam. "You could be lying in a ditch somewhere dead. So you'd better thank God that you had the foresight to come to me. And if you want my help, you had better get a hold of yourself. I won't have you shouting at me every time you hear something you don't like. Am I making myself clear to you?"

"Yes," said John. "I'm sorry about the outburst. I guess sometimes it gets to me. I don't want to die. The idea that some guy used me to kill that poor old lady pisses me off. Why didn't he admit that he was beaten, and die gracefully? I tell you, if it were raining hundred dollar bills, I'd find out at the last minute that I was born without hands."

"That may be true," said Cam. "But you've got to realize that we've got to work this thing out together. No one thinks straight when they are consumed by rage. I need you to be in control of yourself. At all times. Your life may depend on it."

"I understand," said John. "All you need to do is tell me what it is you want me to do. You'll see that I am an eager student. So lead on."

Cam sat back in his chair and stared at John. He felt that he understood the frustration he must be feeling. Cam was ready to start trying to figure out how to beat this demon, but he needed some time alone. He hated to tell John that he had to leave for a while, but he knew that he couldn't do what he had to do with John underfoot. He was about to tell John what he had decided when John said, "I've got to get out of here for a while. It feels like the walls are closing in on me. Do you think you could protect me if I left your house? I really do need to move around some."

"I think we can work something out," said Cam. "I have an amulet that you can wear around your neck. It won't work miracles but it will at least warn you when you're in peril. That and the pouch I gave you earlier should do the trick." Cam went to a large trunk in the corner of the room and started rummaging around inside. Finally, he took out a small tray. John could see all types of things in the tray. Cam chose a beautiful piece connected to a long golden chain.

"You can't be serious," said John. "That thing must be priceless."

Cam chuckled and said, "You're right, it is priceless, but I feel that I can trust you with it. Your life depends on you getting it back to me within three hours."

"Three hours?" Asked John. "Why three hours?"

"This once belonged to the Templars," explained Cam. "They were once a very powerful sect. They were able to do real magic not tricks like most psychics do now days. This amulet was part of their arsenal. It will warn you of danger, and it will give you a little protection. But you must not wear it longer than three hours, because it will start to draw on your life force. The results are almost instantaneous. If you aren't able to fend it off, you'll be dead in minutes."

"Don't you have anything less dangerous?" Asked John.

"Sure," said Cam. "But this is what you need. It's the only thing that I know will protect you." Cam placed the chain around John's neck, instructing him not to try to remove it.

"Why can't I remove it?" Asked John.

"Because it will kill you," stated Cam matter-of-factly. John's mouth dropped wide open. For a moment he was speechless. Then he managed to shout, "Kill me! What do you mean kill me?"

"As long as you leave it alone you'll be all right," said Cam. "Now go. I should have everything ready in a couple of hours. And please, don't do anything stupid, okay?"

"Don't worry about that," said John. "I'm just going to ride around a little bit to try to get my head together. I sure hope this thing will keep that woman away from me."

Cam said, "It won't keep her away from you, but it will prevent her from doing any major damage to you. It should protect you long enough for you to make it back here. Remember, it's okay to touch the amulet, but don't try to take it off. No matter how much you want to."

"I don't intend to touch it at all," said John. Then he turned and headed for the back door. Cam caught up with him at the door.

"You watch yourself out there," said Cam. "You have more people looking for you than one little woman. So you be careful." John told him that he would be back in a couple of hours, safe and sound.

John searched the area before he went outside. He didn't want to walk up on the woman without warning. He didn't think he could take any more surprises from that little lady. But right now he had to put his money away. He had to make sure that if anything did happen to him; his money would end up in the hands of the people he wanted to have it. He didn't want to have gone through all of this just for the money to end up in Dr. Siddig's hands. He checked around the truck, twice. And when he was sure that all was clear, he climbed in and started it up. He sat there for a few minutes taking in the view. Cam had a very nice place. John decided that if he made it through this in one piece, he would buy a place like this. As he drove off, his determination grew. He had to live through this.

# 7

Dr. Johnod Siddig slowly paced around his desk in his office. He thought that he would be able to handle the problem with John on his own. But he had just got word from his partners that they would handle it. Siddig knew that his partners would have John killed the moment he was found.

He had to get in touch with Cooter quickly. He had hoped that he could solve this thing without any bloodshed. But now it looked hopeless. He was beginning to realize that he liked John a lot more than he thought he did. He didn't want him killed. He had to find a way to get in touch with John before anyone else found him. If he could find him and talk him into returning the drugs, he might be able to save his life. But he had to find him first. As he was about the make another circuit around his desk, his receptionist buzzed him. When he answered, she told him that Cooter Cobb was on line two. He snatched up the receiver and said, "Hello?"

Cooter started talking almost before he finished his hello.

"Doctor?" He inquired.

"Yes it's me Mr. Cobb," answered the doctor. "Do you have any news for me?"

"I sure do," stated Cooter. "It's just not the news you want to hear. I know where he has been for the past few days, but I don't know where he is right now."

"Is that why you called me?" Asked Siddig. "Don't call me anymore until you have him. I have better things to do than make small talk with you. And I want you to find him within the next twenty-four hours. Am I making myself clear to you Mr. Cobb?"

After a short pause, Cooter said, "Yes sir, I do." Then he asked, "Hey Doc, are you okay? You sound like you're the one that's in trouble. Did he do something that has put you in hot water? If he has tell me so and I'll rough him up a little before I bring him in."

"You just do what I told you to do!" Shouted Dr. Siddig. "You find him, and then you bring him to me! YOU GOT THAT?"

"Yes sir, I understand that," said Cooter calmly. "Now you understand me. If you ever speak to me that way again, you'll find that you have more problems than some runaway gardener. Do you understand me?"

"Is that a threat, Mr. Cobb?" Asked Siddig. "If it is, let me give you some advice. That had better be the last time you ever speak to me that way. In case you aren't aware of the fact. I could have you erased from the face of the earth before you finish taking your morning dump. So don't think that you're so tough. You do what I hired you to do, and do it quickly before I decide that you don't deserve to live." Then he slammed the phone back on the cradle before Cooter could say anything more. He looked down at the phone on his desk. He was so angry. No one spoke to him in that manner. No one!

Cooter held the phone for a few moments after Siddig had hung up on him. He was quite angry himself. If Siddig thought he could threaten Cooter Cobb, he had better get the damn National Guard to back him up. For a few minutes, Cooter had in his mind to go to Siddig's office and beat the living daylights out of him. But as he hung up the phone, he saw a new Ford Expedition pull into the parking lot of Mac's General Merchandise. Cooter was standing in a phone booth situated at the far end of the lot.

The fact that Mac's was located several miles from town didn't hinder his business any. The parking lot was almost full at all times with patrons moving in and out of the store. Cooter had to crane his neck to see who was in the truck. He watched as the truck continued around the side of the store. Whoever was driving didn't stop at the front as most people would. So Cooter left the phone booth and headed around the other side of the building. After he got out of sight from the rest of the customers he broke into a run. He arrived at the back of the building in time to see the driver get out of the truck.

It was John.

Cooter felt like dancing. He watched John as he got out of the truck and look around. It looked as if he was searching the surrounding area for anyone that looked out of place. Cooter had no doubt that John would flee if he thought he was being watched. Cooter decided to wait until John went into the store. He planned to be waiting for him when he came out of the store.

After John entered the store, Cooter sprinted over to his truck. He opened the passenger side door. It was his plan to be in the truck when John came out of the store. But things didn't work out that way. As he opened the door, he was surprised to see the pretty woman sitting there. Cooter didn't understand why he didn't see her as he ran up to the truck. Cooter's surprise lasted only for a moment. Then he said, "Well hello there darling, fancy meeting you here. Where have you and John been hiding?" She just sat there staring at him. Then he remembered that the girl was a little slow.

"Has he been staying at your place?" He asked. The woman still didn't speak. So Cooter said, "I want you to get out of the truck for a few minutes. I want to surprise John when he comes out of the store."

Finally, the woman spoke, "I told you that he belongs to me," she said. "And I won't have you doing anything to him until I get through with him." For a moment Cooter almost turned to leave. Then he caught himself and said, "Now look girl, I told you to get out of the damn truck. I don't want to have to tell you again." Then he grabbed her by the arm to yank her out. She climbed out without much resistance.

Then she said, "I told you that he is mine." She snatched her arm out of his grasp. "I told you not to ever touch me again. Now I'm going to have to kill you."

Cooter slapped her hand away as she grabbed for him. He jumped back about three feet and said, "Little lady, don't make me have to hurt you. And if you think I'm going to let you get in another lucky punch, you're crazier than I think you are. Now get the hell out of my way."

Sephra smiled and attacked. Cooter threw a solid jab at her face. She dodged his punch and picked him up by the waist. She lifted him over her head and threw him over behind a row of pallets. (The pallets were there because Mac had a sweet potato sorting and packing factory right beside the store. The pallets were stacked with bushels of potatoes as they were picked up in the field. That's how they were brought to the factory.) As soon as Cooter stopped rolling, he jumped up and started running. He didn't know how she was able to pick him up and throw him, but he wasn't going to stick around to find out. He figured he would run up on John later when he didn't have that hellcat with him. Just as he made it around the end of the pallets, he ran straight into her arms.

From that point on, Cooter couldn't tell you what she did to him. All he knows for sure is that she beat him, and beat him, and beat him some more. And when she had beaten him about an inch from death, she stopped. And somewhere out of the fog that was his mind, Cooter heard John's voice. Then he heard a door shut. And a few moments later he heard another door open and shut. Then he heard the truck start up and drive away. Through the fog and pain, Cooter searched for the hellcat. She was nowhere to be found. She had done it to him again. Cooter figured that she must have run back around the pallets and got in the truck with John.

That was the only explanation he could come up with. John must have hired her as a bodyguard.

Cooter tried to get up but found that it felt better just to stay where he was. He had been in quite a few fights in his life, but this was the first time he'd ever been in a fight that he didn't participate in. He hadn't connected a single blow. She had used him like a punching bag. He raised his arms to check if anything was broken. His arms seemed to be fine, so he moved his legs, though painful; they seemed to be all right. He noticed that taking deep breaths hurt pretty badly, so he figured that he must have a broken rib or two. He hoped that no one would find him there before he was able to move. Because there was no way that he was going to tell anyone that a woman did this to him. So he remained where he was for six hours, unable to move. Finally, he managed to get up and make it to his truck. The store was as busy as ever, but no one seemed to pay him any mind.

Coughing up blood, and spitting out what he assumed to be teeth, Cooter headed for the hospital. He hoped one of the broken ribs hadn't punctured his lungs. That was when he decided that he would kill John the next time he saw him. John would pay for this ass whipping. WITH HIS LIFE!

# 8

John came out of the store with his arms full. He saw that someone had been in his truck. The first thought that came to his mind was that someone had found his loot. He walked straight to the open passenger-side door. He said aloud, "Who the hell has been fucking around in my damn truck." As he spoke he was checking out some of his hiding places. Nothing was disturbed. He figured that whoever was there must have seen him coming and ran off. He put his groceries on the seat, closed the door with a slam, and stalked around the back of the truck to see if anyone was close by. He saw no one. He began to relax a little. Maybe everything was all right. He opened the door and climbed in behind the steering wheel. Again he looked around to see if he could catch anyone acting suspiciously. Everyone that he could see was going on about their business as usual. So he started up the truck and slowly drove away. Completely unaware that

Cooter Cobb was less than twenty feet away from him in sheer agony, and very close to death.

As John drove along, he kept checking his rear-view mirror to see if anyone was following him, so far so good. The coast was clear. About two miles from Cam's house, John saw someone reach into one of his bags from the back seat. Startled, John almost lost control of the truck. When he regained control, he slid to a stop on the shoulder of the road.

"What the hell are you doing in my truck," he asked. All the while wondering why he hadn't seen the person when he checked the truck before he left the store. As he turned in his seat to confront his unwanted passenger, it dawned on him who it was. He immediately tried to open the door. It really didn't surprise him when he found it locked. So he turned to face his intruder. She was in the process of peeling a banana that she had taken from the grocery bag.

John asked, "What are you going to do to me this time?"

Taking a bite out of the banana, Sephra said, "I don't know yet. Did you know that an idiot named Cooter Cobb is looking for you?" John was thrown for a loop when she said that. He didn't think she had conversations with her victims. So he jumped at the chance to talk instead of being tortured.

"Yes, I know him," stated John. "We used to work together years ago. We were once friends."

"Not anymore," she said. "He's been trying to find you for the last few days. He intends to kill you, now."

"Now?" asked John. "Why did you put it like that?"

"Because at first he was supposed to find you and take you to the Doctor," she said. "But after today, he's gonna want to kill you. You mortals are so stupid. He thinks I'm your bodyguard."

"What!" said John? "Why!"

"Because I taught him that it is unwise to touch me," she said.

"I don't understand," said John. "When did he meet you?"

"Yesterday," she said. "He tried to convince me that he was your friend. And that he was looking for you for old times' sake. When I wouldn't tell him, he threatened to put me over his knee and spank me."

"Oh no," said John.

"I told him that I would kill him if he ever touched me again," she said. "Now I think he believes me." She began to chuckle.

"But you didn't kill him," said John. "Why?"

"Because as long as I have someone to keep me occupied," Sephra said. "The longer you have to live." This time she laughed outright. When she laughed, John found himself longing to hold her in his arms. Her beauty for a moment made John forget that she was there to kill him. As if sensing what John was thinking, she cut her laugh short. Her mirth seemed to drain away as a look of pure rage took over her face. Then she said in a deep voice, "If you ever think of me that way again, I will kill you then and there." She threw the remainder of the banana at John and vanished. Realizing how close he'd come to dying made John nervous. He knew how she felt about men. All he could do was thank God that she had Cooter to pick on instead of him. He felt that for a minute she was enjoying their conversation. He made up his mind that someway, somehow, he was going to win her over and save his life. So he made his way on to Cam's house, wondering if the woman had a heart that he could win.

# CHAPTER 3

## 1

Floating.........Floating........Floating.......Falling....Falling.......Falling.....
FALLING!!!!!!!!

Cooter Cobb reached out trying to grab hold of anything that he could. His right arm hit something cold and he jerked away from it only to reach for it again. This time he grabbed it and held on until the falling sensation passed. He slowly opened his eyes and through the blur, he saw someone standing over him. It was Dr. Siddig and some guy that he didn't know.

"Well well," said Dr. Siddig, "the sleeper awakens."

"What? Where am I," asked Cobb.

"Where do you think? You idiot", answered Siddig. "You are in the emergency ward at the hospital, recovering from emergency surgery. You've got a punctured lung and four broken ribs. Would you mind telling me how you let something like this happen to you? I gave you a simple assignment, and you screwed it up somehow. And what did John beat you with, a two by four? I've seen car accident victims with less damage."

Cooter tried to remember what the circumstances were that led him to this point. And then in a flash, it all came rushing back to him. John, the girl, and the ass whipping flooded back into his memory. He knew that if he told anyone about the girl, he would be the laughing stock of the whole community.

So he said, "I really don't remember what happened. It all happened so fast. I was talking to John, trying to get close enough to grab him, when somebody hit me from behind. I vaguely remember being kicked from all directions at once. After the blow to the head, I drifted in and out while they were doing this to me. He didn't do this to me by himself, he had help, a lot of help." Cooter looked at the man standing beside the doctor.

"Who's the suit? He asked.

"This is the man that's going to do what you were unable to do," said Siddig, "he's going to bring John to me or kill him."

"If you would have given me that option, John would already be taken care of," said Cooter. "You told me to find him and bring him to you. Why didn't you tell me dead or alive would do?"

"Because," said Siddig, "you're too stupid to be walking around with a loaded gun. There's no telling how many people would be dead or wounded because of your itchy trigger finger."

"If I wasn't laid up here all bandaged up," said Cooter angrily, "I'd bring you John, and then I'd ended your miserable life. But first I'd take the time to teach you that you can't talk like that to me. After all I went through to find that son of a bitch for you, and get myself beat half to death. I'd teach you how to appreciate what people go through for you. You bastard."

Siddig smiled and said, "Be that as it may, but you're going to tell this nice gentleman all that you know, and when you're able to get out of this bed, I want you to take the money I gave you and disappear. If I ever see you again, I'll have you killed. Is that clear to you Mr. Cobb?"

From the way Siddig said that, and the way the guy standing beside him smiled, Cooter decided to play scared. "Hey man," he said, "you know how I shoot off at the mouth sometimes. I meant nothing by it. Forget that I said anything." Cooter knew that if he didn't get out of there the first chance he got, he was as good as dead. So he told the suit all that he knew about John's whereabouts. And after they left, Cooter quietly slipped away from the hospital, slowly forming the plan to take out Dr. Siddig. The man had just pushed the last of Cooter Cobb's buttons.

# 2

Walking the realm of power, Cam slowly drew power into himself. Cam knew that he would need all of the power he could get to handle the demon. He hadn't been aware of this magical realm until his friend in the spirit world informed him about it. Surrounded by fruit trees of all kinds, in a land that was too beautiful to exist anywhere, Cam was told which fruits he would need to absorb to get the power he needed. His friendly spirit told him that some of the fruit was deadly to mortals, and was there to point out which ones were safe. The fruit that Cam picked felt solid, but when he'd try to eat it, it would slowly dissolve in his hand. As that would happen, Cam would feel warmth slowly flow from his head to his feet. He didn't feel any different on the outside, but on the inside, he felt invigorated and stronger than he'd ever felt in his life. He hadn't felt this good as a young man.

When he had absorbed enough power, his friendly spirit told him it was time to go. Cam found out that leaving was going to be one of the hardest things he'd ever had to do. He knew that if he'd come here alone, he would never have been able to leave on his own. With much effort and sadness, Cam opened his eyes in his den. It took a little while for the sadness to leave him, and he slowly came to grips with the fact that he had to leave the most perfect place he'd ever been.

Though saddened, Cam knew he had to pull himself together and get back to the business at hand. He got up and put away his bowl. As he was returning to the den, he heard John drive around to the back of the house. He went to the kitchen window and looked out. To his surprise, John was smiling and walking slowly toward the door. Cam saw that he had some bags in his arms. As he opened the door, John said, "You should have seen her Cam." He walked to the table and sat the bags on the table. "We were talking about Cooter Cobb, that's an old friend of mine, and she looked like she was really enjoying the conversation. Until I started thinking about how beautiful she looked when she laughed. Boy, did she explode. She threw a half-eaten banana at me and told me that if I ever thought of her that way again, she would kill me right then. Can she read my mind or something?"

"I really don't know. But I imagine that she has become an expert on reading facial expressions, yours in particular. You might want to start trying to control yourself. Don't let everything show on your face. It could get you killed," Cam said, as he took a peek inside the bags. Then he turned and removed the heavy chain from around John's neck.

"I agree," Said John, "but I believe that I could love that woman if she was real."

"Oh, but she is real," said Cam. As long as she is after you, she is as real as you and me."

John leaned against the stove and thought for a while. Then he said something that really shocked Cam.

"Cam," he said, "I really think that I've got a big problem. I think that I am falling in love with her. I know that she wants to kill me, but I can hardly wait until I see her again. I've just made up my mind that I am going to win this woman's heart if I die trying." Cam slowly closed his mouth, which had fallen open as John spoke.

"Man, have you lost your cotton-picking mind?" He asked. "How badly does she have to hurt you before you realize that your life doesn't mean shit to her? When she decides that you are going to die, buddy, you're gone. Just like that. GONE!!!"

As he watched John, he realized that nothing he'd said had gotten through to him. Here he was trying to find any way possible to save this idiot's life, and he starts talking about putting his head on the chopping block willingly. For a moment, Cam considered throwing him out of his house. But one look at John told him that the man was hopelessly in love, or just plain stupid. And he didn't think John had a mental problem.

"Will you help me?" John asked. "If it doesn't work out, we'll have a plan B ready to implement and zap her back to wherever she comes from. And since I'll still be alive, she can go on and live whatever type of life she can, because believe it or not, I don't want to see her die. And besides, you could let me borrow that necklace again. I think it really works."

Cam said, "You came to me for help, and I am going to help you in any way that I can. I just hope that you aren't making a mistake. Please bear in mind that her reason for being here at all is because you ran down the only person she has ever been close to. Think about how you would feel about someone that killed your mother, sister, or one of your dear friends. Do you think you could stand to live the rest of your life with that person?"

"God!" John said. "I hadn't thought about it like that. I guess I've got to stop thinking about her in that way. I know that she's dangerous, but I can't help but try. She is too wonderful to let slip away."

"John," said Cam, "you've got to stop thinking with your pecker and start using your brain. Please use common sense when dealing with her. One slip and you are a dead man."

John said, "Cam, I know you may not believe me, but I could live my whole life with her and never touch her in that way. When I see her, I don't think about having sex with her. I just want to hold her in my arms just one time and hear her laugh the way she did a little while ago. If you'd been there and heard her laugh, you would understand. The woman is awesome."

"We'll see," said Cam.

# 3

Bert Jackson (formerly known as the suit) smiled as he watched Cooter leave the hospital through the emergency entrance. Experience had taught him that you always know where a possible problem may be lurking. The doctor thought that Cobb was just another stupid hick. But he knew better. He had watched the man's eyes as he was threatening the doctor. Until Cobb was taken care of, Siddig's life wasn't worth spit. He was as good as dead already. He was just too arrogant to realize it.

He watched Cobb as he limped out of the rear entrance of the hospital, and got into a beat-up red pickup truck driven by a woman. He followed them at a distance, from Betsy Johnson Hospital to highway 301. They turned north on 301 and drove through Dunn, on through Benson, and continued on to Four Oaks. Once in Four Oaks, they turned on a side road heading toward I-95. They crossed the interstate and began taking unpaved roads.

Traveling on dirt roads throws up a lot of dust, so Bert decided to hang back a little more to keep Cobb from noticing the dust his vehicle was turning up. From dirt road to dirt road, Jackson followed Cobb's dust trail. After about twenty minutes of following the dust cloud, Bert decided that he'd had enough. He decided to go ahead and take out Cobb now. If

Cobb would have acted like somebody and just gone somewhere to hide out, he could have lived for another day or two. But now he had pissed Bert off with all of these dusty roads. Now Cobb was going to die, and because of him, the driver of the truck was going to die too.

Bert reached under his coat and pulled out his revolver. He cocked it and accelerated to catch up with Cobb. Being unable to see the truck through the dust cloud, Bert planned to shoot him as he passed him. Waiting until the last minute to roll down the passenger side window, he broke through the dust cloud to find that he was following a different truck. The truck was the same color, but it was definitely a different truck. The old man driving the truck laughed and gave Bert the finger. Angrily he slammed on the brakes. He slid to a stop on the soft shoulder. He almost accelerated again to catch back up with the old man and blow that stupid grin off of his face.

Furious Bert got out of the truck. He could not believe that Cobb had suckered him. He had fallen for one of the oldest tricks in the book. Cobb must have known that he would be followed, so he called ahead and had that asshole waiting for him out here in the boondocks. He knew that if anyone were following him, they would drop back once he hit the dirt roads to keep from being conspicuous. He should have killed him between Dunn and Benson. It would have been a whole lot easier. Now he had to worry about Cobb getting to the doctor before he could get Cramer and collect his money. Cobb had to be in a lot of pain, how could he think things out so clearly in his condition? Most people in the shape he was in wouldn't have been able to even get out of bed. He was looking forward to the killing of Cooter Cobb.

# 4

Sephra was hovering in the vicinity of Cam's house. She was positive that she was in the right place. But something had happened. She couldn't see the house. She could see the boundary of Cam's property, but that was it. He had done something that she had never encountered before. She didn't think that Josephine could have pulled this off. This man is full of surprises. Sephra decided to watch and learn. If he slipped up once, she would pounce, and absorb everything he is. His power would be hers.

After hanging around a while, she decided to go check on Cooter and see how he was making out. She didn't think about it as being odd that she knew where he was, because once she touched someone, she could always locate him with a thought. Now she found herself in a wooded area. It was quite nice actually. Amid the trees was a nice log cabin. And inside she could sense Cooter sleeping in one of the bedrooms. She could tell that he wasn't going to go anywhere for a while. He was serving as a pretty good distraction though. She knew that she should go ahead and take care of John, but she just wasn't ready to leave this world yet. She was having too much fun. And since her master had given her the option to do this any way she wanted, she was going to enjoy this wonderful world a little longer.

She decided to go back to the little house beside the pond where she had the most fun tormenting John. When she arrived she found someone walking around inside. She sat down on what was left of the front porch and waited for him to finish looking the house over. Though she hadn't made direct contact with this person, she felt that she knew who he was looking for. So, she sat and waited, wondering if this guy was going to be more fun than Cooter Cobb.

# 5

Bert walked slowly through the run-down house. He wondered, after seeing the used condoms, paper towels, and old food wrappers, what kind of woman would come to such an awful place to have sex. He didn't think he knew a single woman that would come here with him and get naked. He knew without a doubt that he wouldn't put his bare ass on that filthy mattress. He was amazed at what people would go through for a little sex.

As he walked through the house he could see all the marks left by John when he was hiding out here. In one room it looked like the man had had some sort of fit. Bert could see where he'd crawled from the center of the room to the window. And from the looks of the marks, it looked like he went right on out the window. The grass on the outside of the window was wallowed down, and in some areas, there were clumps of grass pulled completely out of the ground. Bert was beginning to think that maybe this John guy had some mental problems. He'd be sure to ask Siddig if this were true.

He knew that any trail that John may have left here would be cold by now, but he always liked to try to get to know the habits of his prey. This tactic had always paid off in the past, and he'd learned to rely on his gut instinct while surveying anything that he came across. Even if he didn't see anything that he thought was of any value now, events in the future may bring something that he saw now into clarity.

Using contacts he had developed over the years he learned that John always shopped at Mac's General Merchandise. By placing people at strategic points though-out the region; he expected to hear that John was in the area at any time now. Having been in this type of business for many years he'd perfected the art of waiting. He also knew that more than one set of eyes was essential. He had no doubt that he would make contact with John within the next twenty-four hours.

Bert was a very smart man and very good at what he was doing. But he was greedy. More than a few of his jobs ended in the death of the person that hired him. If the stakes were high enough, Bert would always work it out so that he got paid, and delivered whatever he was hired to recover. But he always worked it out so that it looked like someone else did the killing. Then he would let the rest of the people involved know that he was upset and that he was going to take care of the person responsible. He would do this free of charge. After killing some innocent individual he would go back and tell the people that he'd taken care of the problem. And out of gratitude, they would give him a little extra money for doing them such a great favor. That was how he kept getting these big-money jobs. Everyone always gave him good references. He actually turned down more jobs than he took. He was that good.

He tried to retire once, but he found that he was not happy unless he was on the prowl. He really loved to hunt people. His life felt empty without the thrill of the kill. He didn't think of himself as a hitman, he felt that he was more of a clean-up man. He was the one you would call when you couldn't get things done through normal channels. He didn't always get hired to kill someone, but he always found a reason to drop someone along the way. He always got his man. His success rate was 100%, and he intended to keep it that way.

Over the past few years, he'd amassed a small fortune, a fortune that he never really got to enjoy. He never felt the urge to buy a big fancy car or a huge house on a hill somewhere. Those types of things were too mundane to give him much pleasure. The only real joy he ever felt was at the moment when the life energy slowly faded from the eyes of someone he'd just killed. He always felt like God when he was holding someone's life in his hands.

That's why he always made sure that his victims knew who was responsible for their demise. He would always engage the prey in some type of dialog that would ensure him that they knew his name, and knew that this was the day that their lives would end. He enjoyed the look of terror that always surfaced when the prey realized that no matter how much they begged and pleaded, the end result was going to be their death.

As he walked out the back-door of the house, his instincts told him that he was in danger. He walked quietly around the back of the house, checking in all directions to see where the threat was coming from. At first, he thought that maybe John or Cobb had sneaked up on him while he was inside the house. But as he got to the front of the house all he saw was a girl sitting on what was left of the front porch.

The moment he laid eyes on the girl he had to fight the urge to run to his truck. His whole body was screaming for him to run. But years of experience had taught him never to let an adversary know that you were afraid.

With a quick nod of his head, he continued on to his truck. "RUN," his instinct was telling him. But he held himself in check until he got to his truck. As he opened the door to his truck, he ventured another look at the girl. She was still sitting there looking at him. It seemed to him that she had a strange look on her face.

He started up his truck, turned around, and headed for the narrow path that led out to the highway. As he navigated the sharp curve in the path, he almost ran over another girl. He slammed on his brakes and stopped only inches from the girl. He started to get out and give her a piece of his mind when he noticed that she looked just like the girl back at the house. He froze. Either the girl has a twin, or she is the fastest runner he's ever seen. He decided to wait and let her make the first move.

Eventually, the girl realized that he wasn't going to get out. So she started walking around the front of the truck. When she was about halfway down the front side panel, Bert tried to push the accelerator pedal through the floor. The truck fishtailed a little, and then it shot down the path at break-neck speed. When he got to the road he didn't even slow down to see if any traffic was coming.

When the rear tires caught on the pavement, he almost lost control. He managed to keep it on the road somehow. After a couple of miles, he realized that he still had the pedal to the floor. He eased up on it and gradually stopped several miles away from the house.

Sitting on the shoulder of the road trying to get a hold of himself, he realized that his clothes were soaking wet. He got out of the truck to walk around a little. He didn't understand what was going on. How could he have lost control that way when, as he saw it now, there was no apparent danger? He'd never had that kind of reaction with anyone or anything in his whole life. Yet here he was running from a girl. A Girl!!

After about twenty minutes, he had convinced himself that if he didn't go back and face that girl, he would probably be running from women for the rest of his life. He got in his truck, turned around, and headed back to the little house in the woods.

As he got to the path and was about to turn in he almost collided with another truck coming out of the path. The driver of the truck backed up so he could pull off the road. He could see that the man was very angry. His face was cherry red.

"Where the hell do you think you are going," asked the man. "Don't you know that this is private property?"

"I didn't mean to cause a problem," said Bert, "but this place just reminded me of the place I grew up in. And I couldn't resist going up in there to look around."

"Look around my ass," said the man. "I saw how you came out of here like a bat out of hell, what's wrong with you?"

"I'm sorry about that, but I walked up on the biggest damn snake I have ever seen," said Bert. "And I sort of lost it there for a few minutes. If I caused any damage, I'm more than willing to pay for it."

"I don't believe you damaged anything, except the rear end of your truck," said the farmer. "You stay out of here and we'll forget the whole thing."

"Thanks a lot," said Bert. "I really do appreciate that. By the way, you didn't happen to see a girl back in there did you?"

"A girl, you didn't run off and leave somebody down there did you?" He asked.

"No, no, no," said Bert. "I just thought I saw someone as I was leaving, that all."

"No, I didn't see any girl or anything down there but the house," answered the farmer.

"Okay," said Bert. "I'll be on my way then. And again thanks for being so understanding."

The farmer just shook his head and walked back to his truck. Burt got into his truck, backed out onto the highway, and slowly drove away. Wondering where the girl ran off to. He hoped that he would see her again just to prove to himself that his reaction had been a fluke.

# 6

Sephra sat on the front porch of the house waiting for the man to come out. When he came around the corner of the house, he glanced at her, nodded his head, and went on to his truck. That shocked her. She was used to getting a certain reaction from men when they saw her. But this man was different. He hardly noticed her. She could feel the fear leaking off of him like water. She wondered how he knew that she could hurt him, without her doing anything to him.

When the man reached his truck, he looked at her again. Again there was the wrong reaction. He almost ripped the door off the truck.

"What's going on?" Thought Sephra, as she watched him turn around and drive away from the house. Just as the truck was going around the curve, she decided to try again. She materialized just out of sight around the curve. When he saw her he slammed on his brakes. For a moment, she thought he was going to get out. But then he stopped\, and just sat there with both hands on the steering wheel, looking at her. His eyes looked as if they were going to pop out of their sockets.

Finally, Sephra got tired of standing there waiting for him to act, so she walked around toward the driver's side door. When she got about halfway there, the truck did a little dance and shot down the path.

Again, Sephra was surprised by his reaction. She stood there and watched the truck as it entered the roadway, without slowing down and with a lot of noise and smoke take off down the road.

Sephra could only stand there for a few minutes. The mortals of this world were weird. Just when she thought she had them figured out, she would run into someone like him or like that little man John had gone to. She was beginning to see that she had a lot to learn. She decided that since this one was so easily frightened, she would slowly scare him to death.

# 7

Cooter Cobb was almost out of breath. He'd been running for a long time. It seemed to him that he'd been running his whole life. He kept looking back to see what it was he was running from, but he could never see it. But he knew it was following him. He tried to figure out what it was as he ran. Casting back through his memories, he seemed to keep seeing a very beautiful woman. But he could think of no reason for a female to be angry enough with him and be dangerous enough for him to run from her. Because every woman knows that he is a wonderful man and a terrific lover. Yet, he couldn't make himself stop running.

"Cooter," someone said. "Hey Cooter, wake up." The voice sounded like it was coming from a long way off. Then he heard it again. This time it sounded much closer. He felt himself being shaken. And for some reason, the shaking was causing him a lot of pain. He couldn't figure out why it was hurting so bad. Finally, he opened his eyes and saw Becky standing over him.

"Will you please stop shaking me," he shouted. "I'm awake now. God, you're acting like the house is burning down. What's wrong with you woman?"

"That's what I was going to ask you," said Becky. "You're wringing wet with sweat, and you were all over the bed like you were having a nightmare or something. I just wanted to make sure you were all right. It looked like you were going to tear your stitches loose. So I woke you. Forgive me for caring."

"No, you did the right thing," said Cooter, "I'd forgotten about the operation I had last night. How do the stitches look? I didn't tear any of them loose did I?"

"Hold still and I'll look," she said. "Boy, if what you told me is true, I think you'd better lay low for a while. Those people might kill you the next time."

"Not a chance," he said. "I know who to look out for now, and the next time I run into her, uh, them, I'm going to start blasting. And I do plan to see them again. I owe them."

"I hope you know what you're doing," she said.

"Becky you know that I don't take this kind of shit from nobody," he said. "And I am going to make them pay for every stitch and every pain."

"While you were sleeping Henry stopped by," said Becky, "he said that you were right about maybe being followed. He said that the guy got real mad when he saw that it wasn't you in the truck. He said that he thinks he saw a gun in the guy's hand, but he can't be sure. Do you think they really want to kill you?"

"Probably," he answered, "but I intend to get my chance at them first. They don't know where I am right now, so I can take the time to heal a little more. And when I get back on my feet, I'm going to be just like the Shadow. I'm going to ease in and take that damn doctor out first, and then I'm going to find John. I owe him really big."

"John who?" Asked Becky.

"Cramer, you know the yardman."

"Is that who you're looking for? I bet I can find him for you while you're laid up here. What did he do? I always thought he was a real nice guy."

"What he did was sic his goons on me. And for that I intend to kill him."

"Do you want me to see what I can find out?" She asked.

"Yeah, but do it in a way that doesn't look like you want to find him too quickly. I don't want you to get hurt doing this for me, because as you can see, his people like to play rough. And if you see a woman hanging around, get away from there real quick. She's the one that set the goons on me. I think she works for John, and the guys that did this to me work for her. She acts like she's a little slow in the head, but I think that's the way she throws you off. That gal is pure TNT."

All right," said Becky, "as soon as you feel you can be alone for a while, I'll go see what I can find out. And if you'll let me, I'll beat the shit out of that woman when you do what you have to do to John. It's been a long time since I've kicked some ass. It'll be fun."

Becky and Cooter weren't what you would call lovers; they were more like friends that slept together every now and then. They practically grew up together. They lived about a mile from each other all of their school years. And Becky had been your average tomboy. She'd beaten up just about every boy that ever tried to date her. So no one had ever fallen in love with her. She wasn't lonely because she could get a man any time she wanted one. And she had a lot of friends. She wasn't pretty, but with her almost picture-perfect body people seemed drawn to her. The only time she looked pretty was when the light would catch her in a certain way. When that happened she was truly a knockout.

The reason she turned out to be so tough is her parent's fault. Her dad liked to hit her mother, and her mother would let him do it. She watched that happen most of her life. Then at the tender age of fifteen she put a stop to that. Her father was in one of his rages and was beating her mother when she decided to see if she couldn't help her out a little. She knew that her father would probably beat the shit out of her too, but she had to do something to make him stop hitting her mother. She ran into the room screaming at the top of her lungs and attacked with the vigor of a tiger. She doesn't really remember what she did to her father, but she remembers her mother pulling her off of him. He was on the floor and all bloody. As soon as she was pulled off of him he scrambled under the kitchen table to hide. Her mother dragged her out of the house and they rode around for a little while.

"Sweetheart," her mother said. "Your father isn't a bad man. He just gets frustrated sometimes. I appreciate what you tried to do back there, but you may have made matters worse. He never really hurt me before but he just might now."

"If he does," said Becky, "I'll kill him. You shouldn't have to put up with somebody beating on you Mom. You deserve better treatment than that. If he wants me to get out of the house, I'll leave. But I can't let him hurt you anymore."

"You'll do no such thing," shouted her mother. "You will not threaten your father in any way. You will respect him and treat him the way a father is supposed to be treated. I know that he loves both of us. He has always made sure we have everything we needed, food, clothes, and a roof over our heads. And he always made sure that you got everything your little heart desired. When you get older you will see that those things have a lot a value. When I was a little girl, we had to do without a lot of the things that you take for granted. We went hungry a lot of times. And in winter we were cold most of the time. So you should thank God that you have a father that at least tries to do right by you."

"Okay, okay," said Becky. "I get the point. When we get back home, I'll apologize for what I did. I do love dad, but I love you more." She sat slumped against the door. She was trying not to cry. Then she said, "I hope I haven't made a mess of our lives."

When they returned home her father had gotten cleaned up. He met them at the door. He hugged her mother, and then he hugged her. To her surprise, he never mentioned what had happened. And he never hit her mother again. Everything else went on a usual. Their lives were almost perfect from then on.

That was what taught her that if you want to make a point, beat the shit out of the problem maker. It seemed to always work. So that's the way she took care of almost every situation. And this was the way she was going to help Cooter. If she ever ran into that whore she would teach her a lesson. If you don't stop someone from doing you wrong the first time that it happens, they tend to keep doing it every chance they get.

"How about bringing me another one of those pills," said Cooter. "That shaking you gave me has caused me to start hurting again."

"Coming up," said Becky.

Cooter watched her as she moved about the room. It took a while before he recognized the feeling he was having. For the first time in his life he was with someone that was beginning to mean more to him than anyone else ever had. He listened to her as she talked about defending him from that strange woman. The more she talked, the more he was taken with her. She'd always been special to him, and she'd always treated him better than all the rest of her friends. So he decided to keep her away from that strong-ass woman.

"I don't think you want to tangle with that bitch," he said. "She's sneaky as hell."

"I don't care," she said. "The bitch had you beat up. And I want her real bad. I'm gonna show her that she can't do that to you Cooter. You're too nice of a guy to have something like this happen to you. Her ass is mine."

"Just let me be with you when you jump her," he said. "I want to see how she likes having the shit beat out of her. I'll be watching your back. If I see any of the guys that did this to me, I'm gonna shoot the shit out of them. They are like those monsters we saw in that movie. You know the ones that will let you see one of them while the rest sneak up on you from behind."

"You mean Jurassic Park, the one with the dinosaurs in it."

"Yeah, that's the one."

"When I get through with her she'll wish she had been jumped by dinosaurs," she said. "At least they would make it quick. I'm gonna make that bitch suffer."

"I don't see how I've let you walk around single for so long. Will you marry me?" Joked Cooter.

"You know better than to joke with me like that," she laughed. "You know you'll be asleep again in a little while. I'll bundle your doped up ass off to the magistrate's office. If you wake up married it will be your own fault."

As they joked back and forth with one another, as lifelong friends will, Sephra was having a laugh of her own. She was about to have some more fun with John.

# 8

Cam was looking in an old trunk as John talked about the demon. He felt that no matter what he told John, he was going to go on and try to get close to the demon. It seemed to him that John had some kind of death wish. Cam had never heard of a situation like this that the demon didn't kill its target.

"Hey Cam, can I borrow the necklace once more?" Inquired John.

"Yes, you can," answered Cam. "But don't think that if she tried hard enough that she couldn't bypass it. She has a lot of power. She can do things to you that you've never even imagined. And if she happens to get her hands on you while you are away from me, I won't be able to help you. You do understand that don't you? And you do still have the pouch I gave you earlier, right?"

"Yes, I do have the pouch, and I do understand the danger I'm in," said John. "But I really do need to see her again. It seems that I'm drawn to her for some reason."

"I know the reason," said Cam. "It's called stupidity. I don't think that I've ever seen anyone as eager to die as you are. Why on earth do you want to keep putting your head on the chopping block?"

John stood there looking out the window as Cam talked. He knew that what Cam was saying made a lot of sense, but he felt that he could wiggle his way out of anything she put him through now that he was familiar with her tactics. He felt that with the necklace and a little nerve he could survive anything except a deathblow. So he turned to Cam and said. "You will let me use it, won't you?".

"Of course you can use it. But remember that you haven't had enough time to rebuild your strength from wearing it earlier," said Cam.

"But I feel great," said John. "I don't think that it drew much of my energy the last time, because I didn't have to use it. She never got any closer to me than the back seat."

"Okay then, you can wear it. But please be careful. Take nothing for granted while she's around. And don't piss her off again."

"Trust me, I won't," said John, as Cam put the necklace back around his neck.

"I'll be back in a little while," said John, as he went out the back door. He looked all around his truck to make sure she hadn't left any surprises for him. He unlocked the door and climbed inside. He sat there for a few minutes to make sure she wasn't going to appear beside him. Finally, he started the truck and drove slowly around the house and out to the road.

He'd driven about a mile when suddenly she was beside him. He almost lost control of the truck, but he regained his composure and control of the truck. Neither one spoke for about a mile, then John said, "Hi, are you going to kill me this time?"

"I don't know yet," Sephra stated.

"I don't plan to do anything stupid this time," said John. "At least I hope I don't."

"Do you think that whether you anger me or not makes any difference to me?" She asked. "I can kill you any time I please. I might decide to kill you in your sleep or right now if it pleases me. You are mine. You don't have a life unless I decide to let you live. You can go to a priest or that little man back there if you like. But you are still my property, my little cow that I can butcher at any time. Do you understand that, stupid?"

"Yes, I do understand," said John. "My life is in your hands. I give it to you freely and with no strings attached. I'm yours. Do with me as you please. I will not fight or struggle, I will die knowing that what you did to me was just, and that I deserved it."

Sephra sat with her back to the passenger's side window. She didn't speak. She sat there looking at John as if he had a huge bugger hanging out of his nose. She had a strange look on her face. It looked to John that she was in deep thought. Then she disappeared with a pop. Slowly John began to smile. He had crossed the first hurdle.

# 9

Hanging in limbo, Sephra attempted to stop her head from spinning. What was the mortal up to now? Did he think that he could play games with her? Did he think that she wouldn't kill him? His life was over already and he wanted to play games. She decided that she was tired of putting up with his surprises. From the start he had been keeping her off balance. Nothing she did to him seemed to have the right effect. By now he should be on the verge of madness. Most mortals couldn't handle the fact the demons existed at all. Once they found out, they usually went mad or were killed trying to control the demon. But this man was actually beginning to get under her skin. She was starting to get some feelings for the idiot. She realized that if she didn't kill him soon she might find that she couldn't do it when the time came.

Finally, she made up her mind to go ahead and kill him now. But first, she would see how he would react to a few things she wanted to do. She searched for his mind, located it, and materialized thirty yards ahead of him on the shoulder of the road. Then she stuck out her thumb.

# 10

After the woman disappeared, John was trying to think of what to do next. He felt that he had her a little confused by the way he was acting. He decided that he was going to go for broke the next time he saw her. In his mind, he couldn't see himself living any longer without telling her how he felt about her. If she killed him, fine, if she let him live so much the better. He had cared for women in the past but this woman was so perfect that he had to touch her once.

Then he saw her standing on the shoulder of the road hitchhiking. He couldn't believe his eyes. She was actually going to give him a choice. He could stop, or he could keep on going. He decided to stop. He started braking and before he could stop completely, he had traveled fifty feet beyond her. He put the truck in reverse and backed up to where she was still standing on the shoulder.

"You need a lift lady?" He asked.

Saying nothing, Sephra opened the door and climbed into the truck. John watched her as she got in and sat looking out through the windshield. Seeing that she wasn't going to say anything, John put the truck in drive a started down the road.

"Where are you headed young lady?" He asked.

Still she said nothing. She sat there staring out the front of the truck. Every now and then John would look over at her. He could see that her face was going through a lot of changes. First her face was blank, then it looked angry, and then she looked down right mad. Now she looked confused. It looked like she was having a battle all in the confines of her mind. John decided to wait her out. He had the feeling that his life was getting very close to the end. So he waited until she got her emotions together before he said anything more.

Sephra was indeed having problems. She'd expected John to try to run from her again. But instead, he'd stopped to pick her up. And he kept talking to her like she was just another mortal standing on the side of the road. Why couldn't he act like someone who was about to die? Why was he being so nice to her? She wished Josephine were here to tell her what was going on. She felt that she was losing control of the situation. She had to do something to make him realize that she was here to hurt him. Not be a friend.

Finally she looked over at John. She saw that he was looking at her again. So she said, "Now you die." She waved her hands at him and he was blown out of the truck. The blast hit him so hard that when he slammed against the door, he tore it off of the truck. He was thrown over the left lane of the road, across the ditch, and about thirty feet into a field. He landed on top of the door and slid for another fifteen feet before coming to a stop.

Sephra let the truck come to a stop at the edge of the ditch out of the roadway. She got out of the truck and walked back to where John lay in the field. She felt for his mind and found that it was very weak. John was finally dying.

As John slowly drifted towards death, Sephra began to hurt in her chest. It was stronger than the pain that she felt when Josephine died. Why was she having feelings for this murderer? He means nothing to her. She was on earth for only one reason, to make him pay for the death of her master. The pain that she was feeling was far worse than anything she had ever encountered. It felt like someone had injected acid inside of her and it was destroying her from the inside out. Although she knew how to cause immense pain when she interacted with mortals, she had never in her existence felt anything like this. She dropped to the ground writhing in total oblivion, now this was what real pain feels like. She was like that for a while before she began to see a way to think around the pain. It dawned on her that if she didn't stop John's suffering, her's wouldn't stop either.

Now she knew that she had to keep him from dying. She finally managed to get up onto her knees and slowly crawl over to where John was dying on the door of the truck. She reached out to touch him and found that she couldn't touch him. He had something on his person that wouldn't let her put her hands on him. So she grabbed the door he was laying on. Through the door, she sent a pulse of life-giving energy. Although very little of the pulse reached him, she sensed that the trickle that made it through had moved John away from death's door, and it actually eased her pain a little, but he needed more help. Help that she couldn't give him without touching him.

Though she was still in agony, she stood up and picked up the door with John lying on it and transported to the edge of the protective field Cam had put up around his house. Putting the door down gently, she reached out for Cam's mind. She found that she couldn't make the connection. His wards were very powerful. She knew that if she didn't reach Cam soon John would die. In frustration, she sent out a burst of power aimed at the protective field. She felt the field began to weaken at the point of the attack. But then the field regained its former strength, but now she could see the house. She kept pouring on the power until she saw Cam burst out the back-door.

"Attend to him, mortal," she said, "it is not yet his time to die. I have a lot more to do to him before he can embrace death."

Cam saw John lying on the battered door and rushed to him. He kept one eye on the demon as he knelt down to check to see if he was alive. He knew that this had to be a trap. Then he noticed tears running down the woman's face. Shocked, he turned to help John.

"What have you done to him?" He asked.

"I have collected a little of the debt that he owes me," she answered. "And I have much more to collect before I will let him die. You will see to it that he does not die, mortal."

"Why?" asked Cam, "So you can do this to him again? I would be doing him a favor if I let him die now. That way you couldn't torture him anymore for something that was an accident from the start. There is nothing you could do to him, short of death that he hasn't already done to himself."

"If you let him die," said Sephra, "there is no place on earth that you can hide from my wrath."

"Then help me get him inside," said Cam. "He's too heavy for me to carry."

"I cannot," she said. "There is something around him that won't let me touch him. Remove it and I will assist you."

"Not before you promise me that you won't hurt him anymore if I do," he said.

"Do you doubt me, mortal?" She asked. "With a wave of my hand, I could kill you both. I don't have to touch either of you to take your lives. But you have my word that I will not harm him now. But I still have several personal hells to put him through. So remove the wards you have around him and your house and I will help you get him inside."

Cam took the necklace from around John's neck and took the pouch out of his pocket, and lowered the field around his house. Immediately she knelt down and placed her hands on John's chest. As she sent another pulse of power through John, he convulsed like someone getting an electric shock. Cam almost interceded until he realized that she was actually giving John the help he needed to survive. After she finished, they carried John into the house. Cam led them into his guest bedroom and they lowered him onto the bed.

"Now I want you out of my house," Cam said. "I won't let you harm him while he is in my home."

"I told you that I do not wish to harm him now," she said. "But I will not leave until I know that you can help him." Then she turned and walked over to the dresser and leaned against it.

"Begin," she ordered.

Using some of the energy he had acquired in the other realm, Cam began to share it with John. For two hours he worked on John. Finally, John shouted and sat straight up in the bed. When he saw the woman, he tried to scramble off the other side of the bed. He almost knocked Cam down as he tried to get up.

"Stop! Lie back down!" shouted Cam. "She brought you here. She has promised not to hurt you this time. So get back on that bed before you hurt yourself some more. You are still very weak. You have to get your strength back before you try to walk." Then he turned to the demon and said, "Now will you leave my home?"

"Yes," she said.

"Wait," said John. "Why did you try to kill me and then save me?"

"I have not finished with you yet," she said.

Then John said, "Before you go I have to get something off my chest."

"Be careful, mortal," she said. "I can still kill you."

"I think I love you," John said.

Her face clouded over and all of the mirrors and windows in the bedroom shattered. Then she vanished.

Cam, looking at his destroyed bedroom, turned to John and said, "I truly believe that you are the dumbest man I have ever seen. You were an inch from death when she brought you here, and then you say something like that. Do you want to die that badly? If you do, I'll get my gun and shoot you right now myself."

"Sorry about the room," John said. "But I had to say it to her once because she might not give me a chance to say it again."

"I'm surprised she didn't kill you. It could have something to do with the tears I saw outside," said Cam. "I think she was crying out there when she found out that she couldn't reach me in here."

"Crying?" asked John.

"Yes, crying," answered Cam.

"That means that she feels something for me too," said John. "I knew I could get her to care for me."

"Or," said Cam; "it could be just as she said. She told me that she wasn't ready for you to die yet. She said that she had a few more things to do to you before she let you die."

"Oh," said John sadly, "I thought maybe I was getting her to like me a little bit."

"I don't know if that is possible," said Cam. "What we do know is that she was sent here to kill you. Will you try not to forget that?"

"Don't worry," said John, "I'll never forget that. Can you take me to my truck? It's sitting beside the road with everything I own in it."

"Don't worry about your truck," said Cam. "Tell me where you left it and I'll get it here."

John told him where it was, the last time he saw it, and then he stretched out on the bed. He went to sleep almost instantly. He'd lost most of his life's energy and it had to rebuild slowly.

Cam watched him as he slept. He remembered the old saying, "God watches over babies and fools," and he felt that John was really fooling himself if he thought he was winning over that demon's heart. As a matter of fact, Cam didn't know if they had hearts anyway. He went to the phone and called one of his reliable clients, and instructed him to bring John's truck back. After he got off the phone, he went to the kitchen to fix up something to speed up John's recovery. He would need all the help he could get.

# 11

Sephra was in turmoil. She had never felt such pain. How could such pain be possible? She knew that killing John would end her existence, but she had no idea that it was going to be so painful. When her master, (Josephine), died she hardly felt anything. All she remembered feeling was a pinprick to the heart. But this was ridiculous. How could that murderer have such a hold on her? She began to wonder if she'd let him live too long. Was she beginning to form a connection with him? Even now she could still feel the effects of the pain that hit her when she decided to go ahead and kill him. How was she going to be able to kill him if it was going to affect her like this? She decided that she had to find out.

She stood and held out her arms as if she was embracing someone. She closed her eyes and descended into hell. There she found Josephine in her personal hell. She saw immediately that Josephine wasn't enjoying it at all. So she turned to the attending demon and said, "I need to talk to this mortal, stop tormenting her for a little while."

"Just for a short while," said the demon in a low rumbling voice. Sephra waited until Jo realized that the pain had stopped. She watched as Jo looked around to see what was going on. She saw the look of relief that came over her face when she saw her.

"You," she shouted. "I knew you would come for me. Take me away from this horrible place."

"I cannot", said Sephra. "This is your reward for serving my master all those years. This is the way you pay him back for me and the powers you were given in the mortal realm."

"But I thought I was going to have a wonderful place here when I died," said Jo. "But I've been tortured from the moment you brought me here, over and over again. Why didn't you tell me that this was the way that it was going to be? They rip me to shreds over and over again and then they heal me and start all over again. They take away everything except the memory of the agony they've inflicted upon my soul. I wish I had never existed at all. Please use the power I know you possess and destroy me now before the attending demon returns. "It's not allowed," answered Sephra. "Didn't you ever read a bible? It tells all about this. You should have expected this. There was a time after the death of your husband that

I thought you were going to make the change, but you never did. So I figured you knew what was in the bargain."

"I thought he would treat me better than this. I served him faithfully for most of my life," she said. "I deserve better than this. You can talk to someone for me."

"I cannot."

"But you must. I order you to."

"I am no longer under your command."

"Yes, you have to be. You were with me all of my life. You always did what I wanted you to do."

"Think Jo," said Sephra sadly, "why would Satan give you power over the demons in hell? You are here to be tormented for the rest of time. How could that be if you could just order the demons to leave you alone? It just doesn't work that way."

"But you made him stop," she cried. "Just tell him not to do this to me anymore. He'll listen to you. I know he will. Please help me!"

"I am here to get information from you about the task you ordered me to do before you died," said Sephra. "Did you tie me to him like I was tied to you?"

"What are you talking about?" asked Jo. "I need you to get me out of here. If you promise to help me, I'll help you. I can't think standing in this hellhole. Take me away from here and I'll tell you what you want to know."

"Very well," said Sephra. She entered Jo's mind and caused her to see the two of them lying on a beach. Jo jumped up and ran out into the waves. She went out until only her head was above the water.

"Thank you, Sephra," she said. "This feels so good. I know that I'm still in hell, but this feels real. I hope you can leave some of this with me before you go."

"I will see what I can do," answered Sephra. "Now tell me if I am connected to the mortal the same way I was with you."

"No," answered Jo. "In my anger, I bound the two of you together. The two of you are just like twins now. He can't hide anywhere on earth that you couldn't find him. You know that I just couldn't turn you loose on earth without some kind of anchor. You will always be drawn to him until you kill him. And then you will join me here in my torment."

"I see," said Sephra. "Now I understand. I will do what you wanted me to do. I have to, but I wish you hadn't bound us together the way you did. I tried to kill him and it almost ripped me apart. That never happened before. My time has run out. I must leave you now."

"Please leave me with just a little bit of this beach in my mind," begged Jo. "I won't let it show. I'll scream as loud as I always have. He'll never know."

"I'll try," said Sephra. She turned and walked away. As she passed the demon she gave a little nod and kept walking. She heard Jo begin to scream again. She wondered how mortals could serve a master like Satan, and think that he is going to share power in hell with them. Hell is his domain; even Sephra didn't have very much power here in his stronghold. That's why she enjoys the mortal world as much as she does. Hell is hell.

Sephra returned to the little house by the pond. For some reason, she was drawn to this old run-down house. It was the ideal place for her to think a little. She had already decided to leave John alone for a while. She had to experiment a little to find the best way to kill him without it affecting her. There had to be a way, she just had to find it.

# CHAPTER 4

## 1

Bert was elated. He was on his way to the house of a root-worker. Through his network, he had found out that John was seen at that house several times. He was determined that the guy that lived there was going to tell him where John is if he had to beat it out of him.

This was the part of his job that he liked the most. The art of interrogation was a fine-honed tool that you used like a scalpel. If the person possesses the knowledge, you could always get it out of them. Bert felt that he was the best in the trade. He never had to use drugs. All he ever used was pain. And no one could deliver pain the way he could.

He stopped on the shoulder of the road about a mile from the house to make sure he had all of his tools of the trade. He checked to make sure all three of his guns were loaded. He made sure his two knives were where they should be. It was bad business to reach for a knife and find that it had slid around out of place. When you're in a struggle the last thing you need is to have to search for a weapon.

Satisfied that everything was as it should be, he drove on up to the house. He saw John's new truck sitting in the back yard. It looked like he'd already had an accident. The driver's side door was missing. Just for the hell of it, Bert decided that he would shoot John in the foot for messing up such a nice vehicle this quickly. John was clever; he had put the truck in a position that made it hard to see. If Bert hadn't known what to look for, he would have thought it was an old junked vehicle. He pulled in and stopped in the front yard. He got out of the truck and walked up on the porch.

As he began knocking, an elderly man opened the front door. He gave Bert the once over and then he said, "How may I help you?"

Bert said, "How are you sir? I have a problem and I was told that you could most likely help me. I was told that you always get results. May I come in and discuss it with you?"

"Of course, you can," said Cam. "Come on in and have a seat. Would you like something to drink? It's rather hot today."

"No thank you," said Bert as he sat down. "I would like to find out if you can solve my problem."

Cam asked, "And just what is your problem?" Cam knew exactly what his problem was. He knew that he was one of the people looking for John. He wanted to find out how he was going to ask. You learn a lot about a person if you watch and listen.

Bert said, "I'm looking for a friend of mine. And I think you can help me find him. I was told that he was here yesterday, and I saw his truck in your backyard as I drove up. Will you get him for me?"

"I'm afraid I can't do that," answered Cam. "You see someone is out to hurt him, and he came to me for protection. So if you will tell me what it is you want from him, maybe I can help you."

"Old man if you don't go get him right now I'm going to have to hurt you. I have a job to do and I'm not going to let an old fart like you stand in my way. Now go get him!" shouted Bert.

"I see," said Cam. "I know that you're not Mr. Cobb, so just who are you?"

"I'm the one that's about to beat the shit out of an old man. Now go get him!" said Bert.

Cam stood and said, "I'm afraid I must ask you to leave my home, sir. I don't allow violence in my home. You are no longer welcome here." As Cam walked to the door, Bert pulled out one of his guns and was about to pop him upside the head, when Cam turned and waved his arm. Instantly, Bert was picked up and thrown against the wall. He tried to pull his arm away from the wall, but his whole body was stuck to the wall. The old man walked up and started taking away his weapons. He found every one of them.

After he had fully disarmed Bert, Cam said, "I am going to release you now. And when I do, I expect you to leave my home peacefully. Do you understand?"

"Yes," answered Bert. He was starting to feel the same way he had felt around that girl, absolute fear. He wasn't sure but he might have peed himself when he hit the wall. Bert's instincts were telling him to run again. But he still had his pride. When the old man let him down from the wall, he walked slowly to the door.

As he walked through the door his instincts took over and he started running. He ran by his truck and out into the street. He ran for a long while. When he finally managed to stop, he realized that he'd left his truck in the old man's yard. He fell down on his knees, gasping for breath.

He looked up at the sky and screamed, "What the hell is going on? Shit like this can't be happening! I've been in battle with the enemy all around the world, with people dying all around me and I never reacted like this. What is that old man? Is he a warlock or something? I thought root-workers were fakes! I must be going crazy! How am I supposed to get my truck back?"

Then he began to laugh. He didn't know why he was laughing, he just was. He knelt at the edge of the ditch for about an hour. Finally, he decided to try to sneak back and get his truck. When he arrived at the driveway he stopped. The old man was sitting on the front porch, watching him.

Bert said, "Sir, do you mind if I get my truck? And if I offended you in any way earlier, I apologize. Can I have my truck?"

"Of course you can," said Cam. "Take it, and don't come back here again. If you want John, you're going to have to get to him when he is not under my protection. I would have done the same thing for you if I was protecting you."

Then the old man chuckled and said, "I would advise you not to tell anyone about what happened to you here today. They'll lock you up and throw away the key."

"I know," said Bert. "I know." Then keeping his eyes on the old man, he made his way to his truck. Started it up, and back onto the roadway, and slowly drove away.

# 2

Something was wrong. John was having a dream. He was aware that he was dreaming, but he normally had more control over his body than he had now. In his dream, he was talking to the woman that was trying to kill him. This time she was acting like any other woman. She was laughing and talking to him like they were the best of friends. For some reason John felt like he was on one of the outer planets where the gravity was a hundred times stronger than on earth. All he could do was talk. Every time he tried to raise an arm or reposition himself on the couch they were sitting on, he found that it took all the strength he had. Every move required a period of rest. Finally, he decided to sit still and enjoy the dream.

"So," he said, "I guess you have decided to let me live a little longer."

"Why not," answered the woman. "When you die, I die. And I'm not ready to die yet. This is such a beautiful world you have here. I think I will hang around a while."

John sat and watched her as she talked and laughed. He had no doubt in his mind that this was the most beautiful woman on the planet. If there were any way on earth to win her heart he would find it.

Suddenly intense pain ran through his body. His whole body seemed to be a pain repository, and someone had just opened all of the containers. The woman disappeared and he slowly woke up. When he opened his eyes, he saw Cam leaning over him, shaking him.

"Wake up John," he said. "It's time for you to eat a little something and drink some more of this tonic I've made for you."

"Oh man," said John. "What a dream."

"Another bad one, huh?"

"No, not this time. This one was actually a good one. We were having a very good conversation. She was laughing and talking to me like an ordinary woman. I wish she were like that in real life. Then maybe I could get somewhere with her."

Cam said, "Do you know that what you are planning is going to take you directly to hell? You won't pass go, you won't collect two hundred dollars, and you'll be giving yourself over to the dark side willingly. You can't have it both ways."

"What do you mean?" Asked John.

"You are talking about turning your life over to her so you can win her heart over in the long run. Remember, a demon is a demon. It's not like she went over to the dark side by choice. She was created evil and will remain evil as long as she exists. And if you offer yourself to her as a living sacrifice you will become the property of hell. It's that simple," said Cam.

"But what about you? Aren't root-workers the tools of the Devil?" asked John.

Cam smiled and shook his head, "When did you ever hear me say that I am a root-worker. That is a title that most people put on people they don't understand. Folks know that if I can help someone with a problem I will. But the power I have, I hope it comes from the wellspring of God. I actually asked my helper about it once and was told that my purpose on this planet was to help people get *out* of the clutches of Satan. That is what I have been trying to do most of my life. I don't think that I have ever done anything evil to anyone. I try to help people through their crisis without harming the one that is bothering them. I hope and pray that I haven't spent my life on a fool's errand. If I am wrong, I hope God will have mercy on me, because I have always felt that I am working for him."

"Sorry," said John. "I didn't mean to hit a nerve. I didn't mean to insult you. You have been a true friend to me since I showed up on your doorstep, and I hope you'll still help me as much as you can. But will you please try to find out for me if there is a way to convert a demon because if there is the smallest chance that we could do that, we might be saving a lost soul."

Cam said, "I don't think she has a soul, John. You know a soul gives you a conscience, and I don't think demons could do the things they do for people if there were a soul in there. I don't think that I've ever heard of a situation where a demon was conjured up to do something good. I think they are evil through and through."

"But you will look into it for me, won't you?"

"Yes I will look into it, but don't get your hopes up," answered Cam. He fed John and watched him as he fell back to sleep. Cam wondered where helping this man was going to lead him. Although he had only met John a short while ago, he had done things that he had never dreamed of. He now had more power than he had ever had in his life. He understood more about the power within as well as the power without. The new strength was exhilarating. He had no idea how long he would retain the power, but it felt good to have it. And he wondered what toll it was taking on his body and his spirit.

These were the things going through his mind as he sat watching John sleep. He knew that he would have the answers in a little while. He just hoped that he would survive them.

# 3

Bert sat in the waiting room of the office of Dr. Siddig. He watched as the people came and went about their various tasks. He noticed that most of the staff seemed to like their jobs. There was a lot of laughter and joking going on behind the front counter.

"They wouldn't be so jolly if they had witnessed some of the things I've seen lately," he said to himself. He was here to tell the doctor a few things that he felt that he didn't know. The reception nurse told him earlier that the doctor would be in shortly. She said that he had an emergency call from the hospital and had to go there first thing this morning.

Bert tried to think of a way to tell Siddig about the situation without sounding like a total idiot. He knew that he couldn't tell him the whole truth, but he knew that he had to tell him something.

Siddig paged him last night and scheduled a meeting for this morning. He said he wanted a progress report. Bert had sat up most of the night trying to come up with a report that would at least satiate him for a little while.

Bert needed some time to work all of this out in his own head. Things like that girl that scares the living daylights out of him, and the old man that must be Samantha Stevens' son. He could remember watching the TV show Bewitched when he was a kid. He always wished that he could do magic the way she pretended to on that show. Now he had run into a real person that had that kind of power, awesome power. The old man had defeated and disarmed him without even raising a sweat. It was like it took no effort at all to do that to him.

Although there was a lot of fear and confusion running through his mind, way back in the back of his subconscious he was working out a way to get that kind of power for himself. If the old man can do it, he knew without a doubt that he could harness that power and make it his own. The first thing he had to do was to subdue the old man and get him under his control, but how?

"Sir?" said a pretty Hispanic looking nurse. "The doctor will see you now."

"Thank you," said Bert. He stood and followed the nurse as she led him through the maze of offices and examination rooms to a part of the building that looked like it belonged in a futuristic movie. Siding's office looked like a home away from home, mostly glass and corners and curves. Siddig sat behind a desk that was the size of a mid-size car talking on the phone. Bert wondered why he would want a desk that big.

"Have a seat," said Siddig as he hung up the phone. "What do you have for me? I've waited long enough. I have got to talk to John. My life depends on seeing him. And I need to see him now. Well?"

Bert cleared his throat and said, "I found his truck yesterday parked behind a house just outside of Dunn. But I didn't locate John. He must know that we know what type of vehicle he's driving and decided to ditch the truck there. I think that he must be long gone by now. He's probably lying on some beach somewhere living it up. But my people are still looking for him in a one hundred-mile radius. If he is in the area I will find him."

"Did you search his truck?" asked Siddig.

"Of course," lied Bert. "I do know what I'm doing you know. That's why you hired me. I am the best."

"What did you find", asked the Doctor.

"Nothing but the usual, fast food junk that he accumulated on the ride back home," said Bert. "OK then," said Siddig. "Keep up the good work. And keep me informed. My partners are getting a little restless. In fact, I believe they've already taken steps to find John. When you find him get all the info you can from him about my shipment. I must know where he stashed it. I know that he's not stupid enough to still be carrying it around."

"Don't worry," said Bert. "I'll find him for you. And get your shit back."

"Good," said Siddig. "And when was the last time you slept. You look like shit."

Bert just nodded and got up to leave. He stopped and said, "You know,

I'm running out of money on this deal. I've got people to pay. And I don't intend to go in the red over this thing. Your boy seems to be a lot smarter than you thought. You need to get some more money on hand in case I have to call for some more."

"All right," said Siddig. "But you'd better hurry up because I don't like pouring good money after bad. Do what you were hired to do. I'm tired of waiting. He's still just a silly country boy. Don't let him ruin your perfect record."

"Don't worry about my record, it is safe. But John isn't," said Bert. Then he turned and left the room. He was thinking that if he didn't find John soon he would have to take out Siddig. His record would remain intact if he had to take out everybody that knew he was on this case. It's called job security.

Dr. Siddig sat behind his desk watching Bert leave. He was thinking that John might be smarter than all of them put together. But Bert was supposed to be the best. So he would wait a little longer for results.

As Bert left the office, he saw that there was someone leaning against his truck. By the tightening of his gut, he knew that it had to be that damn girl again. He almost turned around, but he decided to go ahead and face this thing and get it over with now.

As he neared his truck, he checked to make sure his weapons were where they were supposed to be. He looked around to see if there were any people nearby. The only person he saw was a young black guy sitting in his car listening to the radio. The way his music was thumping, Bert doubted that he would hear a gunshot or a scream if he had to take the girl out.

For the first time, Bert noticed how pretty the girl was. He decided that he would play on her vanities. All pretty girls are vain. They can't help it. All of their lives they've been told how pretty they are, and eventually they start believing it, and it shows.

"Don't I know you?" asked Bert. "Weren't you in that movie on TV last night?"

"What are you talking about, mortal?" asked Sephra.

"Mortal?" thought Bert. "What the hell was that supposed to mean?"

"So you aren't an actress?" Asked Bert acting surprised.

"No," said Sephra.

"Are you sure?"

"Yes, I am sure."

"I tell you what; you could be if you wanted to be."

"I have no such desires."

"Pity," said Bert.

During this short conversation, Bert had managed to get to his truck. Now he opened the door and climbed in. Then stuck his head out of the window and said, "Well, I'll see you around. It was nice talking to you. Bye." He started the truck and drove away. He never looked back.

Sephra was standing in the parking lot with a look of astonishment on her face. He had done it again. There was something about that mortal that always caught her off guard. She could feel his fear, but his reactions didn't coincide with it. She could tell that he felt one way, but he would act another way. And that was what was so confusing. The longer she dealt with mortals, the stranger they seemed to get.

# 4

Sitting outside of the 8 Days Inn in a new rental car, Bert waited for Jimmy to come out. Jimmy was one of his most faithful employees. He was one of the vets that made it out of Iraq with Bert. Their working relationship was one of mutual respect. There were certain things that Jimmy was good at. This time, Bert wanted Jimmy to silently break into the root-workers house.

The plan was to break in, knock out John, and get him out of the house without the old man ever waking up. This wasn't the first time Bert had used Jimmy for abducting people. Jimmy was good and he was strong as hell. He always completed his missions. He'd never failed Bert.

Bert thought of the conversation that he had, over the phone, with Jimmy after he left Siddig's office. He told him that he had a snatch job for him to do. He didn't mention the fact that the old man could possibly be a problem. He was trying to think of a way to tell Jimmy that the old man was dangerous, without letting him know that the old man had gotten the best of him.

Finally, Jimmy came out of the room and headed for Bert's car. He got in, closed the door, and said, "Hi, Captain. Sorry about the delay, but I was on the phone with Cyn. She's getting up my supplies for the job tonight."

"Fine," said Bert. "Let's ride out and take a look at the place. So you'll know the layout in the dark."

"Great," said Jimmy. "Then I'll know if I need anything extra for the job."

"Look," said Bert. "There's something you should know about the old man. I believe that he was once in the military, possibly in Special Forces. From what I've heard, the old man can take care of himself. I've seen him, and he looks to be in pretty good shape. I want you to avoid him at all costs. If you hear him getting up, get out of there as fast as you can. I don't want you to come in contact with him at all. Do you understand?"

"Yeah, got it," Said Jimmy.

After a ten-minute drive, Bert slowed the car a little as they approached the house. Jimmy leaned forward and gave the house a good looking over. As they passed the house, Jimmy turned and watched the house pass. Bert began picking up speed as they passed, just in case the old man was looking out a window. As they got farther from the house, Bert pulled over and gave Jimmy a pair of binoculars.

"Do you see any place that you can enter without making a lot of noise?" He asked.

"Just one," answered Jimmy. "That back-door seems to be the simplest. Do you know if he has any kind of alarm system?"

"I didn't see one," said Bert. "But I only got into the front room. I don't think he has one unless he always uses the back-door to enter."

"You know," said Jimmy. "That house looks pretty tight. I think I'll knock everybody out and just go in and get the guy. What do you think?"

"That's a good idea," said Bert, smiling. "I hadn't thought of that. That way you won't have to tangle with the old man at all. I knew I was keeping you around for something. You've got a good head on your shoulders."

Jimmy glowed under the praise, but he knew that all he had to do was screw up once and he would be off of Bert's team instantly. They all knew that Bert didn't brook mistakes. He had to get some Halothane and Isoflurane gas added to his list that Cyn was getting up for him. He was sure she could get it before dark. Cyn is very good at what she does.

Jimmy looked over at Bert and said, "I can get some of the sleeping gas that veterinarians use to knock them out. They'll have a hellish headache and may vomit a little bit in the morning, but by that time you'll have your man."

"Fine," said Bert. "I want to be back out here around midnight. That should give you time enough to gather your supplies. And too, that will give them enough time to be in bed. John is going to wake up under my control. Then we all can get paid."

Bert slowly pulled away from the shoulder of the road, and drove to the next intersection, and turned around. He drove back by the house running about half the speed limit so Jimmy could get another look at the house. As they rode along, they talked about the upcoming event as if it were nothing more than a fishing trip.

All Jimmy was sure of was that he was about to get paid. He really didn't care if the person he was to abduct was going to be killed or not. He just wanted to get paid.

Jimmy was about 5'7" and built like a Sherman tank. In service his nickname had been "tank" because of his strength. He got the name from an incident that happened in Iraq. He and Bert were riding with some other soldiers when a tire was blown out by shrapnel from a nearby explosion.

After the dust cleared they found one of the other guys bloody and holding his left arm that had almost been torn off. They knew the guy would bleed to death if they didn't get him to the field hospital quickly. Jimmy jumped out and picked up the front of the jeep, and held it there until the other guys changed the tire. That's how he got the name "tank".

Jimmy had worked off and on with Bert ever since they returned from the war. He'd tried to do domestic work, but he kept getting fired. So he turned to a life of petty crime and dope dealing. His problem was that he kept getting in trouble with his suppliers because he liked the taste of the poison he was supposed to be selling.

Finally, he decided to stick with Bert. He was off of the drugs and was living better than he had ever lived in his life. Bert paid really well. And he was able to travel all over the country. It was almost like he was still in the military.

Bert dropped him off at the hotel. He went inside and put in a call to Cyn. She didn't answer, so he called her cellular number. She answered almost immediately. He told her about the gas he needed, and they agreed to meet at Cyn's brother's house at nine. He took a shower and laid down for a little nap because he had a feeling that tonight was going to be a long night.

# 5

After sleeping all night and most of the day, John was feeling a little bit better. He was sitting up in bed eating supper. Cam had fixed a thick soup for him to eat. It was the best food John could remember ever eating. Though he was still quite sore, he could tell that he was getting a little stronger.

He watched Cam as he moved around the room. It looked like Cam had a lot on his mind, so he said, "Cam, what's wrong? You look like you've just lost your best friend."

"I'm fine," said Cam. "It's just that I don't know what to expect from her anymore. First, she almost kills you, then; she brings you to me crying, and won't leave until she knows for sure that you are going to pull through. I've never heard of such a thing."

"I think that maybe I am getting through to her a little bit," said John. "What if she is starting to care for me a little bit? I could live with that."

"Or", said Cam. "Maybe she found out that if you die, she dies. She may not be ready to leave this plane of existence yet. Or maybe your death causes her pain. I just don't know. And I would advise you to keep in mind that she still intends to kill you. That is something that she has no power to change. She was ordered to kill you, and she will. That is one thing that you can count on."

"I know," said John. "But I hope she waits until I'm old and senile before she strikes the killing blow. Think about it Cam, if she does wait, I could live a full life, with or without her, then she could kill me when I'm on my deathbed, now that would be all right with me".

"Boy," said Cam. "You sure know how to dream. I don't think you are going to see this one come true. I give you maybe a week before she decides to finish the job. She told me that she has several hells to put you through before she lets you die. And I believe her. So if you don't mind, I think I will still try to find a way to protect you."

"OK," said John. "But I still want us to try to find a way to get through to her that I still love her. I must do everything I can do to ensure that she knows that."

"I'll make a note," said Cam. "But as I've told you before I'm going to make sure you make it through this thing in one piece. I'm going to find a way to destroy her first, and then I'll see about the other stuff. Your survival is first and foremost. OK?"

"Yeah sure," said John. "By the way, I thought you said the amulet would protect me from her. It didn't work to well. When she hit me with that blast it felt like I was hit by an eighteen-wheeler. All I remember is her saying that now I die. I thought I was a goner. I don't even know how I got here. I remember waking up, and seeing her, and trying to get as far away from her as possible. I was so scared that I forgot that I loved her for a moment."

"Yeah," said Cam. "But when you got your senses back you were stupid enough to tell her that. Thus, I've got to replace all of my mirrors and windows. If you pull a stunt like that again in my house, I'll kill you myself."

Yawning, John said, "What did you put in this soup? I can hardly hold my eyes open."

"Nothing," said Cam. "Your body is just trying to tell you that you need more time to recuperate. You have no idea how close to death's door you were when she brought you here. I don't think you would have made it if she hadn't saved you herself. Whatever she did, it pulled you from the brink. I wish she would teach me that trick. What I did was nothing compared to the power she used to save you. She is very powerful."

"Well whatever she did, she wouldn't have had to do it if she hadn't tried to kill me," said John. "Maybe now she will forget about killing me. At least I hope she'll see it that way."

"I doubt it," said Cam. "Just don't do anything foolish the next time you see her, OK? You've been lucky so far."

"I know," said John. "I won't press my luck anymore. I don't ever want to hurt this bad again. I feel like I've been rode hard and put up wet. So, what do we do next?"

"Right now," said Cam, "you're going to get some more sleep. I think I will too. Then when we wake in the morning maybe we can come up with something together. I'll have most of our options figured out by then, and we can sort through them and come up with a workable plan."

"OK," said John handing the empty bowl to Cam. "I don't think I'll have much trouble sleeping. I still feel like I've been up for a month. I hope I can pick up the same dream I was having before you woke me up. Now that was a dream."

"Just remember that it was a dream," said Cam. "You are still in danger. Don't ever forget that. One wrong move and you're gone. Sleep well, and I will see you in the morning."

"Good night," said John. "I feel like we may get lucky tomorrow. I'll keep my fingers crossed."

As John was rolling over, Bert was outside of the hotel room waiting for Jimmy.

# 6

Bert watched Jimmy as he came out of the hotel room. Jimmy was dressed in black from head to toe. Bert was dressed the same. They intended to be almost invisible in the dark. This operation would be treated like a major operation in the military, quick in and quick out. And hopefully no dead bodies left behind.

Bert didn't want Cam harmed because he had to get him under his control at a later date to extract the knowledge he had. The old man had something Bert wanted, and he would give it up freely or die. That was the way Bert always looked at things. That power would be his, period.

"Hey Captain," said Jimmy. "I called Vernon a few minutes ago, and he said that everything had been delivered. All we have to do is go pick it up. By the time we go up there and get it and come back, I think everyone in that house should be asleep."

"I think so too," said Bert. "Was she able to get the knockout gas?"

"Yeah," said Jimmy. "Vernon said she was there when the stuff arrived and was certain everything was there. He said that she would meet us there at nine."

The trip to McGee's Crossroads was uneventful. Jimmy talked of old times in the army while they traveled. Jimmy's voice was just a buzz in the background to Bert because he was thinking about the upcoming snatch. He was worried that the old man might not be knocked out when they entered the house. He didn't want to have to hurt the old man yet. That was reserved for some time in the near future.

Bert made a right turn off Highway 50 onto Highway 210. Vernon lived about halfway between 50 and I-40. As he made the left onto the dirt path that led to Vernon's house, he tuned Jimmy back in.

"Where are we going to keep this guy after we get him?" asked Jimmy.

"You let me worry about that," said Bert. "I just want you to do what I hired you to do. The less you know the better off you will be in the future. You know I don't like too many people knowing what I am doing. This job is no different."

"Gotcha," said Jimmy. "I didn't mean to pry. You just let me know if you need me for anything else."

"Don't worry, I will," said Bert.

As they entered the yard, they saw Cynthia come out of the front door. She motioned for them to continue on around the side of the house. She led them to a barn about 50 feet from the house. She opened the sliding barn door and told Bert to drive on in. Bert drove into the barn and pulled up beside a stack of boxes sitting in front of one of the stalls.

"Is everything here?" asked Jimmy as he climbed out of the truck.

"Everything you asked for," said Cyn. "I tried to find the halothane gas in darker containers, but this is all I could come up with on such short notice."

Bert looked at the bright orange cylinders of gas. He didn't think the bright color would be a problem, but he still said, "This is sloppy Cyn. You know the type of work we do. Those things will stand out like searchlights if a car comes by while we're using them."

"Hey," said Cyn. "If you want things just like you want them, give me more time to get it for you. I had to call in a favor to get these damn things. I'll probably have to sleep with the bastard sooner or later. So don't give me that shit. You've got sense enough to put them somewhere where they won't be seen. If not, that's your stupidity."

Jimmy and Bert both laughed and started loading the supplies in the back of the truck. They both knew how tough Cyn was because they had seen her in action before. The woman could be dangerous if you pissed her off. Bert always liked to do something or say something to get a rise out of her. She was used to it.

Bert handed her $25,000. Part of it was for the supplies; the rest was payment for her services. She took the money and stuffed it in the back pocket of her jeans. Bert remembered the story about the New Year's Eve party in which two guys were fighting over Cyn. The story goes that she broke up the fight by beating the shit out of both of them and then leaving with somebody else. It was a story that everyone told, but never in front of her. She didn't think it was all that funny.

Cynthia was 5'11" tall, 160 lbs., and mean as a wolverine. She wasn't a big woman, but she carried herself like a pro wrestler. She never told anyone why she was always like a lit fuse, but it had to be something bad. She looked at the world like it owed her something. And she always collected. Plus, she could always gather everything the team needed to do a job. She was the best.

"Do you need any backup?" asked Cyn.

"Not this time," said Bert. "I'll contact you if I need anything else. You've done a good job here, and I appreciate it."

"Keep in touch," she said.

"You bet," said Jimmy.

On the way back to Dunn, Bert and Jimmy went over the plan for tonight's job. They had everything worked out so that they would not be there any longer than thirty minutes. Jimmy said that while people usually used a mask to administer halothane gas, they had enough to fill the whole house with the gas twice over.

Finally, they reached the spot that they were going to park the truck. Without saying a word they went to work. Jimmy had his glasscutter with the suction cup attachment. They hung their masks around their necks. They took a cylinder each, and quietly approached the rear of the house. Jimmy picked what he thought to be a kitchen window, and began to cut out a circular hole in the glass. He had to do it slowly because cutting glass was quite noisy. Finally he had a small hole cut in the glass. He slid the hose that was connected to the two tanks with a "Y" junction into the hole and pushed in about three feet more. Then he covered the hole with some type of putty to seal the hole to prevent the gas from escaping. When he was sure the hose wouldn't slide back out, he turned the valve on both tanks about a quarter turn. They could just barely hear the gas flowing through the hose. After about a minute, Jimmy turned the valves another quarter turn on each tank. The purpose of this was to prevent anyone from noticing the sound of escaping gas. The human brain is very sensitive to sounds, but if you add a sound gradually the brain will add it to the normal background noises that it normally filters out. But if Jimmy had opened the valves completely the brain would have sounded the alarm and woke them up.

By the time Jimmy had opened up the valves all the way, the gas would have already started taking effect. After twenty minutes, Bert went to get the truck. Then they put on their masks, and Jimmy picked the lock on the back-door. They entered the house quietly, shielding their pin lights with their free hand. When they looked in the room where Cam was sleeping, they saw that the gas had indeed done the trick. After searching the rest of the house, they found John in the second bedroom. He was sleeping the sleep of the dead.

Jimmy lifted John and slung him over his shoulder like a sack of flour. They exited the house and took John to the truck. After they laid him in the seat, they went back and collected the gas cylinders. All that would be left would be the small hole in the window. They doubted if the old man would even notice it until winter.

Bert dropped Jimmy off at the hotel, and headed for the cabin he owned out in the country, it was perfect for this operation. Now things were going the way he liked things to go when he did a job. He would question John and find out where he stashed whatever it was he took from the good doctor, then, he would kill him and keep it for himself. He had no idea that he had left millions sitting in Cam's backyard hidden in John's truck.

# 7

When Cam finally woke up it was well over into the afternoon. The very first thing he did was jump up and run to the bathroom to throw up. His head was pounding like he'd been drunk for a week. Looking in the mirror showed him that he needed a shave so he took four Tylenol and set about cleaning himself up. He was in the shower when he remembered that he had a house-guest. He quickly finished up in the bathroom, and then he went to check up on John. John wasn't there. The only thing out of place was the light blanket he had spread over John right before he had gone to bed himself. The blanket was lying on the floor between the bed and the door. It looked like maybe John had gotten up and just walked away while letting the blanket fall off of him as he walked to the door. "Something just doesn't feel right about this room," thought Cam. "What's going on here?" Then he turned around and went to the backdoor to see if John was outside or if his truck was gone. But his truck was still sitting in the same place the tow-truck driver had left it. And he didn't think that John would drive around in a truck with the driver's side door missing. He was trying to lay low and that would be just stupid.

Cam went to the back-door to go outside to see if John was taking a walk in the yard when found out that the door was open. Now why would John have left the door open? Shaking his head; Cam walked out in the back-yard to look for John. He walked all around the house, but he didn't see John anywhere. As he walked past the kitchen window he noticed a lot of footprints bunched around the area immediately below the window. On closer inspection, Cam saw the small round hole in the bottom pane of glass.

"Now how do you suppose that got there?" He asked aloud. He went back into the kitchen and checked the window from that side. He didn't see anything that would suggest anything had happened at the window, but he knew that perfectly round holes don't just appear in window panes. He decided to do a complete search of the house and he began finding small irregularities from the kitchen to the bedroom John was sleeping in. A vase out of place here, a figurine turned the wrong way there. As he searched he became certain that someone other than John had been in his house last night. So he decided to go to the den and contact his friend on the other side.

As he started concentrating on the bowl of water, Sephra appeared in the room with him. She looked at him with disgust. "All you had to do was watch him and keep him safe," she snarled. "Mortals are completely useless. All of you are a complete waste of space."

"Do you know where he is?" asked Cam.

"Of course I know where he is you idiot," she said. "I always know where he is."

"Then go get him." he cried.

"Not yet, I wish to see what they have in mind for him," she stated.

"And what if what they want is to see him dead?" he asked.

"I won't allow that to happen to him." She said. "His death belongs to me, and I will collect that debt."

As she was speaking Cam was thinking, "Yeah I've heard that before." He wouldn't dare say it out loud because he knew how unstable the demon was. So he just sat there and let her rant. After she finished, Cam decided to do as John had asked him to do. First, he powered up his protective shield and said. "You do know that the fool has fallen in love with you, don't you?"

She glared at him and the lights in the room started to dim.

"Hey, don't kill the messenger, I know how stupid it sounds but I made him a promise!" He yelled. Then he closed his eyes and braced himself for the strike he knew she was about to throw. And he waited, and he waited, but the strike never came. So he opened his eyes and was astonished to see that she was just standing there with a confused look on her face. The lights came back up to their normal brightness and she turned and walked over to the sofa and sat down. She sat there murmuring to herself; ever so often she would give her head a shake.

"I don't understand you mortals not one bit." She said, "I know that I am doing things the right way, but no-one is acting the way they should. He should be trying to get as far away from me as possible, yet he is sending me messages of love. I just don't get it." She looked up at Cam and said, "How can this be happening, you know how they are supposed to be responding to me, tell me what's going on."

Cam cleared his throat and said, "Really? Do you really want to know why they are responding the way they are to you?"

"Yes." She said.

"I think that if you want them to react to you the way you think they should, then you should let them see the *real* you. Not this mask you are wearing, but the real you in all your demonic glory. Have you looked in a mirror? You are probably the most beautiful thing any of us around here will ever see in our lifetimes. John was hooked on you after he saw you the second or third time. After all, he is just a mortal. He's only human." said Cam.

Sephra looked at Cam and said, "But this is not a mask you see before you, this is who I am. I have looked this way through all of my existence. I was there, stored in the back of Jo's mind, waiting to do her bidding. This is the way that she saw me in her minds-eye and this is what I developed into. I cannot change who I am. So you must be mistaken, this is *me* in all *my* demonic glory."

"Then I'm sorry, but it looks like you are going to have to kill John as he looks at you through the eyes of love," Cam said. "And it would truly take a demonic heart to be able to kill someone that is so in love with them. I've seen his face light up and listened to him talk about your laugh and your smile and how if it's the last thing in the world he does, he wants to hold you in his arms, just once, and then he says he would die happy."

*"That makes no sense!"* Sephra screamed. "I am going to kill him, and he knows that. How can you love your executioner? I exist for his destruction. You, you must convince him of this, so I can get on with my work."

"I have tried and I will try again, but I can make you no promises," said Cam.

"You will succeed in this, for I hold you responsible for educating him on this," Sephra said. "And so that you know that this was not a show of weakness on my part, I leave you with this." And every remaining mirror in the house exploded. Cam dropped down on the floor and covered his head as flying glass filled the air. When he looked up again she was gone.

"Wow! He said. "Now that was really weird. A demon, asking me how to be a demon, like I would know. John you have certainly changed the way I see things now. *Cam Suffour, councilor to the underworld!"* He shouted. "Well, at least my headache is gone." He got up and started sweeping up broken mirror pieces. It took him hours to clean it all up.

# 8

John woke up spewing soup and anything else that was in his stomach across the room. He was trying to get up to get to the bathroom, but he couldn't seem to move. His head was hammering away like a steam engine. Opening his eyes only made his head hurt worse. When the heaving stopped, he finally noticed his surroundings. Instead of lying in Cam's guest bedroom, he was sitting in a chair facing a very bright light. As he looked around he noticed that the walls looked strange. They looked like logs stacked on top of one another. And sitting to his right was a man he had never seen before.

"Who are you, and what's going on?" asked John.

Bert sat and watched John as he squirmed in the chair. He knew that he couldn't move very much because he had tied him in the chair himself. To Bert, John looked like any ordinary country hick, but the way he has been operating proved that he has the right connections and the brains to run an operation like he had in secret. No-one was even aware that he was part of an organization that supplied him with muscle when he needed it. It took pros to beat Cooter Cobb that badly. He knew that Cobb was no light-weight; he was quite capable of taking care of himself. It would have helped if Cobb had gotten a head-count of the people that put him in the hospital, that way he would know what to expect from John's camp. And now he would get the information straight from John's mouth.

"What's the name of the organization that you work for?" asked Bert.

"What?" asked John?

"Who are the people that put Cobb in the hospital?" Bert asked.

"Cooter? The hospital? What the hell are you talking about man?" John asked.

"Don't play dumb with me. I know you are smart because there is no way you accomplished all the things you have in the past few days if you were stupid, even with the help of your friends." Bert said. "Now tell me, what kind of trouble am I to expect when they come for you?" he asked.

"Who are you, and why do you have me tied to this chair?" John asked.

"Who I am is not important; who you are is all that matters here." said Bert.

"Look, I'm just a gardener and I work for a lot of people." John said. "Tell me who you need info on and I will tell you as soon as you untie me from this chair. I don't have anything to hide, and I'm definitely not dangerous enough to have to be tied up. I don't know what you are after, but believe me; you've got the wrong guy.

"Like hell the wrong guy, you've pissed off some mighty big hitters, and they want their shit back. Said Bert. "Now tell me what you took and where you stashed it so I can get on with my life."

John said, "You've been misled; I've taken nothing from anyone. And it's kind of hard to stash nothing. You need to go back to whoever hired you and tell them that I have nothing of theirs. You're on a wild goose chase. Now untie me and let me go. I have more important things to do than sit here chatting with you."

"You are a clever son-of-a-bitch; I have to give you that." said Bert. "If I didn't know better I would say that you just told me the truth. I've been in this business long enough to know when someone is lying to me. You really believe what you just told me don't you?"

"Not only do I believe it; it's the truth." said John. "I am not a thief and I don't steal things from the people that I work for. I wouldn't stay in business very long if I did that, now would I?"

Bert watched John carefully as he spoke and he could tell that he was indeed telling the truth. But he also knew that nobody is perfect, everyone has a flaw, and he would find John's before the day was over. Since he was going to kill him anyway he decided to tell him who hired him.

"Look Dr. Siddig hired me to get back what you took from him and he seems pretty sure that you took it." Bert told him. "So whatever it is, just give it back and this will be over."

A look of astonishment came over John's face and he said, "What? Dr. Siddig? Oh no, he has made a mistake, let's go talk to him right now and straighten this thing out before it gets more out of control. What in the world would I steal from his yard? And why would he hire you? He knows my number and where I live. Are you sure he sent you after me?

Damn he's good, thought Bert. Somebody give this boy an Oscar. Yet still it looked like he was telling the truth. The doctor never told him what was missing so he had to assume that it was something of value. Maybe, just maybe this guy didn't know what he was accused of taking. So he said, "Think back to the last time you did a job for the doctor, did you take something to the landfill thinking it was all trash? I don't know what it is but it's about to cost you your life. So think really hard and see if you can remember anything."

John said, "Let's go see him now and we can get this thing taken care of. What are you anyway, a hitman? And what did you do to my friend when you kidnapped me? Is he ok?"

"This is unbelievable, I just told you that this could cost you your life and you're worried about that old man." laughed Bert. "He's alright at this time, but I can't guarantee his future, because if he was part of this scheme of yours then he is just as dead as you are."

"What damn scheme!" John shouted. "I told you that there is nothing going on. I don't have a clue of what you're talking about. And do you have a BC powder or something to take the edge off this headache I can't think straight with my head pounding like this? What the hell did you give me anyway?"

Bert said, "A headache is the least of your worries." Then he got up and walked away. John didn't know that Bert was going to call the doctor and tell him that he had him and give the directions to the cabin. Somebody was going to give up the goods, or Bert was going to be the only person leaving the cabin after this was over.

# 9

Sephra leaned in the corner of the cabin and watched the interrogation as it progressed. She shook her head as the two idiots talked back and forth. Mortals were *so* stupid! When the one that thought he was in control of the situation left the room Sephra allowed John to see her. He jerked around and looked at her in fright. She believed that if he could have run away that he would have. Then to her dismay, she saw the fear drain away from his face and saw the dawning of admiration begin to appear. There was truly something wrong with this fool. For all he knew she could be here to kill him. The stupid look on his face began to anger her again. What was it going to take to get through to this fool? She raised her hand to strike him, but that didn't change the way he was looking at her. The perfect lamb to the slaughter, it made no sense at all. She lowered her arm and stood there looking at him. Then she reached out and laid her hand upon his cheek. Through her palm she felt him tremble and heard a little whimper escape from his lips. Suddenly she felt warmth spreading inside of her and she snatched her hand away from his face and staggered back a couple of steps.

"What is wrong with you mortal? Sephra asked.

"Thank you," said John. "I knew that your touch would be pure perfection and it was. You have just given me the only thing I have craved since I met you. I ask nothing more from you. You just made me the happiest man on earth and now I'm ready to die. I didn't mean to hit that lady with my truck, and if I could take it back I would but I can't, so if my life is forfeit then I accept that."

Something was wrong with her insides. It felt like a bunch of birds were fluttering around in there. She had never felt anything like this. When she tried to reach for her anger and hatred for this mortal, strangely, she found only a shadow of what once had been. When she thought of the rest of mankind her anger and hatred burst out in full bloom, but when she looked at him it dwindled almost to nothing. How can this be? She wondered. What is happening to me? She took another step back and vanished.

John was still floating on the high that her touch had caused. He knew without a doubt that if she had not moved her hand when she did that he would have had sticky semen soaking through his pants right now. Her touch was pure ecstasy just as he thought it would be. He felt like a young boy falling in love for the first time. It consumed his entire mind and body. Then it dawned on him that he was still alive. She hadn't flown into a rage like before. She left without hurting him at all. Was it possible that he was getting through to her at last?

Sephra slowly appeared sitting on the back porch of the little house beside the pond where she'd first tormented John. She didn't know why but this place helped her think. She was still clutching her stomach even though the fluttering had gone away. What had all of that been about? She really needed to know what was going on, but she had no-one to ask. She was here completely alone and she didn't have a clue how to fix this. She knew why she didn't kill him; the pain for her would be too great. She couldn't kill him until she found a way to shield herself from all of that pain. But even as she thought about killing him she noticed that the desire to do so wasn't there anymore. It's like it was some distant dream or a concept spoken aloud by someone else in a crowded room. She thought about Jo who was suffering in hell and realized that she felt very little for all the suffering she was going through because she consciously chose to do the things she did. But this mortal had been misused by another to bring about Jo's death, and now he had to die for it. Was that why she was feeling the things that she was towards him, was he going to be just another innocent victim? And to top it all, he claims to *love* her.

While she was with Jo she never encountered real love. She knew that Jo married Bob just to keep from being lonely, and then he turned out to be abusive so there never was much love in that marriage. So this thing she was going through with John was as foreign to her as anything she had ever known. So to ease her mind she decided to go pay Cooter Cobb a visit and mess up his day.

# 10

Cooter Cobb was laying back in a big plushy recliner watching TV when Sephra appeared in the room. He immediately tried to jump up and run when his broken ribs cried out in protest. He flopped back down in the chair and screamed, "Becky! Becky run! They've found me! Get away from here! Run! Run!"

Of course, Becky, being Becky, was not about to have someone chase her from her home. She ran to the pantry and grabbed the shotgun she kept there for just this sort of emergency. As she ran, she cocked the shotgun, (She always kept it loaded,) ready to unload on whoever it was that had broken into her home. When she got there she was shocked to find only a young girl standing in the room with Cooter. She aimed the gun at the girl and rushed to the window to see if she could see any of the help she must have brought with her. When she didn't see anyone or even a strange car in the yard, she turned to Cooter and asked, "Where are the rest of them? I don't see anybody in the yard, which way did they go?"

Cooter said, "I told you to run woman, what's wrong with you? Now put down that gun and get out of here!"

"Listen to him," said Sephra, "your life could depend on it. I have no quarrel with you, so go ahead and leave."

"Go to hell bitch," said Becky, "this is my damn house. If anybody is going to leave it's going to be you and your bunch. Leave now and maybe I won't beat the shit out of you."

Cooter sputtered and said, "Becky you need to get out of here now, these people play hardball. I won't have you getting hurt on account of me. Now get outta here!"

"No! Shouted Becky, "I won't leave you here in the shape you're in, you can hardly stand up. And I know you can't fight, not with broken ribs. So bring it on bitch, but you're gonna have to come through me first. You'll find that I can play hardball too."

Sephra stood there listening to Becky. She couldn't understand why anyone would risk their life for the likes of this mortal. So she asked, "So you are willing the die for this mortal? He is your mate?"

"What are you talking about?" asked Becky. "No, he's not my mate, he is my friend and I won't let you hurt him again. So leave now. Get out of my house."

While they were talking, Cooter managed to get up out of the chair. It hurt like crazy but he had to get Becky out of harm's way. He made his way over to Becky and gently took the gun away from her. Then he told her, "This is my fight. I won't let you fight it for me. I need you to go to the car and wait there for me. I'll be out in a few minutes. I guess I panicked when I saw her, but I think everything is going to be alright. Just let me talk to her alone."

Becky looked from Cooter to Sephra and back again. Then she asked, "Are you sure you're gonna be alright, what if some of her goons are still in the house?"

"No-one came here with me," said Sephra, "he is in no danger from me at this time. I only wish to speak with him."

"You just remember that I have my eyes on you," said Becky. Then she turned and walked out the front door. She walked over to her car, and leaned up against the front side panel, and waited.

Cooter turned to Sephra and said, "I don't know who or what you are, but thank you for not hurting her."

"I don't hurt women unless they get in the way of me doing my job." Sephra said. "All of you mortals are strange and unpredictable. When you should act one way, you start acting another way. It's confusing and frustrating. You, for instance, work for a man that you know holds you in total contempt, but you work for him never the less. You know that he intends to have you killed, yet you still work on his behalf. It makes no sense."

"I'll tell you what makes no sense," said Cooter, "and that is, *why* did you do this to me. You don't know me, and I've never done anything to you, but you did this to me. And now you tell me that you don't hurt women. Now that makes no sense. What exactly *do* you want to talk to me about anyway?"

"I need to know the reasoning behind this manhunt that's going on for John Cramer." Sephra said. "Tell me what he did to merit such drastic measures. Even now he is in the hands of a kidnapper. Right now he is tied up in a log shack and being interrogated by a thug that means to kill everyone involved including the one that hired him. Tell me what's going on."

"If I tell you will you leave me alone?" Cooter asked. "If it's gotten this fucked up I don't want anything more to do with it. I need to know that you know that I am out of this game."

"I believe you. You have my word," said Sephra. "Now tell me."

"All I know is that John does something extra for the doctor every now and then," said Cooter. "Whatever he did it made the doctor pretty mad. I guess John was stupid enough to steal some of it or something. And by what I heard in the hospital, dead or alive will work fine. I'd hate to be in John's shoes right now."

"Thank you," said Sephra, "if you like I can help you with some of the pain you're going through, but you must trust me." She walked towards Cooter and he back away from her out of fear. "You must trust me," she said. Cooter stood still while she put her hands over his broken ribs. He felt a hot burning sensation and then the pain was almost gone. He stood there with wide eyes as Sephra simply vanish. Now he felt dizzy and very hungry. He called Becky back in the house hoping she had some more food he could eat.

When Becky entered the house she looked around for the woman but she was nowhere to be found. "Where'd she go?" she asked.

"Out the back door," Cooter lied.

"Well, what did she want to talk to you about?" Becky asked.

"She wanted to know some stuff about John." He said.

"But I thought she was working with him." She said.

"I know, I don't know what is wrong with her, I told you that I don't think she is too bright." Cooter said.

"I wonder how she found us out here. I mean, it's not like I live on main street USA. She must have one heck of an organization if she can get info that fast." She said.

Cooter said, "I told you that John was keeping a lot of secrets from everybody. The doctor didn't even know he was this well connected. Whoever they are, they must have some deep pockets." Cooter was glad that it hadn't come out that it was the girl that had broken him up. He didn't know if he would be able to live it down if it ever got out.

"Do you need another pill, or are you hungry again? She asked.

"Yes, I'm starving," said Cooter, "bring me everything but the kitchen sink."

"How about the pill?" she asked.

"Not right now, I guess it's the adrenalin rush that has me all pumped up, but I'm not hurting too bad right now." He said. He stretched out on the bed and wondered what in the world had he gotten himself into. It felt like the girl had made his ribs stop hurting. For some reason, he couldn't wrap his mind around disappearing people and instant bone healing. He felt like trying to figure it out could drive a man crazy. He decided that now was the time to go to Atlantic City for a few days. He had fifty thousand dollars to spend, and he knew that Becky would be glad to help him spend it.

# 11

John was wondering how long he was going to have to sit tied to this chair when Bert came back in the room. "What now?" asked John?

"Now I have to rough you up a little so the doctor will know that I did my job." said Bert. "It won't take long but it's gonna hurt like hell." Then he drew back his arm and punched John in the mouth. The punch was solid and it knocked John and the chair over backward. He walked slowly around behind John and raised the chair back up. He walked back around in front of John and grabbed him by the chin. He looked at his mouth and said, "Not bad, but I need a few more bruises and a lot more blood." Still holding John's chin, he backhanded him, again a good solid blow. But this time John didn't fall over because Bert was still holding his chin. This went on for maybe twenty minutes, and then they heard a car drive up. It was Dr. Siddig. By this time, John was pretty much punched out. He was bruised, swollen, and bloody from the workout Bert had given him.

As Dr. Siddig walked into the house, he paused when he saw how badly John had been beaten up. "What in the world did you do to him?" he asked. "Did he tell you anything? What has he said?"

"Not a damn thing, he keeps saying that he hasn't stolen anything from you." said Bert.

'Alright John," said Dr. Siddig, "I know you haven't tried to sell any of it, so where did you stash it? I know you have my drugs, so just tell me where it is and this will all be over."

Through swollen lips, John said, "My money, my drugs. I haven't stolen anything from you and you know it. You're just greedy and want everything you can get your hands on. But those drugs belong to me. I saved up the money for this deal so I can get away from working for the likes of you. And you can't have it. I'll die before I give you what I earned on my own. So do your worse."

Bert looked from John to the doctor, and said, "I knew he was telling me the truth, I just didn't know the whole story. He didn't steal anything from you, did he?"

Dr. Siddig said, "That's none of your concern. You were hired to do a job, you've done it, now back off." Then he turned back to John and said, "Where is it? Where is my shipment? You know you're going to tell me, so tell me before I have this man start breaking your bones. I think we'll start with your toes."

"Break away then," said John, "hope you enjoy yourself because it's all you'll get from me. Those drugs were paid for with the money I earned from you over the last seven years. The money is mine, and the drugs are mine. Get used to it, you can't have my drugs."

Dr. Siddig looked to Bert and told him to start breaking, but Bert said, "We both know that this man is innocent of what you accused him of, so my price just tripled. I'll break him up when *my* money is in my account."

"Very well then!" shouted Dr. Siddig. I'll pay what you ask as soon as I know where the drugs are. Now get to work." Bert went out to his truck to get the hammer, pliers, and the wooden block that he always keeps in the back of his truck, and headed back to the house. He had no idea that his life was about to change forever.

Sephra leaned against the wall and watched as Bert beat and kicked John. She knew how much it hurt John because she felt every blow. As the beating proceeded she kept trying different techniques to separate herself from the pain. Nothing worked. She *had* to find a way to separate herself from this mortal. Her plans for his future dictates that she be able to do the things that made his life almost unbearable. He'd already told her to kill him, but that kind of death would be too easy for him. He had to suffer for the death of Josephine. He could not be allowed to leave this world until he begged for death and she had the chance to deny it from him, multiple times.

Just as Bert reentered the house Sephra let herself be seen. "I cannot allow you to go any further with this because I feel that it will lead to his death." said Sephra.

Dr. Siddig almost jumped out of his skin. He jerked around and yelled, "Who the hell are you?"

Sephra looked at him and said, "He belongs to me, his death is mine and mine alone. Leave now."

Bert had backed against the door and was looking at her wide-eyed. "Doc I think that maybe we should listen to the lady and leave. My instincts tell me that she is trouble." He said.

"Trouble my ass," said the doctor, "You do as you are told." And he walked over to Sephra and grabbed her arm to shove her out of the door. And that's when his world reverted back to childhood because Sephra beat him like he was hers. First, she broke the arm of the hand that grabbed her, and before he could even start screaming, she broke the other one. And as he turned to try to run away, finally getting around to the screaming, she broke his left leg once, twice, three times. As he fell to the floor, he reclaimed the air that he had expended in the first scream, and started on a new set. And as he screamed, Sephra took her own dear time to slowly eviscerate him. Although completely eviscerated it still took a little time for his screams to completely die away.

Bert, frozen by the pure brutality of the attack, hesitated for just a moment before he flew into action. By the time he regained himself enough to act, the doctor was dead. She had totally destroyed him in less than 15 seconds. Bert knew that if he didn't take her out immediately that he was going to be next. So he drew his knife and threw it at her throat, and at the same time he drew both of his 9mm pistols and began firing. The bullets reached her before the knife, and that's the reason it missed her throat and entered her shoulder. As she jerked from the impact of the bullets, she reached up and pulled the knife from her shoulder. And as Bert continued to fire, she started walking towards him, jerking, every time a bullet hit home.

Bert realized that the woman couldn't be human, and he turned and ran out of the house. As he ran, he kept looking over his shoulder to see if she was following him. To his relief, he made it to his truck. He jumped in and started it up. He stomped the accelerator to the floor, and as he began backing out of the yard, the woman appeared in the truck with him. Without missing a beat, Bert opened the door and jumped out, being narrowly missed by the front tire as it rolled by. Bert rolled away from the truck, and jumped up, and ran towards the tree-line. He figured that if he made it to the woods he would be safe. When he was about 50 feet from the trees, the woman walked out of the woods in front of him. Skidding to a stop, he turned and ran for the highway, hoping that someone would be passing by and would stop to lend a hand. He was almost to the road when she appeared, just appeared, directly in front of him. He slammed into her at top speed, and simply bounced off.

As he got back on his feet, he assumed his martial arts stance, and began delivering nerve punches, and using his hands, elbow, knees, and feet to deliver the worst ass whipping he had ever given. And to his surprise, she just stood there and took it. She didn't flinch or try to avoid any of his punches. She just stood there looking at him. And when he started feeling stupid, he turned and began running again. He saw that his truck had backed into the ditch, so he ran to it and got his shotgun out from behind the seat. It was loaded with double buckshot shells. This baby will stop anything. He dropped and fired twice at almost point-blank range. And as he knew it would, it stopped her. She didn't fall or anything, but she stopped.

Bert yelled, "What the hell are you? Is that guy in there John Connor, and are you a terminator or something? Why won't you die?" He could tell that he had hit her multiple times because her top was blown to shreds, and it looked like the only thing holding it up were her two magnificent breasts and the stickiness from Dr. Siddig's blood. They were poking out of the top like two mountain tops. They looked so great that for a moment his libido jumped up a couple of notches, but his fear beat it back down.

Then he yelled, "Hey, if you want that guy in there, take him, I mean it, take him. I don't want to have anything more to do with him. I'm through with all of this. I mean it. Since you killed the Doc I'm no longer getting paid anyway, my contract is now null and void, just let me go. Please!"

And for some reason Sephra decided to let him go. As she turned to go, he stepped up behind her and placed the barrel of the shotgun against the top of her spine, and pulled the trigger. The gun kicked back against his shoulder and knocked him to the ground. And before he could get up, he yelled, "No", as Sephra turned and reached down and ripped out his heart. "Stupid mortal," said Sephra. Then she went into the house to release John.

John witnessed everything that happened in the house, he was amazed at the brutality of the woman, and at the resilience of her body. He watched as the blade plunged into her shoulder, and then watched as she just pulled it out. And the bullets acted more like paintballs than actual lead, she never even cried out as they hit her. She was an amazing woman. As he watched, he forgot all about his pain, and the stench coming from the mutilated body of Dr. Siddig. As the battle moved outside, he listened to the sounds. It sounded like there was a lot of running, then after a little while he heard what sounded like a shotgun, two blasts close together. Then he heard the man yelling something. And then a single shotgun blast, then a single yell, and then everything grew quiet.

As Sephra entered the house, John looked at her through his swollen eyes and said, "You are absolutely amazing. There is no way there is anyone else anywhere that is as amazing as you. You just keep enriching my life experience every time I see you. Is that man alright?"

"He lied and broke a promise, he is no more." She said. As she bent down to untie his feet, John couldn't keep his eyes off of her exposed breast. They were the most perfect things he had ever seen in his whole life. When she finished untying his legs she stood up and noticed where he was looking. She just shook her head and thought, "Stupid mortal." After she untied his hands, she picked him up like he weighed nothing at all, and poof they were in Cam's den again.

## 12

Cam leaped up from his sofa when they appeared in the room. Then he yelled, "What have you done to him this time? I don't know if I can fix this. What did you do throw him in front of a truck?" He was stunned when he saw how she was covered in blood and other unidentifiable things. She carried herself like this was an ordinary occurrence, something she was accustomed to.

"Silence fool," said Sephra, "I did not do this to him. Another mortal did this. You mortals are so destructive to everything and to yourselves; I don't see how you've survived this long. Now I will do what I can to fix this, but I will need you to tend to him until he is healed."

Cam said, "And if I say no?"

She looked at him and said, "Don't try me human."

Cam swallowed and told her to put him on the bed. He watched her as she did that thing she had done when she healed him the last time. Then she turned to Cam and said, "Tend to him until I return." Then she vanished. Cam saw that John was already looking better than he had a moment ago. He wished he could learn that trick.

Cam walked over to John and that's when the smell hit him. "Good God!" he yelled. "Where did they have you, in a slaughterhouse?"

John just shook his head and said, "I think what you smell is the remains of our good doctor Siddig. She pretty much turned him into sausage right before my eyes. He made the mistake of touching her. I don't think she likes to be touched. So whatever you do, don't put your hands on her."

"So that's the reason she looked like she'd been in a zombie movie. Do you think you can make it to the bathroom to clean up, or am I going to have to wash the stink off of you myself?"

"I got this. You know, I should be in shock right now after what I just witnessed, but I don't feel hardly anything."

"You *are* in shock son; just give it a little time to sink in. It will probably hit you about the same time the pain returns. If you are hurt as badly as it looks like you are, you are in for a world of hurt. She must know how to dull your pain, because from the way you look you shouldn't even be able to carry on a conversation, much less walk."

John slowly got up from the bed, and gingerly walked to the bathroom. As he entered the bathroom, he glanced over at the mirror and almost fainted. His face was a swollen mess, everything was swollen. If he didn't know who he was, he wouldn't have recognized himself. He had been aware of the beating he had gotten and it had hurt like hell, but he had seen corpses that looked better than he looked right now. As he stood there looking at himself Cam tapped lightly on the door and brought in an armload of towels and washcloths.

"You can use as many of these as you need because I'm probably going to have to throw them all away. I doubt if I'll be able to get the stink out of them. You get cleaned up and I'll fix us something to eat. If you think you can hold it down. Then you can tell me what happened and how they got you out of the house without waking me up." He said.

John took a long hot shower, scrubbing himself as firmly as he could stand. The hot water had brought a lot of the pain back, never the less, he stayed in the shower until the hot water ran out. After drying off, he wrapped a dry towel around his waist and stepped out of the bathroom. When he did, the first thing he saw was the overnight bag he had packed for himself when he had stopped by home to get the rest of his money. He'd been going through so much lately that he had forgotten the money he had placed in the false bottom of the bag. A twinge of apprehension caused an increase of blood flow, and the pain intensified all through his body. As he doubled over in pain, he realized that he couldn't start mistrusting Cam now. Not after all Cam had helped him through. The apprehension was replaced by shame as he picked up the bag and placed it on the bed.

After he got dressed, he checked the money in the bottom of the bag anyway. Then he joined Cam in the kitchen and sat down at the table. He watched Cam as he dished out the food, which consisted of grits, bacon, and eggs. It was strange eating breakfast this late in the day, but it was delicious. John felt like it was the best bacon, eggs, and grits he'd ever had in his entire life. After he knocked the edge off of his hunger, he began telling Cam all he could remember from the time he woke up tied to the chair until Sephra brought him back here.

Cam sat there amazed as John recounted his tale of pain and suffering. He decided to let John finish his story before asking any questions. There were times through the story that he had to bite his tongue to keep from speaking. As John was finishing up, Cam could understand the motives of the doctor and his hired muscle, but he couldn't seem to wrap his mind around the motivations of the demon. What game was she playing? She had made it clear that she was here to kill John for accidentally running down her master, but her actions seemed to indicate a different agenda altogether. It seemed to Cam that she was playing a cat and mouse game with John, one minute she's trying to kill him and the next, she's standing in his home healing him. Basically preventing his death, it made no sense to Cam. Why not go ahead and get it over with? Cam was beginning to think that maybe John's stupid crush on the demon was beginning to get through to her. Was she slowly changing her mind? Was she losing her resolve?

# 13

Lying across the bed, Jimmy was relaxing watching a porno flick when the phone rang. He answered it thinking it was Bert calling to tell him that the job was done and he could break camp and go home. Instead, it was a hysterical Cyn yelling about something on the news. He sat up in the bed and said, "Now hold on Cyn, I can't understand a word you're saying."

"I think Bert is dead," cried Cyn, "there's a news report about some murders out at the log cabin. Bert's truck is in the ditch and they are saying that they found two mutilated bodies out there. I think we need to go see if Bert is all right."

"Bert can take care of himself," Jimmy exclaimed. "He's one tough son of a bitch. I saw the guy he was hunting, and trust me, that asshole couldn't hold a candle to Bert. Bert probably had to get rough with him and he probably died on him. You just wait and see, in a few days Bert will be contacting us about another job."

"I hope you are right Jimmy," she said. "But I don't see Bert leaving his truck there for the cops to connect him to the crime scene. It just doesn't add up for me, so if we haven't heard from him in a few days, humor me, and let's go find him. Ok?"

"All right, all right." he said. "I'll see you in a few days, and we'll go have a drink with Bert, and you'll see that he is all right."

"Thanks," she said. She hung up the phone and watched the rest of the news to see if they would tell any more about the bodies found out at the cabin. Bert was at best, a solitary man, but he was always true to his word and true to his friends. If anything has happened to him someone was going to pay. As the end of the newscast came and went, she was making her list of the equipment she would need to facilitate a rescue operation or a get-even campaign. Either way, she was going to be prepared.

Jimmy sat on the bed flipping through the local channels trying to see if he could catch anything about the happenings at the cabin. When he could find nothing, he got out his laptop and powered it up. He went to his browser and typed in the name of one of the local TV news stations and typed in the search word "mutilations" and got well over million hits. When he found the one he was looking for, he clicked on it and watched the news story firsthand.

In the clip, the news reporter said, *"In what appears to be the most gruesome murder case ever to happen here in rural Johnston County, the authorities tell us that they were notified by a passing motorist that an accident had occurred here this morning. Upon arriving at the scene they told us that they found one body beside a vehicle that had apparently backed into and gotten stuck in the ditch. According to our source; the first victim had severe chest cavity damage, it looked like something had pierced the chest cavity and caused a lot of internal damage. Our source seems to think that the victim died immediately. And as for the second victim, our source tells us that the only way they are going to be able to identify him is through dental records. They don't know what happened to him. But I can tell you this, while we have been here, multiple people from the police departments and rescue squads have been seen running from the premises white-faced and throwing up as they ran. We have reported on some pretty bad accidents, but this is the first time I have personally witnessed this kind of reaction from such a well-trained and seasoned staff. At this time the authorities are with-holding all information about the victims until the next of kin can be notified. We will keep you updated as we learn more. Tracy Johnson reporting for WRAL Channel 5 Eyewitness News."*

Jimmy began to think about some of the things that Cyn had said. She was right about the fact that Bert wouldn't leave his truck at the scene of a crime. As he shut down his laptop and put it back in his suitcase, he began formulating a plan to go see what really happened out at the cabin.

He decided that he would drive out that way and see what he could see. As he drove, he started thinking about all the money he had made with Bert since leaving the military. With the skill-set he learned in the military he was well suited for the kind of jobs Bert contracted him for. He could enter a building without making a sound or he could take out a whole wall if that was what was needed to get the job done. He is the best, and everyone in the business knows it. As he came to an intersection about a mile from the cabin, he ran into a roadblock. There was a police car parked diagonally across the road and a young uniformed police officer was redirecting traffic and giving directions on how to go around a short detour to get to the other side of the incident. He told Jimmy that no one was allowed back in there yet, and he said he didn't think the road would be open again until way over in the night.

"Officer," said Jimmy, "that cabin I saw on the news belongs to a friend of mine, do you think you could let me go in there and see if I can identify either one of the bodies? I sure hope that my buddy isn't one of the dead. I think your superiors would like to know the identity of those poor bastards as soon as possible. I really might be some help to them if they let me."

Young officer Perry was just fresh out of the academy. He'd joined this police force three months ago and was still learning the ropes. So he told Jimmy to wait right here and let him speak to his Captain about it. He went to his cruiser and raised his boss on the radio. He explained about who Jimmy was and asked if he wanted him to send him on through. His superior said, "Negative, we don't need help identifying these men, they both had their wallets on them. We know who they are. Now get back to your post and keep those lookie-loos out of here!"

"Roger that," said Officer Perry. He turned to get out of the car and almost bumped into Jimmy. "Sir, I need you to get back in your vehicle and turn around and leave. They don't need your help."

"I heard that," said Jimmy. "They know who the people are; they just aren't going to tell anybody. I understand that, but I'll give you a hundred dollars right now if you will find out their names for me. It's very important to me to know that my friend is all right."

"Sir," said Officer Perry, "I'm not going to tell you again. You need to get in your car and leave *now!*" The reprimand from his Captain had caught the young officer by surprise. That was the first time anything like that had ever happened to him since putting on the uniform. And he never wanted it to happen again. His anger was evident on his face, so Jimmy held up both hands and backed away. And per instructions, he got in his car and left. Officer Perry had made up his mind that nothing was going to make him get on that radio again until this thing was over.

"What if Cyn was right," he thought as he drove back to Benson and his hotel room. Bert had told him that John seemed to have a lot of powerful friends around here, could someone have done the impossible and got a jump on Bert? Nah, Bert was a fine-tuned killing machine; there was no way these country bumpkins had the skill to do that. Not without more bodies on the scene. There was no way they got Bert and he didn't get even one shot off, no way.

Sheriff Mitch Bennett believed that he had seen everything in the twenty years he had served on the force. But this case was beginning to make him reconsider the advice his wife, Mary, had been giving him for the last six months. Retire and let the young men worry about all those sickos that keep coming out of the woodwork. He was sure that he had thrown up his breakfast, supper from last night, and lunch from yesterday. He felt like he had nothing more to bring up. He had gagged so hard that his stomach was still sore. He watched as the forensic team literally scooped up what remained of the good Dr. Siddig from the cabin floor. He wondered what kind of sadistic bastard could do this to another human being. I mean, how dead can a person be? He was sure that Siddig was dead long before he arrived at the condition he was in now. But it looked like the killer had kept on hacking on him just for the hell of it. And that guy out by the road, all the plumbing that ran to his heart looked like the heart had just been yanked out. How the hell do you yank somebody's heart out? And why? And where in the world is the heart. Did whoever did this take it with them for a souvenir? What are they going to do with it, mount it or God forbid, eat it? There are, without a shadow of a doubt, some sick people in this world.

Captain Bennett had watched, over the years, as young aspiring officers in the sheriff's office and the SBI had started investigations on Dr. Siddig only to be turned aside by their higher-ups, or their files disappearing or their witnesses mysteriously contracting amnesia. It seems that most in law enforcement knew that there was something fishy about him, but no one could ever prove it. Now it appeared that whatever he was involved in finally caught up with him. But the Captain still felt sorry for both of them, because no one deserved to die like this. And the thing that bothered the Captain the most was the fact that the killer was still out there somewhere, and no one has a clue of who it is.

# 14

Sephra sat on the porch of the little house by the pond. She sat there with her legs hanging over the side. And she was swinging them back and forth. She was still hurting from the beating that John had taken, but it was getting easier to bear. The pain wasn't what had her sitting here like this. What had her sitting here was her own actions over the last eighteen hours or so. She couldn't understand why she was going around healing people, and what was up with the caress she had given John in the log cabin? Why had she touched him like that? And what was that strange feeling she felt in her stomach as she touched him? And what happened to all the hatred she had felt toward John after he had killed Josephine? How can she possibly tolerate being in his presence? Killing him is the most important thing in her existence, and yet she keeps bringing him back from the edge of death. She didn't understand what was going on, and she had no one to talk to. There is no hotline for demons in distress. She knew that she couldn't ask the All-Father because his Son would probably destroy her on sight because she knew that her kind had lost all privileges in The Fall during the age before this one. She envied mankind for the relationship they have with the All-Father and his Son. It amazed her how many humans never take advantage of that relationship. And there was no way she was going to involve her boss in this. He would probably take over the whole thing and kill her and John in one stroke. So that left her on her own.

# CHAPTER 5

## 1

"Hey Cam!" shouted John, "come listen to this! That's the cabin they took me to this morning. I don't know who that guy was that had me tied up, but I think Sephra must have really done a job on him too."

Together, they watched the newscast and heard as much information as they could give. But John had already given a better account of what went on out there. John hadn't seen what Sephra had done to the man outside but it sounded like he had put up a good fight.

"So, are you feeling better?" asked Cam.

"Yeah, I still look like shit, but I'm actually doing pretty good."

"Are you hungry again?"

"Sure I could eat. Maybe not as much as you brought me earlier but I could eat."

"Do you need anything for the pain? It's been a while since you had anything.

"Nah, just the food, I feel like I'm mending pretty good."

"So tell me," said Cam. "What have you decided to do about your demon problem? You know that she's not going away. Her only purpose is to cause your death. I don't think you should forget that."

"Oh, I haven't forgotten. I know my lifeline probably looks pretty short right now, but I really don't care. When she put her hand on my cheek, I thought I could see compassion in her eyes. For a moment I thought she might actually kiss me. It was just for a second, but I know what I saw."

Cam sat there and watched the stupid grin slowly spread over John's face. All he could do was shake his head and think about how dumb love can make you. Love can make you do some of the stupidest things. Then he got up and went to fix John something to eat.

# 2

On the six o'clock news they told the names of the dead men out at the cabin. Jimmy sat at the foot of the bed watching the news with a heavy heart. Before the story finished, the phone rang. Jimmy fell back on the bed and picked up the receiver from the nightstand. "Hello?" he said.

"Did you watch the news?" asked Cyn.

"Yeah I watched it."

"You do realize that we've got to fix this. I don't know who this dude is that he picked up, but we have to leave a message to everybody out there that think they can get away with something like this. We've got to put that bastard in the ground. And I mean *now*! With Bert gone, it's up to us." Said Cyn.

Jimmy thought for a minute and said, "Ok, let's get together and put something together. I don't know where he lives, but I do know where we picked him up from. I'm sure the old man that lives there must know where he lives. See you in a bit."

"Ok," said Cyn. After she hung up she went out to the barn and started putting together the equipment they would need to give somebody a bad day. While she was in the barn, her brother Vernon drove around the house to the barn. When he got out of the truck, he walked around the back of the truck and got out two green ammo cans, with a thousand 9mm rounds in each can. In the back of his truck he had ammo cans with 308 and 30.06 rounds in them also. As he walked into the barn, he said, "I don't know how many rounds you're gonna need to send down range, but I got enough to overthrow a small country. I heard on the radio that they identified Bert as one of the dead men out at the cabin. I figured you would want to go ahead and even the score as soon as possible. What else do you need? Tell me and I'll have it here by sundown."

"I have all I need." said Cyn. "If I understand it correctly this guy is just well connected. I'm going to cut off his connections and show him what the real world looks like. When I finish with him, he'll wish he were never born. Then I'll kill him." Then she turned and walked into what used to be the tack room. At the back wall under the desk was a trapdoor. She slid the desk out of the way and opened the trapdoor. She descended the little ladder and turned on the light. Arrayed around the walls were a whole lot of guns, guns of every make and model. One wall held handguns, another held assault rifles, another held shotguns, some legal and others not so legal, and the last one held knives of all categories. And propped up in one or two corners were RPGs. Standing in this room made Cyn a very dangerous woman. She feared no man, and truth be told, she felt that there were very few men that she couldn't handle in hand-to-hand combat.

After choosing which items she would use in the assault, she climbed up out of the cellar to find Jimmy standing there talking to Vernon. As they talked Jimmy was looking over the duffel bag filled with guns and ammo that Cyn had prepared for him. He glanced up at her and smiled, saying, "You always did know how to pack for a party. I can do a lot of damage with the contents of this bag."

"You bet your sweet ass," replied Cyn. "When we walk away from that bastard, he's going to look just like Bert looked. I'm going to personally cut his heart out and feed it to Vernon's dogs."

"We're going to have to question the old man at that house where we picked him up from last night. Bert had me knock out everybody in the house because he thought the old guy was Special Forces or something. He just looked like an old man to me. But be careful around him, he could have some skills."

"I've got that old fart's skill right here," said Cyn, brandishing a KA-BAR. "We will get the information out of him, I guarantee it. Just get me to him, he'll talk."

Within the next twenty minutes they had the truck loaded and were heading out to Cam's house. This time it would be a frontal assault instead of a sneak attack. The trip to Cam's house was quiet, because each of them was preparing their minds for the violence ahead. Jimmy drove right up to Cam's front door and gave his horn a light tap.

Before Cam went to the front door to see who was out there, he went to check on John. John was sleeping like a baby. When Cam opened the door, he found a couple, and man and a woman, standing on his front porch. The moment he saw them, the hairs on the back of his neck stood up. His senses started sending out warning signals, and before he could react, the man stepped up to the door and shoved the door hard enough to cause Cam to stagger back into the center of the room.

Cam shouted, "What do you think you are doing? Why are you barging into my home like this? What's wrong with you?"

"Shut up old man and sit down, said Jimmy. "All we want from you is some information about that fellow we took out of here this morning and we will leave you alone."

"John?" asked Cam. "Why in the world are you looking for John here, didn't you just say you took him away from here this morning, it doesn't look like you brought him back, so I suggest that you look for him wherever you left him. Now get out of my house before I call the police."

"Not before you tell us where he lives old man," said Cyn.

"How should I know, he came to see me. And I didn't ask him where he lived." Said Cam. "It's not like we are friends or anything, he was just another client."

"The organization the two of you are in killed my friend and gutted him like an animal," said Jimmy. "You're gonna tell me where they took him after they killed Bert. I know that you know, so don't lie to me, or I'll gut you where you stand."

"What are you talking about? What organization?" asked Cam? "You people are working off of some wrong assumptions. Number one; I am not affiliated with any organization, two, I am not in anything with John. I'm just here trying to help out someone need. That's all. You need to go update your info, because you have your wires crossed."

"I don't think so," said Cyn. "And I think I'm going to enjoy getting the truth out of you. So sit down and let's get started."

"I'm going to ask you good folks to move on one more time, and then I'm going to have to get ugly." said Cam. "Leave now!"

Cyn started to laugh when the door to the next room opened. And out walk the sorriest sight she had ever seen. It looked like the guy had been beaten with a two-by-four, twice. Cyn looked at Jimmy and saw the look of recognition on his face. She asked, "Is this him, is this the one that killed Bert?"

"He's the one that we took from here, but he looked a hell of a lot better than he does now. What the hell happened to you mister," asked Jimmy.

"I guess this is what happens to a man when he gets kidnapped from his bed in the middle of the night," said John. "What I want to know is why you and your friends would think that I was important enough to be taken and severely beaten. If you can tell me that, then maybe all of us will know."

Cyn walked over to John and said, "Why don't you sit your ass down and tell us what you did to our friend."

"What I did to your friend?" asked John. "Does it look to you like I had any say so about what went on in that cabin? I woke up tied to a chair and that's where I stayed the whole while I was in that hell-hole. I had to sit there and watch what happened to the doctor, and trust me that is something that I'll never forget for the rest of my life. I can tell you this; you people have some dangerous enemies. I guess they didn't kill me because I was already almost dead. I guess they figured I'd die soon enough on my own."

"You're telling me that you didn't have anything to do with killing Bert? Asked Jimmy. "Then how did you get here, did you walk?" Then he looked at Cam and asked, "Who brought him here? Or are you the one that did all that damage? Bert told me that you were some kind of super soldier or something."

"What?" exclaimed Cam? "I was never in the military. The only time I've ever picked up a gun was to shoot a stray dog. Your man lied to you. Super soldier, hah! I think that maybe some of the things you've done to people over the years just finally caught up with you. If I were you two, I'd hit the road running and not look back."

"Bull-shit!" shouted Cyn. "Both of you know who killed Bert and I'm not leaving until I know the truth!" She walked over to Cam and said, "You know old man, now talk!"

"You won't believe me if I told you," said Cam.

"Try me."

"Ok, it was a demon."

"Do I look stupid to you old man? Don't make me hurt you."

"I told you that you wouldn't believe me," said Cam.

Cyn drew back her hand to strike Cam, but found that she couldn't move her arm any farther. She tried and tried, but she couldn't bring her arm down. Cam stood up and took her by her shoulders and turned her around. With a gentle push he started walking her to the door. To her surprise her legs worked just fine. He walked her right past Jimmy, who was standing there with a startled look on his face, and then she realized that he couldn't move either. Cam walked her out the front door over to the truck and left her standing there. All she could do was stand there with her arm still raised; she couldn't bring her arm down. It wouldn't move an inch. She watched Cam walk Jimmy out of the house and make him walk to the truck.

Cam positioned Jimmy next to the driver's side door, and then turned and walked back to the porch. When he reached the porch he turned and said, "You two idiots have no idea what you have walked into here. This situation is way over your heads. If you are smart, you will get in your truck and go home. If you choose to come here again, I can't guarantee that you will survive. *Don't come back!*"

Cyn's arm dropped and she could control herself again. She looked over at Jimmy and saw that he was just standing there. "What the hell just happened?" she asked.

"Damn if I know," said Jimmy, "but I think we need to regroup. That was some weird shit that went on in there. I was stuck to the floor; I couldn't even raise my arms. Who is that old man? How could he do something like that to us?"

"I feel violated," said Cyn. "Nobody should be able to take over someone's body like that. I feel dirty, I need a shower. Take me home."

They got in the truck and Jimmy slowly backed out of the yard, because he wasn't sure he was fully in control of himself. After about a mile he finally sped up to the speed limit. They didn't talk anymore until they reached Vernon's house. They both headed for the liquor cabinet as soon as they were inside. After they both had downed the first drink, they both got a refill and walked over to the couch. Neither one wanted to be the first one to start talking.

Vernon watched them when they came inside the house. Then he said, "Well, *now* I've seen everything. Did you mess the guy up so badly that it has upset you? Sis did you go *too* far?" They sat there and said nothing. "Come on guys," said Vernon, "you guys are scaring me. What happened?"

"We didn't touch the guy," said Cyn, "it looks like Bert beat the shit out of the guy, but he was back at the house where Jimmy helped Bert kidnap him. We don't know who brought him back there, and we couldn't get any info from either one of them."

"What? What happened? asked Vernon, "you mean to tell me that an old man and a man already badly beaten out maneuvered the two of you? No way!"

"You had to have been there," said Jimmy. "We just got handed our asses and they didn't even break a sweat. We walked in there unprepared. We had no idea that they had that much power. The old man is a witch or something; he took over our bodies and just walked us out the door. Things like that are not supposed to happen in this day and age." As he was talking, Cyn got up and went to the bathroom. After a little while, they heard the shower start up.

"Now that *is* weird," said Vernon, "I've never seen my sister stymied by anything. When we were kids, she was always on top of the situation. Nothing ever *"got her goat "*, actually she's always sort of been my hero. To see her like this is scary. A witch? We both know that there is no such thing."

"Like I said," said Jimmy, "you had to have been there to believe the shit we've just seen."

As he talked, Jimmy got up and got himself another drink. He was slowly beginning to regain control of himself. Then he had a silly thought, *"now is the time to call in Bert, he would know how to handle this."* But Bert was gone. Now he would have to be the boss. With that thought he started smiling. That is until Cyn returned to the room. She was freshly showered and dressed to go to war. She stopped in the middle of the room and looked at Jimmy and Vernon, then she said, "Alright boys, saddle up! We're going to kick some ass!" They all walked out to the barn and started planning their assault.

# 3

John was standing at the front door watching Cam as he gave the man and woman instructions not to come back. As he watched, he asked himself who or what is Cam Suffour? Who had he come to and asked for help? First he found out, the hard way, that demons are real, and now he just watched someone take complete control over two people's bodies and lead them around like sheep. Where was all of this going to end? How can a person wrap their mind around the fact that he now knows a woman or creature that can teleport him from one place to another in the blink of an eye? And to top it all off, he was at this time hopelessly in love with that very creature. He felt that he was getting pretty close to losing his mind, or had he already lost it and was not aware of the fact? When Cam turned to come back inside, John walked back over to the sofa and sat down. He felt that he had to have some answers before his head exploded.

When Cam was back inside, John asked, "How in the world did you do that?"

"I don't really know," answered Cam, "all I know is that when she went to strike me, in my mind I yelled, *"Freeze!"* and that's what happened! Then I just winged it from there. I've been going through a lot of changes since you walked into my life Mr. Cramer. I have met a demon that seems to be bipolar, my friendly spirit that has helped me for years has taken me to a place more beautiful than all creation and taught me that there is a reservoir of power that I can tap into to give me more power than I ever dreamed of, I am learning that I can facilitate healing just by having the desire to do so! I need a vacation just to have time to sort all of this out before I lose my mind!"

John sat and listened to him rant. When he finished John asked, "Do you need a drink? I know I do. You know, watching the demon do the things that she does is easier to digest than seeing that thing you just did to those people. That was just scary; no one should be able to do that. Do you realize that you could have told them to kill themselves and they probably would have done it without protest? Please tell me that you've never done that to me." John got up and walked over to Cam's liquor cabinet to get that drink.

"I told you," said Cam, "that I had no idea that I could do that. It just happened. My friendly spirit told me that I have gained enough power to help you fight your demon, but he never said I could do stuff like this. I mean, think of all the good I can do in the world with abilities like this. The possibilities seem endless."

John hated to burst his bubble, but he felt like he had better help him slow his roll before he talked himself into a world of trouble, so he said, "Whoa Cam, think about what you are saying. If the world ever finds out what you can do, they will either want to control you or study you. And if you choose not to be handled, then you would become public enemy number one. You know that if they couldn't control you they would want you dead. You know how our society works, you would have no peace, no privacy, and they would take away all that you hold dear. Don't let that happen, man, you are too decent a man to become what they would make you become, a villain. It would be their way or no way."

Then John had a thought and he asked, "Hey, do you think you can make her love me back? I mean, from where I'm standing it looks like you can do pretty much anything. Do you think you could?"

"Now look who's jumping the gun," said Cam, "I told you that I don't know what I can do, but I don't think that the first thing I try to do should involve matters of love. Matters of the heart are tricky in the best of circumstances and now add in the demon and her purpose for being here, which is to kill you, I don't believe I can safely touch that. I think trying that might end up with both of us dead, and right now I hope the goal is just to keep you alive. And as for what I'm learning to do now, I believe I'm going to keep it all quiet and learn how to use what I have slowly. That is if I survive this thing with you and your demon. I don't think we've seen the worst of what she can do to you or me yet."

"To be honest with you Cam," said John, "if I can't have her in my life, I don't know if I even want to live. Now that I've felt her touch and seen the compassion in her beautiful eyes, I don't want to go back. Even though I am independently wealthy, my life without her in it would be almost like being in a coma. I love her Cam, I really, really love her. I'll make you a promise, if you can pull this off, I will give you all the money I have and that's over two and a half million dollars. It's all yours if you make this work."

"What would I do with that much money?" asked Cam, "I don't need it, and I don't want it. And besides, you have more people looking for you than just that demon. You need to be figuring out how you're going to get away from them. They've already proven that they can get to you whenever they want to, even here at my house."

# 4

Sephra stood leaning against the wall as Cam put the whammy on the two mercenaries and led them out the door. She almost let John know she was there, but then decided to wait and see what he had to say about what Cam had just accomplished. She didn't know the mortal possessed that much power. She decided that he might be worthy of her attention after all. She listened to the banality of the conversation and was astonished at how mortals trivialized everything. She was amused by the conversation until John started confessing his love for her. When he started she just laughed at how stupid he was, and then the words began to have an effect on her. The warmness was slowly creeping back inside her stomach, and a pressure started building up in her chest area. It was like someone was slowly putting the squeeze on her heart. The more she heard the more discomfort she felt, so to ease her discomfort, she dematerialized again and went back to the little house at the pond.

"What is wrong with me?" she screamed, and then she started walking around the bank of the little pond. As she walked she pondered her situation. What steps had she taken that led the events to happen the way they had? She realized that her decision not to kill the murderer immediately had apparently caused a ripple in this timeline, and it was changing the way that she perceived things, and it was apparently changing her as well. So the best thing for her to do was for her to carry out her mandate and get it over with. No matter how much pain it caused her, she knew that she had to go ahead and do it. She realized that if she didn't do it now, eventually it would become too painful to do it at all. She deliberated back and forth, the rest of the night, trying to figure out how to handle the situation. The longer she waits the worse it was going to be for her. So as the sun began to rise, she headed back to confront John and end him.

When Sephra materialized in the room, Cam instantly put up a ward around John and himself. John was asleep and Cam had been sitting there, overnight reading, and watching over John. When she moved towards John, Cam asked, "And what are your intentions this time? Are you going to break him up and then expect me to mend him up again? Because I'm tired of your games, make up your mind so we can get on with our lives. All of this popping in and popping out is starting to get boring."

GERRY MCDOWELL

Sephra looked from John to Cam and said, "Now he dies. And if you interfere you die too. Is that clear enough for you?"

"Then Houston we have a problem," said Cam, "he hired me to protect him from you, then the fool fell in love with you. If he was awake, he would probably tell me to let you do whatever you want with him, but he hired me before he went insane, so my job is still the same. I won't let you harm him anymore."

"Then you both die," she said, "problem solved." Then she leapt at Cam with the intent of killing him, so he wouldn't interfere with her as she tortured and killed John. But this time the wall she hit, struck back. She was flung back and pinned to the wall. And she found that she was unable to move. As she hung there Cam stood and leisurely walked over to her.

When he got about a foot from her, he stopped and said, "I told you that I won't let you hurt him anymore. And besides, you don't really want to hurt him anyway. I can sense a change in you, you are not the same demon you were the first time you came here. According to my source, your essence should project nothing but the single minded desire to carry out your master's last command. But I sense in you something different, is that compassion I sense? Is it possible that you are beginning to be changed on the inside because someone loves you? Through all of history has anyone ever fell in love with the demon that was sent to kill them. I don't think so; I believe we are in uncharted territory here. I believe that having, and feeling the love that he has for you is changing who you fundamentally are."

"You don't know what you are talking about mortal," said Sephra, "I cannot be changed. My kind are the same as we have always been. We are unchangeable. In the age before this one when my kind were bound, we were made to be subservient to the ones with the strength to bind us to their will, thus, we only follow the mandate given to us by our masters. What you speak of is impossible, total nonsense."

"Really?" asked Cam. "Then what is the fire I sense in you when you look at John? And why the caress in the cabin when you found him beat to a pulp? And why, for the love of God, have you healed him right here before my eyes, twice, when his death is your mandate. Answer me these questions, truthfully, and I will free you and let you do whatever you want to do to him. Answer me demon!" As he spoke Cam began feeling the

120

pressure of her struggles against the wall he had put up between them start to lessen. By the time he demanded an answer, there was no pressure at all. He also noticed that the look on her face went from rage to confusion, if he didn't know better, he would say that she was almost on the verge of tears.

"I cannot give you answers that I don't have," she answered, "I have been trying to figure this out myself. The simple truth is that I don't know love. My master, Josephine, had only fear and revulsion for me, and only called on me twice in her whole life to manifest. She did not love me or really want me, for that matter, I was there only to facilitate her wishes. I don't know love!" She glanced over at John asleep on the bed and said, "That mortal has infected me with something that I don't know how to deal with or control. My hatred for him is gone, and the pain of his suffering is almost debilitating. I know I can endure the physical pain of his dying, but this other pain I feel is so much stronger, and feels like it's going to rip me apart. I don't know what I'm doing half of the time, do you know that I stopped a man named Cobb from hurting John by almost beating him to death, and then I went to him and healed him just like I've done for John. This thing called compassion is destroying who I am, and I must find a way to work around this because I must do what my master ordered me to do. It was her dying wish, and I must obey her."

Cam was about to try and answer her when the front door was blown off of its hinges. And when the smoke cleared Jimmy, Cyn, and Vernon stepped into the room. They all had multiple weapons strapped to their bodies. Cyn stepped around Jimmy and shot Cam with a Taser, and smiled with satisfaction as he writhed on the floor. She shocked him for so long that she saw his bladder release and urine colored the front of his pants. When she released the trigger, Cam was unconscious.

"Try that voodoo shit on me now, you bastard." She growled.

The explosion woke John up in time to see Jimmy and Vernon rush him and snatch him off the bed and slam him in one of the straight-backed chairs in the room. Disoriented, and hurting again, he felt himself being tied to another chair; his attempts to struggle are totally useless. When he looked around the room he saw Sephra standing against the wall looking down at the floor, it looked like she was ignoring everything that was going on in the room. As he was about to shout at her to do something, Vernon stuffed a gag in his mouth and tied it off with a hand towel. He saw that Cam was bound and gagged just like he was. As he watched, he saw Cyn take Sephra by the arm and sit her down in another chair and tie her up too.

Cyn said to her, "Hon, we're not going to hurt you, but I need to keep you from running off and calling the law, so if you just sit there and be quiet no harm will come to you. Ok?" Sephra didn't say a word; she just sat there looking at the floor.

"Maybe she's slow or something," said Jimmy, "don't worry about her, these two are the ones we need to worry about." He walked over to John and squatted down in front of him, removed his gag, and said, "Ok fellow, you seem to be the one with all of the info, so we're gonna have a little conversation. First of all, I want to know what you did to Bert, so start talking."

"Who is Bert?" asked John.

"He's the one that beat the shit out of you, that's who," said Jimmy.

"Oh him" said John, "the last time I saw him he was running out the front door."

"Who was he running from?"

"Retribution," said John.

"What the hell is that supposed to mean?" asked Vernon.

"It looked to me like somebody was calling in his accounts," said John, "the doctor got his called in too. The killer was the most vicious person I've ever seen, and if you people value your lives, you'll all walk away from this now and call it even. That bunch plays for keeps."

"He's lying," said Cyn, "I know that you know who it was because after they killed Bert and the Doc, they brought you back here. Strangers don't do that. We know about the organization you work for, so stop lying and spill the beans."

"Organization? What are you talking about? I don't belong to any organization," said John.

"Somebody is covering your ass, and we wanna know who it is," said Cyn.

John noticed that Cam was finally awake, and saw that he was looking at Sephra with a strange look on his face. He (John) wondered why Sephra was still looking at the floor and not doing anything. He knew that she could wipe the floor with these people, yet, she was doing nothing.

"If I told you who did all of the killing out at that cabin you wouldn't believe me," said John. "I wouldn't believe it if I hadn't seen it myself."

"Alright mister wise-guy, tell me why Bert was hired to find you in the first place," said Jimmy.

"A mistake," said John, "someone thought I had taken something from them, but they were wrong."

"And what was it that you were supposed to have taken?" asked Jimmy.

"That is none of your concern," answered John, "all you need to know is that they were mistaken. I am not a thief."

"I don't care if you're a thief or not," said Jimmy, "because whatever it is its mine now so where is it?"

"I'll tell you just like I told Dr. Siddig, it's my property, bought and paid for, and you can't have it," said John. "Now untie us and leave."

"I ain't going nowhere until I get what is mine," said Jimmy. "You owe me for Bert."

"You people sure have a weird way of seeing things," said John. "Your friend brought everything he went through down on himself. He could have just walked out of the room when the killer was working on the doctor, but he chose to stay and fight. That's what cost him his life; he was too stupid to run. Just like the three of you, all of you can survive today if you just walk away now."

"So now we are supposed to be afraid of this nonexistent organization of yours." said Jimmy. "I don't scare that easily. Me and my friends here have been trained by the United States of America, they taught us a whole lot of ways to kill, and you and your friends are about to find out just how well we were trained." He looked over at Cam, and said, "I don't know what kind of friendship you have with this guy, but it's about to get your little girl hurt. We're gonna start with her, and then work our way around to the rest of you until I get what's mine. Do you understand me?"

Cam nodded his head and started looking at Sephra again. John just shook his head; he was thinking about how he could convince these people that their lives were in danger. He didn't want to sit, tied to another chair, while she mutilated another group of people.

Jimmy stood up and walked over to where Sephra was sitting tied to the chair. John knew that if he touched her that he was as good as dead. Sephra would tear him apart. So he yelled, "Alright, I'll tell you what it was that they were after. But I don't have it anymore. I left it with some friends in Iowa."

"The state of Iowa?" asked Cyn. "You expect us to believe that you let Bert beat you like he did and let us do this to you for something you don't have anymore? Just how stupid do you think we are?"

"Pretty stupid after what Cam did to you yesterday," stated John, "most people would still be running, but you smart-asses came back for more. And look, you've got him gagged, but did he say anything to you earlier when he froze you in your tracks? No, he did not! Yet you're standing here thinking that you are in control of this situation. Now that's just stupid! The only reason any of you are still standing is because we are not murderers, but you are pressing your luck. Untie us and leave. That's the only way you're going to get to see tomorrow!"

Jimmy pulled out his gun and placed it an inch from Sephra's head, then he glanced at Vernon, and Vernon walked over and put his gun at Cam's temple.

"Talk now," he said, "or she goes first. I know you don't know me, but I don't bluff, so don't try me. I will blow this bitch's head off if you don't talk. Then we'll do him next, and save you for last. But you won't go as quickly as these two." He looked over at Cam and said, "Mister, do you believe I'll blow your daughter's brains all over this room?" Cam nodded again. "Then you better tell your boy to start talking." He looked back at John and said, "Well?"

John looked up at him and yelled, "Go to hell!"

**Bam!!!**

He shot Sephra point-blank in the side of her head. He didn't even look at his handiwork; he just started walking over to Cam, looking at John the whole while. "Now do you...."

"Jimmy!" yelled Cyn. "Jimmy! Loo...." Jimmy spun around to see what had Cyn so excited and saw that the girl had stood up and lifted Cyn clear off the floor. She had Cyn by the throat and was just standing there holding her in the air with just one hand. And Cyn was kicking her and hitting her trying to make her let go, but to no avail.

Jimmy turned and opened fire on the girl as he ran to help Cyn. To his surprise the girl just jerked as the 9mm slugs tore into her. She waited until Jimmy was close, and she flung Cyn away and grabbed him. Before he could realize what was happening, she lifted him from the floor and held him there. Jimmy knew that he was all muscle; he knew that he could break this girl's neck with a single jerk. But he also knew that there was no way that he could lift her up with one arm and just hold her there. So he reached down and grabbed what was left of her head and gave it a bone-breaking yank. He thought he heard her neck break, but she didn't drop him; instead she reached out with her right hand and ripped his left arm off at the shoulder. Then she flipped the arm around and caught it at the elbow, and began beating Jimmy with it. And that's when Jimmy began to scream. Vernon jumped back from Cam and stood up straight, and snapped his heels together like a German soldier in one of those old movies; and his eyes rolled up in his head, and just fell over in a dead faint.

Cyn watched the girl tear Jimmy's arm off, and she watched her brother faint. Then she recalled that John said Bert would have lived if he had just run away, so screaming at the top of her lungs, she jumped up and headed for the nearest exit. She hated to leave her brother in there, but she knew he was out of the game until he woke up and she sure couldn't carry him. As she burst out the back door she could still hear Jimmy screaming, and the sound of meat banging against meat as the girl beat him with his arm. Along with Jimmy's screams she heard a pitiful whimpering sound coming from somewhere and it took her a minute to realize that the sound was coming from her. All of her military training hadn't prepared her for what she had just seen. No one is prepared to see something like that. She ran through the woods until she reached where they had parked the truck earlier. She didn't have Jimmy's keys, so she used her KA-BAR on the key cylinder and popped it out. Then she started the truck with the knife and quickly drove away. She had the feeling that she needed to be far away from there when the girl finished with Jimmy. How can a girl that young have that much strength? She had lifted her with one arm like she weighted nothing at all. What the hell is going on? She had to stop three times on the way to Vernon's house to lean out the door and throw up. By the time she reached home her throat was burning from all the stomach acid she'd vomited up.

She sat there in the truck crying for a good while because she realized that she had lost two of her best friends in less than two days. She hoped that her brother wouldn't become number three. She was torn between going back out there and trying to free Vernon, and the preservation of her own life. She had little doubt that that woman could kill both of them if she wanted to. So she sat there in the truck and cried.

Jimmy knew that he was dying, he knew that if the beating he was getting didn't kill him, (he was being beaten with his own arm), that he would bleed out soon. The blood was spraying out of what was left of his shoulder like a fire hose. He was getting faint from the loss of blood and that made the beating he was getting less painful. He also knew that one of the reasons he wasn't hurting as badly as he should have been was because when she ripped his arm off he heard and felt his neck break. Ripping his arm off had basically hung him, because she was still holding him up in the air. As his vision began to fail him, he watched as what was probably the most beautiful creature on earth continued to beat him with his arm. His last coherent thought was that he finally knew what had happened to Bert.

John and Cam were both screaming at Sephra, pleading for her to stop what she was doing to the man. They had no doubt that the man was already dead, because no one could survive that much blood loss and live. But she kept on beating the man long after he had stopped screaming. Since this was the first time Cam had seen her in action, he was the one that was almost in shock. The brutality of the attack had taken Cam completely by surprise. The doubts started filling his head with questions, like, "How am I supposed to be able to fight something this violent? Why in the world had he let John waltz into his life bringing this thing with him? And had he really just had this thing pinned to the wall? It was all he could do to not faint dead away like that other fellow over there. At least he hadn't had to witness the mutilation of his friend. As Cam watched the mutilation unfold, tears began to flow from his eyes, because no one deserved to die like this. And he felt that he was watching the prelude to what was going to happen to him and John. And now he felt completely helpless to do anything to stop it. Everything he was able to do with his abilities depended on his confidence in himself, and that had just been ripped out of him when the demon had ripped off the man's arm. He felt with confidence the he and John were toast.

Though John had seen Sephra in action before, the viciousness of the attack took him by surprise. And as the spattered blood began to coat the room and everyone in it, he realize how big a fool he had been to ever think that the creature standing before him beating another man to death could ever love him. He understood his love for her, but he didn't think that she could ever be won over. He tried to look away, but his eyes were glued to Sephra's face. Her expression never changed, it was as if she were just standing there doing nothing. There was no anger on her face or pain from being shot in the head, and as he watched, the holes that were blown on both sides of her head were beginning to close up. The damage that had been done to her head would have meant instant death to a regular person, but she carried on like nothing had happened at all. And with the violence she was dishing out on that man you would expect to see anger or satisfaction on her face, but her face was just blank. She basically had the same look she had when she was staring at the floor. He didn't understand how she could seem so detached from what she was doing, she was killing someone, but it didn't seem to bother her at all. So as she kept beating what was now quite evident a dead body, John began to be afraid for his life. He saw Cam sitting there crying and realized that they could be next. Who or what in this world could stop her if she decided to close out all accounts when she finished with the man? He began to tremble when the demon lowered what was left of the man to the floor, and turned to look at him. It really surprised him when he saw the vacant look on her face change into one of fear.

More was revealed to Sephra in the short conversation she was having with Cam while pinned to the wall than the whole time she was walking around the pond last night. Her conviction to kill John had been absolute when she had returned to Cam's house. But she had been surprised when Cam had stopped her cold. Never had she encountered a mortal with such strength and single minded dedication to someone they hardly knew. She now knew that he would do anything necessary to protect John from her wrath. She struggled to break through the barrier that had her pinned to the wall until she realized that what he was saying was the truth. She didn't feel the way she should towards John; it felt like his slate had been wiped clean in her mind. It felt like the order that Josephine had given her when she was dying had been rescinded. It was almost like she had been released from the mandate. She felt free, for the first time in her existence. Free to act anyway she chooses. She could let this man live and not be destroyed for failing to fulfill her mandate. And as she pondered these things, Jimmy and his crew blasted their way into the house. She was deep in thought and didn't really pay any attention to what was going on around her. That's why she let Cyn walk her over to the chair and tie her up. She didn't really start paying attention until Jimmy tried to blow her brains out. In response she had grabbed the one closest to her, and that had been Cyn. She snatched her up just to stop her from interrupting her train of thought, but then Jimmy started shooting her, so she threw Cyn away and grabbed Jimmy. He attempted to break her neck, and out of reflex she tore off his arm and started beating him with it. Still deep in thought, she just beat Jimmy until he stopped squirming. When she realized that he was dead she put him down, and glanced over at John. Seeing John covered in blood snapped her back to the real world. She ran over to him and asked, "Did I hurt you? Where are you hurt?" And she knelt down in front of him and started feeling all over him trying to find out where he was injured. The strange inner feelings that she had been experiencing lately had returned in full force. As she knelt there in front of John she was wondering what the feelings had to do with her. She asked herself, "Is this what love feels like? Am I even capable of following through on them? I know that I should break his neck right now and be finished with this. That is what I exist to do, yet touching him even while he's coated in blood, feels right. I hate to even take my hands away from his face, because it feels like this is what I should be doing. But, I know what my orders are and I will carry them out."

"I'm not hurt," said John with a startled look on his face. He thought when she ran to him that she was about to kill him, but when she reacted the way she did, he didn't know what to think. It took a moment for him to realize that she was concerned about him. Then he said, "I'm all right love."

When he called her "love" something broke inside of her, she didn't know what it was, but she felt something change inside of her, so she said, "I don't know love, all I've ever known is what my master let me know, so stop wasting your time with that. I could never love you because I don't know how." Then she turned to Cam and said, "Are you hurt?" She reached over and pulled the gag out of his mouth.

"No," Cam said, "but I sure would like to get untied from this chair so I can go wash some of this blood off of me."

"Very well," said Sephra. Then she untied John and walked over behind

Cam and did the same. Then she went over to Vernon where he was passed out on the floor, as she knelt down to see if he was all right, he woke up.

"No! No! No!" he screamed backpedaling away from her as fast as he could. "I just came along for moral support; I don't have any reason to be here at all! I just came along for the ride! I wasn't going to do anything to anyone! I thought we were here just to get some information from the old guy, I didn't even know *that* guy was here! I promise you, if you'll let me go, you'll never see me again! I give you my word!"

"Then go," said Sephra, "and don't ever bother him again. I hold you to your word. Go!"

Still covered in blood on one side, Vernon burst through what was left of the front door, ran around the house and ran through the woods to where they had left the truck. He was shocked to see that the truck and Cyn were gone. He couldn't believe that she had left him here. So he took out his cell phone and called her. She answered on the fourth ring. "Hello?" said Cyn. "Is that you Vernon?"

"Hell yes it's me," he yelled, "where the hell are you?"

"They let you go?" she asked?

"Yes they let me go," he yelled! "Come and get me right now. How could you leave me back there in all of that mess? I could have been killed!"

"Where are you now?" Asked Cyn?

"Where we parked the truck," he said, "I can't go walking down the road with all of this blood on me."

"Blood?" asked Cyn, "are you hurt?"

"No, it's Jimmy's blood," he said, "The place was covered in it. And in case you don't know, Jimmy didn't make it. From the looks of it I would say she beat him to death with his own arm. What kind of woman is she? Nobody is supposed to be able to do that to anybody."

"I don't know, "said Cyn, "I'll be there in a few minutes. Don't move!" Fifteen minutes later Vernon was in the passenger's seat headed for home. He looked over at his sister and said, "You and Jimmy knew what those people were capable of, didn't you? That's why the two of you were so messed up when you came home earlier. But what I don't understand is why you would want to go back out there again. And why did you take me along?"

"We didn't know about the girl", she said, "All we saw was the old man doing some weird shit. He caught us off guard. We figured we'd go back, disable him, and find out what John had done to Bert, and take whatever he had that everybody wanted. It was supposed to be so simple. I don't know what that girl is. She must be one of those Kung-Fu types, you know, the ones that can break boards with their fingernails. If I had known that it was going to turn violent, I never would have taken you with us." She confessed.

"Kung-Fu my ass!" screamed Vernon. "Jimmy blew her brains out, you saw it. You saw the big hole that that 9mm slug took out when it left her head! You know she should have fell over dead, but she didn't. Instead she stood up, and lifted you up off the floor and held you there, with one hand, until Jimmy started shooting her again. Don't you remember how many bullets Jimmy pumped into her? Kung-Fu can't make you that tough! That woman was not human! If you plan on going back out there again, you can count me out!"

"I've lost enough friends for one day, thank you." said Cyn. "I don't know if I'll even drive on that road again. I intend to stay as far away from that house and those people as I can, they are way out of my league." They remained quiet the rest of the way home, silently mourning the loss of their friends Jimmy and Bert.

## 5

Cam called John and told him that the bathroom was free. He hoped that he'd left enough hot water for John to get all of the blood off of him. He walked into the kitchen and got the mop bucket out of the pantry, and went to the sink, and got his cleaning supplies from underneath it. He filled the pail with lukewarm water and headed for the guest bedroom. As he walked by the bathroom he heard John talking to himself in the shower. He wondered how John was holding onto his sanity after going through all he'd been through for the last few days. He was trying to figure out how he was going to dispose of the badly mutilated body in his guest bedroom when he stepped into the room. He dropped the bucket splashing water everywhere. Sephra was standing in the middle of the room with not a spot of blood on her. Her bullet-riddled clothes had been replaced with new clothes, and the room was also spotless. And when he looked for the body, it was also gone. If you had not been there, you would think that nothing untoward had happened in this room.

"How did you do this?" asked Cam.

"It's just something I do," answered Sephra. "It's not that hard to do. I'm sure you could do it. I've seen what you can do. Once you mature, you will be a formidable adversary."

"I hope I never have to use these abilities ever again." said Cam. I've seen enough death and destruction to last me a lifetime. Can you tell me what you have decided to do about John? He really is *too* in love with you to even have sense enough to run when he gets out of the shower. I hope you and me don't have to go toe to toe, because I honestly don't think I would stand a chance against someone as powerful as you. But I still have my obligation to John, he did ask me to protect him from you. Are you going to kill him?"

"For some reason," she said, "I don't feel the compunction to kill him anymore. I think that I can walk away from him without being drawn right back to him. Neither of you has a need to be afraid of me anymore. I have no desire to hurt him or kill him. For now he can go on with his life, just like I no longer exist."

"No!" shouted John, stepping into the room with a bath towel around his waist. "I can't live without you in my life. I don't care where you intend to go, but I know that I want to be there with you. Living without you would be just like trying to live without air. I know that I will wither away and die. Please don't leave me! Please!" Then he stopped abruptly when he noticed the room. "Wow," he said. "How did the room get cleaned so fast?"

"Sephra did it," explained Cam. "She is truly amazing. We were just talking about your future John. It looks like you're going to get a reprieve. I think she is going to let you live. But I don't know if she is going to be able to hang around, you know you did kill her master, and she'll probably remember that every time she looks at you. Her hatred of you will more than likely start to come back, and you don't want to be there when that happens."

"Will you give me two weeks?" Asked John? "Just two weeks, to give me a chance to show you that my love for you will help you overcome any animosity you may have toward me. You already know that I was a pawn used by someone else to kill your master. If I could change that, I would in a heartbeat. But what I can do for you is love you so much that even though you don't know what love is, you will be able to tolerate my presence enough for us to spend some time together."

"I will give you no promises," she said, "But I will try to do as you ask, but if I start to feel the urge to kill you returning, then I must leave and stay away from you. Because right now I do not want to see anything bad happen to you. I cannot explain why I feel this way, but I do."

Cam sat there with a big smile on his face because he could sense the changes that were happening to her as they spoke to each other. He was beginning to think that John had stumbled upon something that had never happened before. John was actually melting a demon's heart. Cam felt that if John kept at it, that he might just win her heart. Cam knew that it would be touch and go for a while, but if Sephra would stick with it, it just might work. Who would have thought that falling in love with the demon that came to kill you could actually save your life? Most of the time, well, all of the time, demons strike immediately upon wrestling control from the one that called it here. Death was usually instantaneous; they never gave you the chance to regain control over them. But Sephra's master had given her enough leeway that it gave John time to interact with her and fall for her. This is truly amazing!

# 6

Assistant District Attorney Robert Beasley was beside himself. He'd just learned over the news that Dr. Siddig had been murdered. He knew that he should have insisted on taking care of the Cramer problem, but the doctor had told him that he would take care of it because he was the one that hired John in the beginning. He had the feeling that the doctor was going to go light on Cramer because he thought of him as a friend. But he had learned long ago that you can't run an operation like the one that they had going if you couldn't dump an employee when he screwed up. It's hard to be tough when you are dealing with a friend; you always want to give them a chance to explain when they make a mess of things. But that isn't good business. When you treat an employee like that, then you end up with a situation like we have with Cramer now. He was truly baffled that Cramer could keep his association with the organization he was in a secret for so long. Nobody had any idea who the leader of the organization was. He doubted that Cramer could be the mastermind behind it because he'd always come across as a little dense in the mind department. He just didn't seem to have what it takes to control killers as well trained as the ones that were doing the killing around here lately. The viciousness of the attacks proved that they were highly trained and very dangerous. There was no way that they were from around these parts. He was aware that there were local people that could be just plain mean, but he didn't think any of them could bring themselves to mutilate bodies the way these had been done. The murders were almost like animal attacks, and the way they had beat old Cobb was just wrong. If you are going to beat someone that badly, then you should just go ahead and take him out of his misery. He had no doubt that Cobb would be laid up for months recuperating from all of those broken ribs.

As he sat there thinking about finding a solution to his problems, the phone rang, "Hello?" he answered.

"Hey Bob, didn't you tell me that old Cooter Cobb was busted up pretty bad?" asked Deputy Stuart Warren?

"Yes, he's in a mess, a lot of broken ribs I hear, why?" asked Robert?

"I'm looking at him right now, down at the Carlie C's gassing up his truck, and the way he just ran from the store don't look like a man with a broken anything," said the deputy.

"What do you mean running?"

"I reckon he'd just paid for his gas, but he don't look like he's hurt to me."

"Bring him to my office; we have some things to discuss," said Robert.

"Do you want me to arrest him?"

"No, just tell him that I need to talk to him, and be discreet; don't draw any attention to yourself." said Robert.

"Ok, I'll see you in about thirty minutes," said Deputy Warren.

Cooter was about to get into his truck when the deputy pulled alongside his truck. He suddenly felt very cold inside. He knew that this couldn't be good. He glanced at Becky who was sitting on the passenger side and shook his head. He looked over at the deputy and said, "Hey Stuart, what are you up to?"

"Robert wants to talk to you," he said, "so hop in and we'll run up there and see what he wants."

"I got somewhere I need to be," said Cooter, "tell him I'll be back in a couple of days, and that I will swing by and see him then."

"Sorry buddy, but he wants to see you now."

"Alright then," he said, "go ahead and we'll follow you. I know where his office is, I'll be right behind you."

"Ok, but no funny business, we want to keep this friendly," said the deputy, "Don't get no bright ideas."

"Ideas about what?" asked Cooter. "You think I don't know how to get to Smithfield? And what would Robert want with me that I should be getting any *ideas* about anyway?"

"Damned if I know," said Deputy Warren, "he just told me to bring you to him, so let's go!"

Cooter walked around to the driver-side door and told Becky that he thought she should wait here until he gets back.

"Hell no!" she yelled. "I ain't letting you out of my sight. I'm still expecting you to fall over from the pain of those broken ribs; you need to be in bed!"

"I told you that I'm feeling alright," said Cooter, "this meeting with the ADA might not go so well, and I don't want you caught up in the middle of it."

"Don't tell me," she said, "he's mixed up in this mess with John too, isn't he? You can't take a breath around here without hearing John's name. I'm sick and tired of John Cramer, let's just find him and put him out of my misery?"

"Trust me; you don't want to get involved in this thing any more than you already are. Your life could depend on it. And I won't stand by and let you walk into something that you don't understand."

"Then enlighten me Cooter, tell me what John has done to everybody around here that's driving them crazy."

"All I know is that there are some pretty bad people involved in this and that they don't mind killing. You know that report we heard on the news last night, the one where the doctor and that other man was killed?"

"Yeah."

"John did that or had it done. I think he has lost his mind or something. He has brought some people to town that will kill you in a heartbeat. They are cold-blooded killers, and John is part of their organization. Has been for a long time I think. John has become one of the most dangerous people I've ever met, and I don't want you on his radar. I don't want you getting hurt!" He said as he pulled away from the gas pump and began following the deputy, because he could tell by the set of Becky's jaw that she wasn't going to get out of the truck. And trying to make her get out was a fight that he felt that he was not up to yet. She could be as stubborn as a mule at times like this.

"You must be wrong," stated Becky, "I've known John most of my life, and there is no way that he can be behind all of this killing; it just ain't like him to do something like that."

"I told you that he has changed," said Cooter, "you never know what people will do when their backs are up against the wall. I told you that the doctor said he wanted him dead or alive, wouldn't that change the way you operated, if you learned that someone has people looking for you with orders like that?"

"Well yeah, I guess," she said reluctantly, "but mutilation? That seems a bit overboard to me. I know some folks that I would like to beat the shit out of, but I wouldn't kill and mutilate them, I mean, what's the point of kicking their ass if you ain't gonna leave them around so you can gloat every time you see them?"

"These people don't think like you and me Becky," said Cooter. "It's almost like they have no humanity in them or something, they just beat you until there is nothing left. I got lucky when they jumped me; they said that whoever beat the doc to death kept beating him long after he was dead, who would do that? It's like there is nothing there but uncontrolled rage.

Cooter followed the deputy all the way to the County Courthouse in Smithfield and parked across the street in the parking lot. He turned to Becky and said, "Will you at least stay here in the truck until I get this straightened out?"

"I'll be right here, that is *if* you don't take too long," she answered.

"Be right back," said Cooter. He turned and crossed the street and joined Deputy Warren at the courthouse steps.

"For a man with broken ribs you sure do get around good," he said.

"Misdiagnosed," answered Cooter. "You know that if I had broken ribs that I would be in bed somewhere all doped up."

"I reckon so," said Deputy Warren as they started up the steps. He knew what he had heard, and the people that should know said that his ribs were busted up something awful, yet here he is walking up these steps better that he was. Something fishy was going on here and he would get to the bottom of it.

"Mister Beasley will see you now," said the pretty secretary as she walked towards them to guide them to the office. The deputy looked over at Cooter and winked, and nodded towards the secretary's full-figured behind. Her stride was almost hypnotic; it was a beautiful thing to see.

Cooter dropped his answering grin when she opened the door to the ADA's office and announced them. She pointed to the chairs in front of the large desk behind which the ADA sat speaking on the phone. Both of them sat down and waited for Robert to get off the phone. When he finally hung up the phone, he looked at Cooter and said, "You look awfully good for a man that was almost beaten to death, what's your secret?"

"No secret," answered Cooter, "just a misdiagnosis, there's no way I could be walking around if I was in as bad a shape as everyone is saying that I should be, now is there?"

"I guess not," said Robert. "I need you to tell me what the hell is going on down there. How could Doc Siddig end up dead when all we are supposed to be dealing with is just a country hick gardener? I want some answers and they better be good. This thing has gotten so out of hand that it's starting to border on stupid."

"All I can tell you is what happened to me," said Cooter, "I don't know what happened to the doc, or who did it to him. But I can tell you that the crew that John is using is the best I've ever seen. They had me down and were kicking the shit out of me before I was even aware that they were there. Then they were just gone. I sat up and looked around and they were gone, just like that. I figured that they got in the truck with John when he left, but that's just a guess."

"How many were there?" asked Robert? "Or did you miss that too?"

"I don't know," answered Cooter, "when someone is beating you and kicking you from all directions all you want to do is cover up your head and pray that they hurry up and get tired."

"I guess you have a point, I wouldn't know," said Robert. "Do you think you can find John again?"

"Don't know," said Cooter, "I guess I could try, but I give you no guarantees. He has turned out to be a slippery bastard. But if you want my advice, I would tell you to accept your losses and leave him the hell alone. How many more have to die before everybody realizes that he has all the right connections to turn all of our worlds upside-down. I wish I had never met him."

"So you are saying that you're afraid of him, right?" Asked the deputy?

"No, I'm not afraid of John, but I have firsthand knowledge of what his people are capable of doing to someone that gets in their way. I might be a lot of things, but suicidal is not one of them," said Cooter, "all these bruises you see on my face are nothing compared to the rest of my body. My ribs may not be broken but that doesn't mean that I got away without a whole lot of hurt.

"Do you want the job or not?" asked Robert.

"I believe I'll pass on this one, but whoever you send in there, be prepared for more losses," said Cooter. "You may think that you are safe sitting here in your office, but you ain't, because they can find you no matter where you are. That boy has got connections like I've never seen before. You want to know who is in his organization, just look around and you're probably looking at a couple of them right here in the courthouse."

"Bullshit!" yelled Robert. "I know my people here. I may be just an assistant here but I know my people are loyal to me and to this office. You go crawl back under whatever rock you climbed out from under and let the big boys handle this. Your services are no longer required. Good day gentlemen." With that he swiveled his chair around and began to stare out the window as they left. He was sick of dealing with stupid people, first the doctor and now that idiot Cobb. So he began putting together a list in his mind of some of the worse criminals in the area that owed him a favor, the list was quite long.

Four hours later Assistant District Attorney Robert Beasley was standing at another window, this one was looking out at highway 301 down what was known as tobacco row, waiting for the four men he had summoned to get seated and settled in. This warehouse belonged to his family and had for as long as he could remember. He often used it for meetings that he wanted to keep private. After they got quieted down, he turned and addressed them as if he were in a courtroom.

"Gentlemen," he said, "I have a problem that I need you to solve for me. It's not really a complicated thing, but several people involved in it have died. I imagine their deaths were the result of underestimating our quarry or just plain stupidity. First, I want you to find someone for me. Second, I need you to detain him until I get to talk to him, or if he puts up too much of a fight kill him. Does either one of you have a problem with that?"

"No", they answered in unison.

"Very well, the man I want you to find is named John Cramer," he said. "He has taken something from me and I want it back. Barring that, I want his life. Now how simple is that, even an idiot should have been able to carry that out, but as you can see there has been screw-up after screw-up. It even cost Dr. Siddig his life, I'm sure you've heard about his death on the news. He underestimated John and it cost him his life. I trust that each of you will have better sense than to think that John is just another good ole boy. From what I know so far is that he is connected to some group or organization that is supplying him with muscle, I guess to give him time to move the product he stole from me. They have proven to be merciless when it comes to protecting him. There seems to be nothing they won't do to keep him safe, so when you encounter them don't hesitate, shot first and ask questions later, your life could depend on it."

Charlie Barefoot glanced around the room at the other men sitting with him. He knew Walter McNeill and Liam McLamb, but he didn't know the other fellow. So he looked at him and asked, "And you are?"

"Sam Peacock is my name and kicking butt is my game," he said. Then he turned to Robert and said, "What kind of deal do we have here? Do we work as a team, or are we to go after this guy separately? Personally I like to work alone, you don't have people getting in your way and you don't have to share to pot."

"That is for you guys to figure out," said Robert, "but I'd recommend that you stick together because you need someone watching your back. I told you that these people play for keeps; if you encounter any of them they will hurt you. All of you have gone through the court system frequently enough for me to know that each of you can be dangerous, and I want you to use that this time. Do what you need to do to subdue John, or kill him before his crew can react. I do need to find out what he did with my property before you put him down though. It's very important that I get my property back. Understand?"

"Yeah, we understand," said Walter, "how much information can you give us about this guy and his crew? Are they local or imported, military or mercenaries? We need to know this kind of stuff so we'll know how to handle them. Are they always with him, or do they wait for him to call them into action?"

"I can't answer any of those questions because my partner was handling this end of things," said Robert. "He thought he knew John well enough that he could talk him into giving our property up willingly, and it cost him his life. I don't know if you know what happened to him, but it was beyond anything anyone around here has ever seen. I was told that it looked like he had been put through a meat grinder. They had to use shovels to get him up off the floor; I don't want to see any of you in that condition. So, the choice is yours, if you want to walk now, there is the door and you won't hear anything from me again. But if you decide to stay know that there is a whole lot of money waiting for you after this thing is done."

"I'm in," said Charlie.

"Me too," said Sam.

"Count me in," said Liam.

"Yeah, I'm in," said Walter.

"Good," said Robert. "Now, how many of you know who John is?" Everyone nodded their head; it's hard to not know basically everyone when you live in small tight-knit communities like these. "Good, at least we don't have you looking in the dark. Since you all know him, maybe you have some idea where he might be hiding. At this point I don't have a clue about his whereabouts. He may be being sheltered by the organization that's supplying his muscle, I just don't know. If that is the case I want you guys to come on back in and forget about the contract. What he has is not worth your lives to me. I want you to engage him only if he is alone. Make sure that he is not being covered covertly; in other words, make sure you check your surroundings before you engage him. Their response seems to be swift and deadly, I don't want you taking any chances. Clear?"

They all agreed and formed a circle of their chairs and started making their plans. Liam said, "Let me know what you need in the weapons department and I'll have it for you the next time we meet. Just give me a list."

"I have access to heavy ordinance that we might need," said Walter. "You name it and I can get it. Tell me where they are and I'll blow them all to hell. Problem solved."

Robert stood looking out the window and listening to his new team plan their mission. He already has everyone in the tri-county area looking for John and he was sure that he would be located before long. John couldn't hide from everybody, he had to eat and sleep somewhere. But at this moment it seemed that he had dug a hole, jumped in, and pulled the dirt back in over him. Somebody was coaching John, telling him how to lay low, and when he is found, they have the muscle to protect him and put him back into hiding. They are resourceful, intelligent, and very dangerous. Robert was making sure that his new crew couldn't be traced back to him; he had taken every precaution to ensure that as far as these men were concerned he was not here. If they got killed, they couldn't be traced back to his office. And too, if they died no-one would miss them, they were just criminal scumbags.

Sam, Liam, Walter and Charlie were fully aware of the type of man they were working for. They knew that if the shit hit the fan he would drop them like a hot potato. They knew that right now there were at least ten people that would state under oath that he is with them this afternoon. Although they were planning this job together, each one had a side plan to make sure that he came out on top. If John had something that was valuable enough for the doctor to die for, then it must be something good.

Robert turned from the window and said, "Gentlemen, it seems that you four can work together without killing each other, so I'll leave you to your planning. If I locate John before you do I'll let you know, and if either of you find him let me know before you confront him. I need to talk with him before his people find out that we've found him. Do not, I repeat, do not tangle with his people, if you are compromised get out of there as quickly as you can. Enough people have died over this thing."

Then he left the room. Leaving them to decide what method they would use to apprehend the elusive John.

Headed for I-95 Cooter filled Becky in on the conversation he'd just had with the Assistant District Attorney. "Robert doesn't have a clue about what he's walking into, and he wouldn't take my advice to let it go. Mark my words, in a few days you'll hear on the news about some tragic thing that has happened to him. Some people always think that they are in control of a situation when they don't even know what they are doing. I'd bet you money that he's in his office right now thinking that all he has to worry about is John and a couple of thugs, he's not aware of the resources John has at his disposal. That girl you saw and her men will chew him up and spit him out before he even knows what's happening."

"I'm glad you decided to stay out of it this time," said Becky, "because sometimes it's better if you just walk away. Are we still going to Jersey?"

"Yeah," answered Cooter, "and I think it might be best if we go somewhere and lay low for a while. Do you think you can stand to hang with me for a couple months or three until this thing blows over?"

"Sure," said Becky, "if you start getting on my nerves I'll just kick your ass." And just like that Cooter Cobb made the best decision he had ever made in his life, because he saved his life and possibly Becky's life too. As Cooter merged onto I-95 north he laughed along with Becky as they started their journey to a new beginning and a new life together.

# 7

Sam Peacock was what most people would call a man's man. He was 6' 5" tall and weighed in at 290 pounds. He was as strong as an ox and had the temperament of a pit-bull. Back in the day, he ran his own liquor still. He had to carry all of his ingredients to the still by hand. He had it well hidden on land that belonged to his aunt Gertrude and had to make sure that he left no tracks or trails that led to his still because she would have a heart attack if she found out that he had a still on her property. Carrying two 100lbs cylinders of gas on your shoulders through the brush trying to leave no evidence of your passing is nearly impossible, but he'd managed it for years. He had over the years built his upper body strength into something quite phenomenal. He was a dangerous man to make angry; though he was slow to anger, a few poor souls had found out that angering him was probably not a good idea. He had put the few that had chosen to confront him in the hospital. Most folks just left him alone. He worked his still until he walked up on an ATF raid in the process of destroying his still. They were all over him before he even knew they were there. He put four of them in the hospital before they could subdue him. He broke them up pretty bad. Robert had worked out a deal that kept him out of prison and wiped his record clean. As far as he was concerned; Robert could ask him to do just about anything, and he would do it. Robert was the *man*. His aunt Gertrude was still angry at him for putting that still on her property though; and she still wouldn't speak to him.

The six years he had spent as a Marine sniper had taught him the value of patiently waiting on his target. Though not the top sniper in his sniper squad, he could drop you at a mile and a half. He knew this because he had done it multiple times in the service of his country. His strength made him more than capable of hand-to-hand combat, but his shooting skills made that fact superfluous. Why waste time slugging it out when with just one bullet he could solve the problem for good. As they sat there making their plans he hoped that he would get the chance to put down another target.

Walter McNeill was the person that Cyn and Vernon had always used to get the arms *they* needed. He could put together a small arsenal in just a few hours. His years as a procurement officer in the Army had set him up to be the one to see if you needed anything. Upon leaving the military he had made sure that he stayed in touch with the suppliers he had befriended while keeping his base fully stocked. They'd all made a lot of money working together to keep the people that came to him happy. There was nothing that he couldn't get for you if you had the cash. That's how he ran afoul of Robert three times. Each time he was caught Robert would always pull some strings and either get him off or get him a reduced sentence. Robert was very good at what he does; he knew all of the judges and they would always come to an agreement that he requested. Robert knew that Walter was still running guns, but he made sure that he kept him advised of any raids or investigations that were coming his way. That's why he was sitting here making plans with these guys to mess up somebody's day. Just like Vernon, he also had a hidden cellar where he kept all of his weapons and ammunition. That was why he was able to deliver to his customers so quickly; he knew what most people wanted so he kept an abundant supply ready for shipping. He was sure that he had in stock what the team would need to facilitate the rounding up of John.

Liam McLamb was the transportation man; he owned and operated a garage that pumped out most of the highly modified cars and trucks you see around here today. He and his staff could trick-out anything brought to him. He'd started out running a chop-shop and soon found out that that was not such a good idea. People seemed to get angry when someone stole their cars, and that's how he wound up in the judicial system, he had bought one too many stolen cars. The last one had been a plant, and he walked right into it. Actually, that happened to him a couple of times, but the last time was enough to convince him that running a chop-shop was the wrong life for him. So the last time he got out of prison he decided to run a legitimate operation. To his surprise, he was making more money working on and modifying cars than he had ever made on the wrong side of the law. And now here was this crooked attorney asking him to pay back a favor. Robert had made sure the last time he had prosecuted him that he served only a portion of the time he was supposed to have gotten; thence the favor.

Charlie Barefoot was the man in the know. He had more connections than the CIA. If you need information on someone he was the one to get it for you. Basically, anything that was about to go down on the criminal side of things in the region he was aware of it. He even had his hands in a few of them. As a young man he had blindly joined a few jobs that weren't thought out very well and wound up going to prison three times. In the pen, he learned from some of the best con-men on the planet how to gather and use information wisely. They went through their mistakes one by one teaching Charlie the dos and don'ts of a criminal enterprise. When Robert helped him out the last time he went in he promised him that if he ever needed anything from him, all he had to do was call and he would be there. So here he is sitting here getting ready to do something that could probably wind up putting him back in prison. But to him a promise was something that you kept, period.

They decided to split up to give Charlie time to put his skills to work. Charlie assured them that he would have the info they needed first thing in the morning if not sooner. He actually found out in less than an hour that John was last seen at some old guy's house on the other side of Dunn. They agreed to meet at the Hibachi Grill in Dunn at eight o'clock to decide how they were going to carry out the capture. Charlie decided to ride out that way and have a look at the house so he could fill the guys in on the logistics of the place. As he was riding by the place, he saw a guy run out of the demolished front door covered in what looked like blood. He slowed down so he could see where the guy was headed. He had never in all of his experience seen someone run that hard. The guy was picking them up and putting them down so hard that you could see the jarring effect it was having on his clothes and body. The guy's ears were actually flapping with each step; it was a weird thing to watch. The man ran around the house coming towards Charlie and went right on into the woods at the back of the house at top speed. Charlie hoped he didn't run into anything because at the speed he was running he could possibly kill himself if he hit a tree.

Charlie saw a dirt path up ahead on the left and slowed and pulled into the path that led to an old dilapidated tobacco barn. He turned around and pulled up just far enough to see the old man's house, plus he watched to see if the running man was going to come out of the woods and run down the road. After watching the house for about fifteen or twenty minutes he heard a car coming from the opposite direction. The truck slowed and pulled into another dirt path about a hundred yards on the other side of him. He was actually close enough to hear the people shouting at one another but he wasn't close enough to make out what they were saying. Shortly after the shouting stopped, the truck pulled out of the path and headed away from the house and where Charlie was sitting. On a whim, Charlie decided to follow them; because the whole while he'd watched the house no one had come or gone. So he figured that maybe the bloody man could tell him whether John was inside the house or not. Charlie felt that luck was smiling on him to let him drive by right when the man was running from the place. Questioning him would probably give them all the info they needed to find John.

Following them at a discrete distance, Charlie trailed behind them as they got on I-95 north and continued to the Benson exit, then he saw that they were headed towards Garner on highway 50, he held back when they made the turn on 210 headed towards I-40. When they made the left turn to go up to Vernon's house Charlie started smiling because he was an associate of Vernon's. They ran in some of the same circles. He wondered if that had been Vernon running from that house covered in blood. He wondered if that had been his sister Cynthia driving the truck that picked him up.

He called his crew and told them to meet him at the restaurant at McGee's Crossroad as soon as possible. He told them to be prepared for an interrogation session. He suggested that they arm themselves because Vernon and his sister weren't pushovers. He knew that if they didn't want to tell him what he wanted to know, that he would have to hurt one of them. And he didn't want to do that because he knew both of them so well. The way the guy was running, he doubted if he would try to cover up for John or anyone else. Charlie had never seen anyone that frightened before; he wondered what could have scared him that badly. And as bloody as he was, Charlie was surprised that he had the strength to run at all if that was his blood all over him.

Vernon and Cynthia were sitting in his living-room sipping from their third or fourth refill. When they'd first gotten home, after Vernon had gotten cleaned up, they were taking the shots straight-up. But now they were drinking scotch and soda because they didn't want to get totally drunk while trying to piece together the thing they had gone through out at Cam's house. The loss of Jimmy and Bert was something that they couldn't seem to wrap their minds around. Cyn felt that Jimmy was dead because she wanted to vindicate herself after Cam had humiliated them so thoroughly the first time. She had felt like she had been violated and she wanted to balance the books with that old man. Looking back, she wished that she had just let it go because now Jimmy was gone and that was something that she couldn't undo. They had eventually talked about it so much that they really didn't have anything more to discuss on the subject. Cyn had convinced herself that with the old man and that girl working together, that there was no way anyone was going to get John to give up whatever it was that he had taken from the man that Bert was working for. She knew that if it were left up to her, she would just put two or three RPGs through one of the windows and solve the problem once and for all. Except for the fact that she didn't think RPGs would hurt the girl, you might be able to blow up John and the old man, but she had seen the girl take a bullet to the head, plus all the rounds that Jimmy had pumped into her after she had picked her up. The way she reacted to being shot was just unreal, who can remain standing after you have taken eighteen or twenty 9mm rounds to the body? Things like that are not supposed to happen in a rational world. The way she had ripped his arm off without any apparent effort was supposed to be impossible, no one is supposed to be that strong. After witnessing all she had seen today she didn't know if she would ever feel safe and in control of her life ever again. Someone with that much power could pretty much make you do whatever they wanted you to do.

Vernon, on the other hand, hadn't actually witnessed all of the things the girl had done to Jimmy. Just the sight of her ripping Jimmy's arm off was enough to cause his brain to have an instant reboot. To him it was like everything had happened very quickly. He went from seeing Jimmy lose his arm to waking up seeing the girl come for him. He had almost fainted again when she reached for him but realized that he had to talk fast to make her understand that he had nothing to do with any of this. When he realized that she was going to let him live his body just took over and got him out of there. When he reached the clearing where they had parked, he had almost fainted again when he realized that his sister had left him. That's why it took him a few minutes to call her, first he was relieved to know that she had made it out of the house alive, but he just couldn't believe that she had left him.

Now he was trying to come up with a plan the ditch Jimmy's truck, because once it was found out that he was missing they were going to look awfully guilty with his truck sitting in his backyard, especially with all of Jimmy's blood smeared all over the passenger side seat. He was about to mention it to Cyn when there came a knock at the door that caused both of them to almost jump out of their skins.

Vernon jumped up and slowly walked to the door, thinking that there was no way that anybody could have located Jimmy's truck this fast. When he opened the door he sighed with relief when he saw that it was just Charlie Barefoot.

"Hey Charlie," Vernon said to the man standing on his front porch, "What are you doing here? Come on in."

Charlie saw the relief that came over Vernon's face when he saw that it was just him at the door. He had stationed the rest of the guys around the house just in case they tried to run. So he just smiled and said, "Hey Vern, I just need to get some information from you, I won't be long."

When he said that, Vernon's insides started quivering. His first thought was that he was here to find out about what happened to Jimmy. He knew that with Jimmy's truck in his backyard he couldn't deny knowing where Jimmy was. So he walked over to the liquor cabinet and mixed himself another drink. He turned to Charlie and asked, "Would you like a drink Charlie? Come on over here and fix your own poison." He tried to laugh at his own joke but found out that he couldn't get one to come up. So he went back to his chair and sat down while Charlie fixed his drink.

"Ok," Vernon said, "what can I do for you?"

"First," answered Charlie, "I'd like to know what in the hell were you running from a little while ago. I've never seen anyone run that hard."

"You were out there?" asked Vernon? "I didn't see you, but my mind was on getting away from that house, at the time, I probably wouldn't have seen you if you were standing right in front of me. Why were you out there anyway?"

"I've been hired to find John Cramer and I have information that he is at that house," answered Charlie, "is my info correct?"

"Oh yeah," answered Cyn, "he's out there alright. But trust me, you do not want to go out there and stir up that hornet's nest again."

"Who hurt you and where are you hurt, Vernon?" asked Charlie. "As much blood as I saw on you when you ran from that house looked like they had hit a main artery, but looking at you now, it looks like you're not hurt at all."

"Wasn't my blood," said Vernon. 'That blood belonged to Jimmy, you remember Jimmy don't you? There was a girl out there that literally ripped him apart as we watched; it was the scariest thing I have ever seen. And if she is still there, I recommend that you give whoever hired you their money back and stay away from that place. Nothing good will come out of you going back out there. Only pain and death are waiting for you at that house."

"Listen to him Chuck," said Cyn. He ain't lying about that girl. She picked me up with one hand and just held me there, and that was after Jimmy had put a 9mm slug through her skull. She kept holding me there while Jimmy emptied both magazines into her body and all she did was jerk when the slugs hit her. Then she threw me away and picked Jimmy up the same way she had me. Jimmy broke her neck; you know how strong Jimmy was. I know this because I heard the bones in her neck crack and saw her head turn almost all the way around, I know he broke her neck, but she just reached up and snatched his arm off and started beating him with it. That's how she killed him, beating him with his own arm. So I just ran because I knew that I was next. That ain't no way for anybody to die."

"Just how stupid do you two think that I am," asked Charlie, "yall been drinking too much of your whiskey Vernon. Nobody can do the things you just told me. How much did they pay you to tell a lie like that?"

"But you said you saw me when I ran from the house," exclaimed Vernon. "Do you really think that we could fake how scared I was and all the blood that was on me? Do you want to go out and take a look at Jimmy's truck and see how much blood came off of me just on the ride home? Every word we've said is the truth, and if you go out to that house thinking that you're gonna get John you might as well put your own gun to your head and pull the trigger because either way you're dead meat. She does not play. She can kill you without breaking a sweat. No gun can kill her, if you go out there with anything less than a cannon you're just wasting your time. No handgun made will kill her."

"I hear you both, but I've been hired to do a job, and that's what I'm going to do." Charlie clarified. "I'm going, and if you two want some payback, you're welcome to come along for the ride. As much as I'm being paid, I have enough to cut you two in. What do you say?"

"You haven't heard a word we've said, have you? If you go anywhere near that house with the intent to do John harm, then I hope you have your insurance paid up because somebody's gonna collect," said Cyn.

Vernon looked up at Charlie and said, "You and me we go way back and you know that I shoot straight from the hip. As your friend, I beg you not to go anywhere near John. She will protect him, violently."

"Alright guys," said Charlie, "I believe you believe what you've told me, and I appreciate your concern for my wellbeing, but you know that once I take a job I'm going to finish it. That's just who I am. After I get this job done, I'll come back and let you guys tell me some more tall tales." He put down his unfinished drink and left.

Cyn looked sadly over at Vernon and said, "It looks like we are about to lose another friend." Then she got up and refreshed her drink. It was going to be a long evening.

"We got him," said Charlie to the rest of his crew as they climbed in the truck down the road from Vernon's house. This was the spot that they agreed to meet if everything went all right inside the house.

"That was Vernon I saw running away from that house covered in blood," said Charlie, "he claims that he had just witnessed some girl killing Jimmy, single-handedly. They claim that Jimmy put a bullet in her head, and when that didn't stop her he broke her neck and she still killed him."

"But she's dead now, right?" asked Walter. "Maybe it was a reflex type of thing; you know how the body can do some pretty strange things when under duress. I mean, how do they expect us to believe that she can possibly be alive after taking a bullet to the head and having her neck broken? I mean come on, let's be real."

Charlie said, "Both of them were pretty stoned back there. They were working on a bottle of scotch and it was almost empty. We'll just have to read between the lines. What we know now is that John has a highly trained bodyguard that knows how to handle herself. Now that we know, we can plan around that. We know that to get to John we are going to have to take the girl out first thing. I was hoping that we wouldn't have to kill anyone to get this job done, but this Amazon has changed the playing field. We drop her, grab John, and clear out before their reinforcements can get there."

"Just get me a clear line of sight and I'll put her down before you guys ever enter the house," said Sam. "A 30.06 to the brain should put her down for good."

"I agree," said Walter. "With her down it should be a piece of cake. I don't see her guarding him all by herself though. The way people are dying here they must think that whatever it is that John took is mighty important, so I don't see leaving one person to guard him. There has got to be some more guys stationed around there somewhere. We're gonna need to reconnoiter that place real good. Three people as we know of have died over this thing, and I don't want to be number four."

"Amen brother," said Liam, "we've got to make sure that we have control over the whole situation before we bounce in that place. What are the odds of you finding out what organization he's being protected by Charlie?"

"So far pretty low," answered Charlie. "It's almost like they are ghosts, if I didn't know better, I would say that there is no organization. You know like maybe John went out and hired this killer on his own. But I don't believe that there is an assassin out there that nobody but John knows about. If she is as good as everybody is saying she is, then I should be able to get some information on her. But I get nothing, nobody knows who she is or who she's working for. You heard what Clutchfield said about her a few minutes ago on the phone, she doesn't exist. You know our government keeps track of every contract killer in the business, except her. I tell you, there is something fishy about this whole operation. Somebody is withholding vital info on what's going on here. I refuse to walk into this mess without knowing everything I can about everyone involved in it. Do you gentlemen agree with me on this?" They all were in full agreement with him.

"So what are we going to do?" asked Sam. "Put her down, or disable her so we can find out who she is working for?"

"One of us has got to go up to that front door and knock," said Liam. "If they let us in, we'll know more about the situation than we'll ever be able to figure out by just riding by the place. We have to put boots on the ground."

"Good luck on knocking on the front door," laughed Charlie, "because it looked like Vernon and his crew blew the damn thing off its hinges. There is nothing there but a gaping hole. And according to Vernon there is so much blood all over the place that there is no way you could walk in there without leaving some trace evidence. We have to make sure that the cops never know we were there. That means that we are going to have to gain entrance another way."

# 8

Deputy Stuart Warren was cruising by Cam's house when he noticed all of the damage that had happened to the house. He stopped and backed up to pull into the driveway. He tapped his siren for a second to get the attention of anyone in the house and got out of the car. As he walked up to the porch Cam stepped through the sheet to meet him.

"Good afternoon officer," said Cam. "What can I do for you?"

"Sir," said Deputy Warren, "I can't help but notice that your front door has been blown off of the house. Would you care to explain how that happened?"

"Officer," said Cam, "I figured it was some kids playing a prank on me. I was away from the house only a little while, and this is the way I found it when I returned. Because of the kind of work I do, helping people, I've picked up the name of "root-worker" and that makes the kids think I'm weird or something, so every now and then they come through and tear up something of mine. You know how kids are and how they react to anyone they think is different from them."

"That's vandalism sir," said the deputy, "have you reported this to our office?"

"No, not this time," answered Cam, "I figured what was the use. I've called you guys on several occasions and you couldn't find enough evidence to tell you who did it. It's just a waste of time bringing your office into this. I'll just get it repaired just like I always have. What are you going to do? They're just kids."

"Be that as it may sir," said Deputy Warren, "do you mind if I take a look around. It's my job to make sure that things like this don't happen to the good people of this county. It looks like they used a lot of dynamite on your door here, and I wonder where would a bunch of kids get that much dynamite. That alone is reason enough for my office to investigate this incident. It's kind of scary to me to think that children can get a hold of enough explosives to do something like this."

"Of course you can look around sir," said Cam. "And yeah, it is scary when you put it that way. I wonder who would sell explosives to children anyway, an adult should know better."

Cam stepped back and pulled the sheet over so the deputy could enter the house. As the deputy entered the house the first thing he noticed was all of the empty mirror frames hanging on the walls. The next thing he saw was a man who looked like he had been badly beaten, and a woman sitting on opposite sofas. They looked like they had just finished having a heated discussion and stopped talking when he entered the room. He nodded his head towards them and moved on through the house. He noticed that every mirror in the house was missing the actual mirror. When he went into the guest bedroom he saw that not only were the mirrors gone but so were the windows. He looked around at Cam and asked, "Sir, can you tell me what happened in this room, where is all the glass?"

Cam smiled and said, "I guess it was sonic resonance from the blast that took out my door. This room seems to have taken the brunt of the explosion's concussion wave. I was cleaning up glass most of the day."

"Uh-huh, I see," said the deputy. "The people in the other room, is this their residence too? And was the guy with all the bruises hurt during the explosion?"

"No, they are just friends that came to help me clean up the mess. At times like this you need good solid friends that you can rely on. No, we weren't here when they blew up my door, and the best I can tell you about his bruises is I guess someone said shut-up and he thought they said stand-up, and that is the result," joked Cam.

"Very well then," said the deputy, "I'll file a report about this but if you don't want to find out who did this then we can't do anything about it. But I'm gonna talk to my boss and see if we can't get a team out here to get some samples of the explosive residue to see if we can pinpoint where the stuff came from because somebody is playing with some very dangerous stuff. And sir," he said to John, "you might need to go get checked out at the hospital because you don't look so good." He nodded to John and Sephra again as he ducked back through the sheet to leave. As he stepped through the sheet it hit him who the man sitting on the couch was. He went on out to his cruiser and backed out of the yard. As he drove away he used his cell phone to call Robert to let him know that he had found John Cramer.

"Do you want me to go back and arrest him?" he asked?

"No, but I want you to get someplace that they can't see you and watch the house until I get there," ordered Robert. "If you see him trying to leave arrest him, but other than that, just sit there until I arrive."

The deputy drove into the same dirt path that Charlie had used to watch the house earlier. As he sat there Charlie and his crew made their first pass.

"Now that is what I call connected," said Walter as they rode past the place Deputy Warren had chosen for his lookout post, "it looks like he has gotten a Sheriff Deputy watching the place. Guys it looks like he has some friends way up the ladder. I can't think of a better partner in crime to have than someone in the Sheriff's department. I wonder if the ADA is aware that his boy looks like a mole because he is either working for the cops or they are working for him. Either way, it makes our job that much harder. Charlie we need to have another confab with Robert before we step into something that we can't wipe off of our shoes. I don't plan on going back to prison for nobody, not even the Assistant District Attorney." They all agreed to wait until they had a chance to talk to Robert before they went any farther.

Charlie was about to call Robert when his phone rang. "Yeah?" said Charlie.

"I know where John is," stated Robert. "I need you to get your crew and meet me at 132 Warren Rd. It's right outside of Dunn. The guy that lives there is named Cam Suffour and folks call him a root-worker. I don't know why John chose that place to hide out but we'll know in a little while."

Charlie let him finish talking then he said, "I know where it is. In fact, that's where I am right now. We just finished casing the place, and in case you don't know it, I think he has someone from the Sheriff's department on his payroll because he has a deputy watching the place as we speak."

"No," said Robert, "that man is mine. He is there on my orders, so you need to get with him and wait for me to get there. I'll be there in about fifteen minutes." Then he hung up before Charlie could say anything more.

"Well guys," said Charlie with a laugh, "we don't have to worry about the cop watching the place because he's in Robert's back pocket. I hate crooked cops. Since the law is already involved in this, we're gonna have to play this thing by ear. When we show up and the cop realizes who we are, he might want to get a holier than thou attitude, so watch your backs and don't let him see you actually commit a crime. Any rough stuff is going to have to come from him first. We don't lay a hand on the guy until the cop does, that way, we'll be covered because we'll have some dirt on him. And remember, Robert is not our friend; I imagine that we are all here because he did us a solid when we were in court. So don't let him talk you into doing anything that he can hold against you in the future. He is a snake, and the only person he's looking out for today is himself."

Deputy Warren had to back up so they could drive in, turn around, and get around behind him. After they pulled up behind him and shut off their engine, Deputy Warren got out and walked back to their car and asked, "What are you thugs doing here?"

"We're here because Robert told us to be here," answered Charlie.

"Well I don't need your help apprehending John, so as far as I'm concerned you can go and crawl back under the rock you crawled out from under," said Deputy Warren. "As far as you people are concerned this is a police matter, and you can't do anything here but get back in trouble with the law again. So, why don't you just leave and let the good guys take care of this."

Walter leaned over and told him, "We will just as soon as the good guys get here, you're just as crooked as a seven dollar bill, and just about as useless."

Since Deputy Warren couldn't come up with a snappy return, he jerked around and went back to his cruiser and sat there as mad as he could be. What made those criminals think they could talk to him like that? He is an officer of the law and therefore deserved respect from lowlifes like them. How dare they? As he sat there stewing, he started thinking of ways to make all of them pay for disrespecting him. He would show them, just wait and see.

Sephra was sitting at the dining room table with John as Cam fixed supper for everyone. She had told them that she didn't need to eat food the way mortals do because her sustenance came from the terror she induced from her victims as she tortured them. She fed, she told them, on the emotions of the people she terrified. That's the reason demons loved to scare people, it was their food. John and Cam had finally talked her into trying some real home-cooked food. She had agreed to at least give it a try. Cam was cooking three beautiful steaks on the griddle on his stove. He also had three large potatoes baking in the oven. They were convinced that she would like eating food like everyone else.

As the day progressed they had finally worked out why those people had returned after Cam had shown them the door. Their conclusion was that they were just simply idiots.

"How are you still living after taking a 9mm slug to the head?" asked John, "and how did it heal so quickly?"

Sephra said, "Me and my kind were kicked out of paradise in the form of spirits. We were allowed, in some instances, to choose the form we wished to use to interact with the ones that called us forth. I know that before I was placed inside of Josephine to be her servant that I was someplace else doing something else; I just can't remember what it was that I was doing. There is nothing new; everything that is and is going to be has been here since it was first created in the age before this one. The body that I am using now is not anchored to this reality as the souls that are born of a woman. Once a spirit is brought into this world through the human birth cycle, they are tied to the ravages of time and last only an eye blink in the scheme of things. In the past when one's body died, the souls were returned to the pot to await rebirth. But since the Son came and gave everyone options, the soul now is stuck for eternity experiencing whatever choice the host body has made. Yet spirits like me are destined to roam the halls of time indefinitely. When this is finished, I will move on to become whatever the creator has in store for me."

"This body I inhabit now is completely under my control," she continued, "I can heal it if it is injured, and nothing that happens to this body can truly destroy it. It was given to me for the sole purpose of being a servant under the control of Josephine. Whatever healing or hurting that Josephine dished out came directly through me. I was Josephine's power plant; anything that she commanded to happen, I carried it out. Josephine was in control until she called me to manifest and do things with my own hands, then I could handle it in whatever fashion I wished as long as I was doing what Josephine had called me here to do."

Cam brought two plates to the table and placed one in front of John, and he placed the other one in front of Sephra. Sephra looked at the food on her plate and leaned over it and took a big sniff. "It sure does smell good," she said.

"Go ahead and take a bite," said Cam, "and let me know what you think."

She reached out and picked up the steak and started to lift it to her mouth when John jumped up and told her to wait. "Let me show you how to really enjoy a steak," said John. He walked around behind her and took her steak knife and cut off a small juicy piece doused it in A-1 sauce, then he put it into her open mouth. When she bit into the meat her face lit up like a light bulb.

"Ummmm", she said, "this is delicious!" She took the knife and fork from John and began devouring the steak. While she was demolishing the steak, John split her baked potato and inserted a dollop of butter and he sprinkled some bacon bits inside. Then he scooped a spoon full of potato and stuffed it in her mouth between the bites of steak. She was ecstatic; all of the flavors mixing together in her mouth almost overwhelmed her. It took her hardly any time at all to clean her plate; the only thing left was the bone from the steak and the skin from the potato. She looked over at John's plate and said, "Are you going to eat that?"

"Go ahead," laughed John, "enjoy yourself." He looked over at Cam and said, "You wouldn't happen to have another one of those would you?"

"Here take mine," said Cam as he headed back to the refrigerator to get himself another steak.

# 9

As they enjoyed their meal, Robert and his crew were getting ready to pay them a visit. When he finally joined them at the tobacco barn down the road from Cam's house, he found that deputy Warren was upset that he had to work with known criminals.

"I don't need their help to get John," he said, "I've known him most of my life, and I don't think he is capable of doing all the things that you say he did. He ain't killed nobody, that's just not the John I know. As bad as he looks, it looks like somebody's been using him for a punching bag. I'd be surprised if he can walk out to my car on his own. He is so fucked up that I didn't even recognize him until I was leaving the place. And I had talked to him some. I was trying to talk him into going to the hospital so someone could check him out. John looks in bad shape, he ain't going to hurt anybody."

"Tell that to Dr. Siddig and the man that was with him out at that cabin," said Robert, "John isn't the one we have to worry about according to Cooter Cobb; it's his bodyguards that are dangerous. Cobb said they are led by a young woman that won't hesitate to kill you if you threaten John. Make no mistake, they are deadly. I don't know if you're aware of it, but they had to scrape Dr. Siddig up off the floor with a shovel; they do not play. I'd prefer it if all of us walk away from that house tonight in one piece. If I tell everyone to leave; I expect you to obey me without hesitation."

They were just finishing up their steaks when they heard a light tap at the front door. Cam got up and went to the front door to see who was there. He pulled back the sheet that was covering the large hole that once was his front door; and standing there was a man that he had never seen before.

"What can I do for you tonight sir?" asked Cam.

"You can tell John that Assistant District Attorney Robert Beasley would like to have a word with him if you don't mind," said Robert.

"I will get him for you," said Cam, "Please come in and forgive the mess my front door is in, I've had a little problem with some of the local kids."

"I understand," said Robert, although he was fully aware of what happened to the door. "Tell John that it won't take long. I am just looking for a few things and I think he can help me." Cam led him to one of the sofas in the front room. Then he said, "Give me just a moment and I'll let John know that you are here."

Cam entered the kitchen and motioned for John to come join him at the sink.

"I think you have a new problem sitting in my front room," said Cam.

"Who is it?" asked John.

"He says that he is the District Attorney," said Cam, "but I think he is after the same thing everyone else looking for you has been looking for. I think you should look out for yourself because this guy has probably got some clout. Do you want me to tell him that you have stepped out for a little while?"

"No," answered John, "I'm ready to get this stuff behind me so I can go on with my life. I think that if we could have just a little more time to work on her without being interrupted every few minutes, we might just get through to her."

"I think so too," said Cam, "but you know if this fellow intends to hurt you that he is a dead man right?"

"Yeah," said John, "let's see if we can't keep that from happening. Maybe this one has sense enough to walk away. I'm going to give him that chance to leave, hopefully he'll listen." John turned and walk away from Cam. When he entered the room, he stopped, because he felt like he should know the man sitting there, but he wasn't quite sure so he asked, "Do I know you, sir?"

"Not first hand," answered Robert, "but you have been working for me for the last seven years. I am or was Dr. Siddig's partner. We've never met because I let him handle the transportation part of our business, I handle the financial part. And my books are coming up short because we didn't get the last shipment you picked up, and I'm here to give you the chance to help me balance my books. Now, what do you say? Are you going to help me? Or are we going to have to get physical with you? And just so you know, I'm aware of the security you've placed around yourself, and I know that they killed the doctor. But know this; I'm not going to give you this opportunity again. The next time you see me I will be bearing arms, and I'll have some professional gunmen with me. You will return what is rightfully mine, because if you had not been working for us, you wouldn't have known where to get that much product at one time. So technically anything you have gained from our working relationship belongs to me, understand?"

"No", answered John, "what I have I paid for with my own money. Money that I saved up from working for your group for the past seven years. I've purchased a new truck and that was made possible because I worked for you. Are you claiming that my new truck is yours too? Or for that matter, anything that I've bought with money I've made working for you, do you feel like that is yours too? I'm going to tell you the same thing I told Dr. Siddig, it's my property, bought and paid for with my money and you can't have it."

"Don't be ridiculous", snarled Robert, "you know that's not what I'm saying. You are going to try to sell it and that is going to take away from our bottom line. And simply because you have a lot of the product, you are going to have to undercut our prices so you can move it quickly. So don't stand there and pretend to be naïve, you know exactly what I'm talking about."

"If that is all you're worried about", laughed John, "then I can put your worries to rest because I've already sold the entire shipment to a buyer out of state. It's far enough from North Carolina that you will never feel the effect of it being sold. So you can go back home, and not worry about me bothering your bottom line. You know, it's a shame so many people had to die over this thing. You know all I have done is the same thing you are doing, trying to make enough money to make a clean break away from this kind of life. All I'm trying to do is raise enough money to live off of for the rest of my life. I want to retire, that's it in a nutshell".

"You should have come to us John, we could've set you up in a nice place and made sure you had enough money to retire peacefully. You could have been living the good life in a few years".

"Yeah", said John, "living under your thumb always being obligated to do you just one last favor, no thank you! When I walk away from this I'm going to be gone for good. I refuse to live a life where people can always pick up the phone and mess up my day any time they feel like it. When I leave here I leaving as a free man. So you need to forget about my property and go on with your life because I am not sharing this with you or anyone else".

"I was afraid you would feel that way", said Robert, "but the part that you don't understand is that you don't have any say so when it comes to your life or your plans. You don't walk away from this until I say that you can. And the money you made off of the shipment that you bought and paid for is mine too! You're just going to have to get used to the fact that I own you, lock, stock, and barrel. So sit your dumb ass down and tell me where I can go pick up my money. And if you think you can try the same stunt you pulled with Siddig take a look out the door. There's a deputy sheriff waiting out there to arrest you on any charges I can make up. And I can make the charges stick too. You talk about me messing up your day, hell son, I can mess up the rest of your pathetic life, so where is my money"?

John couldn't hold back the laugh that popped out of his mouth. He knew that Robert thought that because of his position in politics and the fact that he had always been rich made him immune to the realities of life. He actually believed that bullshit that he had just said. And what made it funny to John was that Robert didn't have a clue that unless John said so, he probably wouldn't be leaving this house alive. So John enjoyed his laugh as Robert slowly turned cherry red. He didn't know exactly what John was laughing about, but he was sure that he was laughing at him, and that infuriated him. Nobody made fun of him. He is the assistant district attorney. He is in control of this situation, not John. He jumped up from the sofa and stomped over to the sheet hanging where the front door should be and yanked it aside and motioned for the deputy to come inside.

Deputy Warren saw Robert gesture for him to join them inside. He climbed out of the car and made a big show of rearranging his badge and gun. Then he strutted up to the house like he was John Wayne coming to take out the trash. As he stepped into the room, Robert said, "Deputy, I want you to arrest this man for drug trafficking, maintaining a vehicle for that purpose, and first-degree murder, is that clear"?

"Yes sir", answered Deputy Warren. When he took a step toward John to handcuff him, he realized that they weren't the only people in the room. He looked to his right and saw that there was a girl standing there. He didn't know how he had been unaware that she was standing there, but there she was, and man was she pretty!

He looked at Sephra and said, "Don't be afraid ma'am, I'll have him out of your house in just a minute". He turned back to John and said, "You can make it easy, or you can make it hard, either way, is fine with me. You already look like you've been through the mill, but I will bust you up, don't try me".

Then he stopped because John was holding out his hands indicating for him to stop. John told him, "You know that if you arrest me you're going to have to arrest Robert too. Because I was working for him, I have documents and recordings of all of our transactions, including the conversation we just had. And the sweet thing about this conversation is that it was videoed too. So there is no way for him to weasel out of it. I can tell from the look on your face that you are well aware of his illegal lifestyle and that you are working along with him in this unlawful activity". That brought the deputy to a complete stop. He remembered the statement about the camera and quickly amended his statement.

"Mister Beasley", he said. "I would have to have more than just your word about his wrongdoings before I could arrest him. You know the law better than I do so you know that I can't just violate his freedom on just your word". As he was talking he was putting his cuffs back in the pouch on his gun-belt.

"What do you think you are doing"? Robert shouted. "You do as you're told, I want him arrested and in cuffs now"! He looked at John still red-faced and shouted, "You think you know how to play with the big boys, but you don't have a clue what I can have done to you. I can make you and everybody in this house disappear before the sun sets this afternoon. And so you know, thanks for letting me know about the recording because no-one is leaving this house until I get that tape. I'll have everybody in here killed and burn the damned place to the ground if I don't get that tape right now. It would be wise to not doubt me on this because I brought enough manpower to accomplish anything I have to do to get what is mine, so where is my money? I know it's not in your truck because Bert told Siddig that he searched it thoroughly when he found out that you weren't here. So it has got to be in this house somewhere. And we are not leaving until I have it in my hands".

"You're wrong", said John. "The money isn't in this house. Do you think that I would ride around with that much money on me, you do think I'm stupid don't you? I've already placed my money in accounts and safety deposit boxes all up and down the eastern seaboard", he lied. "If I should turn up dead or just happen to go missing the entire amount goes to charities of my choosing. Trust me, the best thing for you and your crew to do is just go home. You are not getting my money. Learn to live with that fact and you may live a long life. But carry on the way you are right now and I doubt if you leave this room in one piece".

"Are you threatening me John", sputtered Robert. "Have you forgotten who I am"?

"No", answered John. "I don't need to threaten you. You have put your head in the noose, and the only thing left for you to do is to step off the bench. You have never in your life been this close to death, and you are strutting around here like you own the world. Now be smart and take your men and leave. Forget that you have ever known me because pursuing this can only end in one way, and that is with someone scraping you up off of this man's floor. Go home, Robert, and live to see another day".

"That is probably the best advice you've ever gotten", said Cam as he entered the room. "The amount of hurt you are opening yourselves up to is indescribable. I have witnessed things over the last couple of days that if I had not seen it with my own eyes, you'd never be able to convince me that it was happening. Right now each of your lives is balanced on a razor-thin edge. And the decisions you make in the next few minutes will determine your future or the lack thereof. Gentlemen, I am not being melodramatic when I tell you both to turn around and run out of here as fast as you can, because once you pass a certain point there will be no way to turn around. So please, just leave and enjoy the rest of your lives".

"You called them", said Robert. "You called them while we were in here talking. You have alerted the rest of her men and they are on their way as we speak. I should have never let you walk out of this room. I should have the deputy put a bullet in your head right now you son-of-a-bitch"!

"I assure you", said Cam. "I have called no-one. You were in danger the moment you walked through the sheet".

"What"? Asked Deputy Warren. "You would have us to believe that we should be afraid of a badly beaten man, an old man, and a pretty little girl. I don't know what yall been smoking, but I want me some of it". As he spoke, he reached over to stroke Sephra's hair, but before he could, she punched him in the chest, and luckily he flew out the front door, taking the sheet with him. He hit the ground and bounced and finally landed in Cam's garden thirty feet away. He quickly scrambled onto his hands and knees struggling to take a breath. He had not been able to inhale since she had punched him. The bulletproof vest he was wearing had kept the punch from breaking his ribs, but it still hurt like hell. As far back as he could remember, he had never been hit that hard in his whole life. As he struggled to breathe, he saw Walter break from cover and sprint across the yard up onto the porch and through the hole in the wall before he could shout any warning. Walter had been hiding in the brush beside the road waiting for the signal from Robert or that dumb cop to come on in. When he saw the cop come flying through the hole in the wall, he figured that was the signal and broke cover. When he arrived in the room, he quickly accessed the threats in the room and found that there were none. All he saw when he got there was Robert, and the old man that lived there, a badly beaten John, and a young woman. His training told him that he had missed the guy that had thrown the cop, out the door.

So he asked, "Where did he go, quickly, which way"? He couldn't figure out why they were looking at him like he was an idiot.

John shook his head and said, "No-one has left this room except the deputy". He looked over at Robert and said, "Tell your man that everything is alright so he doesn't get hurt like the deputy". Robert was still trying to regain his composure after seeing the girl knock the deputy through the remains of the front door with only a single punch. After he got control of himself, he said, "Hold on for just a minute Walter, I need to get my information lined up in the correct sequence. I know what I think I just saw, but I know that what I think I saw couldn't have happened". He looked over at John and asked, "What did you see? Did you see her hit a man hard enough to make him go flying out of the house"?

"Of course", John snickered. "And if you don't want to experience the same thing, you and your man should leave now. There is no reason for this thing to escalate any further. Be smart, and just leave. Your life really does depend on your next decision"?

"What"! Laughed Walter. "The two of you expect me to believe that this child did that to the cop? Very funny". Then he turned to Robert and said, "What do you want me to do, you are the boss".

"Just shut up and give me a minute"! Shouted Robert. He turned to Sephra and said, "Do you know who I am? Do you have any idea of how much trouble you are in for striking an officer of the law? They are going to lock you up and throw away the key. The only way you are going to get away with it is if you walk away from here, this minute".

"No"! Said Sephra. "I don't know who you are, and I don't fear your justice system. I feel that you think that you have some kind of power over me, but you are wrong. Your corruption makes you unworthy of any respect that I might have for the office you hold. You think that you are better than this man you brought here with you, but your moral values place you lower than this man, and the other three you have waiting outside. They at least, know who they are and their place in society. While you walk around all day claiming to be a just man when in reality, you are lower than scum. Killing a fly on the wall would affect me more than killing you would. You have no respect for the law you claim to represent. If you did you wouldn't be out here trying to take something that doesn't belong to you. If you are a smart man, you would take John's advice and leave now".

Walter snickered again. He was amazed that it looked like Robert was about to believe all the bullshit these people were spouting. He stood there looking from one to another trying to decide which one he was going to take down first. As he stood there Liam, Charlie and Sam entered the house with weapons drawn. And each one picked out a target and froze.

Liam felt a little strange to be pointing a gun at such a young-looking woman. But he held his stance anyway. No-one moved.

Finally, Robert cleared his throat and said, "As I was saying, first, I want the video that was taken while we were talking, second, I want my money, John, and third, contrary to everyone's belief, I am in charge here. I decide who lives and who dies". While he was talking Deputy Warren entered the house again. When he saw what was going on, he quickly drew his sidearm and shouted, "Everybody freeze! I want you criminals to lower your guns and put them on the floor. You are felons and are not supposed to have guns. Drop them now! If I have anything to say about it, all of you are going back to jail"!

"You'd better put a lease on your dog Robert before I put him down", Sam said coldly.

Deputy Warren began to sputter again and Robert realized that he had a volatile situation on hand, so he said, "Everybody, lower your guns, and I'm talking to you too, deputy. All of you are working for me, now do as I say"! He glanced around the room and saw that no-one had moved. "I said drop them now, damn it"! He yelled.

Charlie saw where this was going, so he said, "We have a job to do boys, lower your guns so we can finish this and get the hell away from here".

"Lower them my ass"! Shouted Deputy Warren. "I said drop them on the floor, and assume the position. All of you are under arrest"! Robert rushed over to Deputy Warren and punched him in the mouth.

"Do what I say, now"! He yelled.

Taken by surprise when Robert punched him, the deputy fell flat on his ass. He dropped his gun and it slid over beside Sephra's foot. When she reached down to pick it up, Cam stepped over and kicked it away from her.

"Why did you do that, mortal"? She asked Cam.

"To keep this from getting more out of hand", he answered, "if you would have picked it up, all the guns in the room would be pointing at you. And I know how you would handle something like that, I've seen enough bloodshed to last me a lifetime".

"He's right", said Robert. If you had picked it up you would be dead now".

Deputy Warren looked up from where he was sitting on the floor and said, "Robert, what the hell? If you put your hands on me again I'll kill you myself. I agreed to help you out, now and then, but you striking me is way over the line. And I won't have it. You can do anything you want to these criminals, but don't you ever do anything like that to me again, are we clear"?

"Crystal", said Robert, "but I had to do something to break this stalemate. If I hadn't one of these boys would have put you down. So basically I just saved your life".

"Bullshit"! Said Deputy Warren as he climbed to his feet.

"Why don't all of you just go home and let this thing go", suggested Cam. "Nobody has to die here today. And trust me if you don't leave, and if you keep pestering John I don't see any of you leaving here alive".

"There you go again", said Walter. "Acting like we are supposed to be afraid of that little lady over there. I'm gonna tell you what is going to happen. Robert is going to get what he came for, and when I leave I may just take this little lady with me and show her what a real man feels like up in her". Everyone in his crew laughed at that and the tension began to ease off a little in the room as they each began to lower their guns and relax.

"Finally", exclaimed Robert. "Now let's get back to the business at hand, John, where is my money"?

"I guess your money is in your bank account", said John. "I told you that you can't have my property. I don't know what I'm going to have to do to convince you that I am not going to give it to you. I know you're not stupid, but damn. Somebody has got to leave here and if you won't I will. I'm tired and I'm in pain, and all I want to do is get some rest".

When John said that he was in pain Sephra started walking towards him and asked, "Are you in a lot of pain? I can help you with that".

When Robert saw her headed toward John he stepped in between them and placed his hands on her ample breasts. "Hold on there little lady", he said. "You can comfort him after I get what's mine". As he finished his statement Sephra slapped him. It was just a simple backhanded slap. But the result of the slap sent Robert flying into Deputy Warren and they both ended up tangled on the floor. As they got untangled, Robert was going to tell his men to restrain her when he realized that his mouth wouldn't work. When he reached up to inspect the problem the pain arrived. He found out that the girl had broken his jawbone. The entire lower half of his face was just hanging there. He turned to the deputy to tell him to get him out of there. But since he couldn't speak, everyone thought he wanted them to take action on his behalf.

Charlie and his crew could tell that Robert's jawbone was crushed. And they all reevaluated the threat the girl posed. As they all reacted Liam was closest to the girl so he reached out to restrain her. He intended to slam her down on the floor and hold her there until everything could be sorted out. But it didn't work out quite the way he had planned it. When he grabbed her lower left arm to pull her around to force her to the floor she reacted instantly by bringing her arm across her body causing him to lean farther than he had intended. Which caused him to be off-balance. She used his momentum to throw him around and send him head-first into the door facing that led to the guest bedroom. The crack of his neck breaking could be heard all over the room. Before the body could fall to the floor, Sam had unloaded half a clip from his forty-five into her back. The impact of the forty-five caliber slugs slammed her into John. Upon impact, she wrapped her arms around John and instantly teleported the two of them into the kitchen. As they arrived, she spun around so that her back would slam into the wall, thus preventing John from hitting the wall.

"Are you alright"? She asked him.

"Yes, are you"? He returned.

"Yes, I am fine", she said. "I now must go finish this. Do not leave this room until I tell you that it is safe".

"But", John began.

"No buts", she said. "They are going to try to kill you now, and that is something I cannot allow. Stay here and be safe, please"!

Seeing the look in her eyes made John reconsider going back into the fray. The worry he saw on her face made him realize that he had through some miracle gotten through to her. The compassion he saw there almost made him weep. When she released him he slowly slid down the wall and sat there with that stupid grin on his face again. And this time Sephra didn't think to herself, "stupid mortal". She gave him a big smile before she vanished. John remained sitting there as Sephra returned to the room of death. And he listened to the sounds as the carnage unfolded.

"What the hell", yelled Walter, when Sephra and John vanished. He looked around at the rest of the crew and saw that they were as stunned as he was. He turned to Cam and yelled, "What's going on here man? Where the hell did they go? What kind of trick are you people trying to pull here"?

"I tried to warn yall", said Cam. "You've pissed her off now and there is no turning back. If you are smart you'll start running now and hope that she spins enough time on whichever one she catches first to give the rest of you the time to escape her wrath".

The only one to run was the deputy, he dashed to his cruiser, quickly started it up, backed into the road, and floored it. After the tires stopped squalling, he turned on his siren and headed for I-95 planning on going to Fayetteville just to be in a crowd. Thinking that the crowd might hide him from that hellcat. He knew how hard that bitch could hit, so he wasn't going to hang around and let her do to him what he'd seen she'd done to Dr. Siddig out at that cabin. He knew now without a doubt that the gang of people Cooter Cobb had told them about was a flat out lie. Cobb just didn't want anybody to know that he got his ass kicked by a girl. And the organization that John was supposed to be in didn't exist either.

The speedometer of the cruiser was reading 105 miles per hour when the deer sprinted across the road in front of him. By pure instinct, he jerked the steering wheel sharply to the right to miss her and the car went into a sideways slide. All Deputy Stuart Warren was able to say before he broadsided a 250-year-old oak tree was, "well, shit"! And just like that Deputy Warren went to meet his maker. He was the lucky one.

Cam watched the deputy get up and run out of the house. He turned to Robert and said, "You had better get your people out of here now. You stated that they work for you. It is your responsibility to tell them to go. I don't believe they will leave until you tell them to. Don't let any more people die over this thing. You can stop all of this right now with a nod of your head for a couple of them. I don't know about the fellow that just shot her in the back, but I think that maybe the rest of you might make it if you leave now, Go"!

Charlie turned to Robert who was moaning on the floor and said, "I didn't come out here to die for you today. I appreciate the favors you've done for me in the past, but none of them are worth my life".

Robert was sitting on the floor moaning softly holding his broken lower jaw. He looked up at Charlie and shook his head negatively and pointed toward the door. Charlie and Walter were helping Robert up from the floor when Sephra reappeared in the room. She went straight for Sam. Having reloaded after shooting her in the back, he was loaded for bear. Taking a shooter's stance he began to shoot her. And this time the rest of the crew joined in, incidentally dropping Robert as they drew their guns. She ignored every shot as if they were insect bites. She walked up to Sam and yanked the gun out of his hand. And then she grabbed him, spun him around so that his back was to her. She placed the gun in the exact spot where he had shot her at the base of the spine. And began to fire. By the time the gun was empty, she had cut Sam in half just above the waist.

The bullets ripping through Sam prevented anyone from leaving by the front door. So they all, having had a change of heart about staying, made a break for the kitchen door at the back of the house. Amazingly Robert jumped up without a single soul helping him to lead the charge. The only thing that kept them from being successful was Cam. Somehow he knew that Sephra had taken John to the kitchen when she removed him from this room. Cam knew that if they ever got their hands on John they would use him as a shield to make their escape. He didn't think John would survive that. Robert had already stated that if he didn't get what he wanted he would kill everyone in the house and burn it to the ground. There was no way that Cam was going to let them get to John.

He stood in the doorway with his arms outstretched and said, "I'm sorry guys but this way is off-limits. If you wish to leave you must use the same door you used coming in". To everyone's surprise, Robert lifted Deputy Warren's sidearm and shot Cam in the forehead from about 18 inches away. Imagine everyone's surprise when the bullet never reached Cam. But ricocheted up into the ceiling. Cam never even blinked. He had raised his shield the moment Charlie and his crew had entered the house with their weapons drawn. And now, he did a pushing motion with his hands and Robert and the rest of his crew slid back into the center of the room. It took all the will power Cam had not to break out laughing when he saw the look that was on all their faces.

They had just run into something that they never really believed existed and it had shoved them back into the room. They were looking at Cam like he had grown another head. And Robert with his noggin already rung had finally reached his breaking point. He flopped back down on the floor and began to cry like a baby. Full throated sods were coming from his vicinity. He emitted them loudly and proudly showing not a bit of shame at the display. Charlie and Walter felt like they could join him, but they were the type of men that had no idea how to give up when their backs were against the wall.

Resigned, Walter turned toward Sephra and decided to take her on in hand-to-hand combat. She had just dropped Sam's body and was turning toward them. When she was straight on to Walter he hit her with a flying tackle. His shoulder made contact with the upper thigh of her right leg. When Walter hit her he heard his shoulder pop as if dislocated. At the moment he didn't feel any pain, but he knew that he had ruined his shoulder. He managed to get himself centered enough to get back on his feet. It shocked him to realize that the blow that had broken his shoulder hadn't even made her stagger. He yanked his K-BAR from its sheath and squared off with her again.

"I don't know who or what you are girl", he said, "but you're my kind of woman. Come on, let's dance". Then he waded in slashing the big knife left and right. He managed to land several deep cuts across her bosom before she managed to grab his wrist. With a sudden twist, she snapped his left hand completely off of the arm, and with a deft flip, she turned it around and began slashing Walter to pieces. She grabbed his now useless left arm and used the knife to sever his forearm at the elbow. And as Walter tried to turn away she grabbed that same arm just above the elbow and chopped with the knife again. This time severing the rest of the arm off at the shoulder.

Blood was gushing from his shoulder like a fire hose. Slipping and sliding on the coating of blood that coated the floor Walter almost made it to the gaping hole where the front door used to be. He was stunned when his knees buckled. Somewhere in the back of his mind, he knew that he had lost too much blood to survive much longer. So he tried to turn and face the girl again so he could tell her that he would see her in hell. But before he could speak the room went dark and he heard as if from a great distance the thud of a falling body. That was the last thing he heard. He passed away due to severe blood loss.

When Sephra turned to face Charlie and Robert she still had Walter's upper arm in one hand, and the hand holding the K-BAR in the other one. She looked at Charlie and then glanced down at the whimpering Robert on the floor. She waited for one of them to attack her. When no-one did she said, "The two of you have two choices, you can continue attacking me and die, or you can go out that door and live. But the condition for letting you live is if you forget that you know John and Cam. If either one of you interferes with either one of them I will find you and end you. If you hire someone to do them harm I will kill the one you send and then I'm going to find both of you and kill you. It won't matter if one of you is innocent of the deed, it will only take one of you being stupid to cost the lives of both of you. Now, do either of you doubt me"?

"No, I don't doubt you", said Charlie.

Robert couldn't speak, but he was shaking his head hard enough to make her understand what he meant.

"Then go", she said.

Charlie reached down and grabbed Robert by the arm and began trying to rush out the door. Though he was slipping and sliding pretty badly, he made it out the door dragging Robert like a sack of potatoes. Robert was screaming the best his broken mouth would allow because Charlie was dragging him over the rough front yard and then down the road to where they had parked their vehicles.

When they reached their vehicles Robert had abrasions over most of his body. Charlie asked him, "Can you drive yourself to the hospital"? Robert shook his head yes after Charlie helped him get into his car. Before Charlie closed the door for Robert he told him, "If you ever contact me again to do your dirty work, I will kill you. Do you understand me"? Robert nodded yes again. After Charlie closed the door he said, "I am aware of all the criminal activity around here. And I'll know if you try to hire somebody to get revenge on John. The moment I find out that you are stupid enough to do that after all we've just seen here tonight, you are a dead man. And you can take that to the bank".

Then he walked to his truck and climbed in. Wondering if he was making a mistake by letting Robert live. He knows for sure that he is not going to bother John, but Robert is greedy, he may not be able to let John get away with millions of dollars. He motioned for Robert to go ahead so he could follow him to make sure he could drive. He followed him to Pope Rd, and turned to the left, and crossed I-95, and continued to follow him to where Pope Rd turned into a four-lane street.

Robert took the inside lane, Charlie stayed on the outside lane. Charlie sped up to pass Robert and as he came even with him, he stuck his 9mm out of the driver's side window and opened fire into Robert's car hitting him multiple times. And to his surprise, he felt the bullets tearing into him as they entered his door and window as Robert opened fire on him at the same time. Charlie's truck drifted up on the right-hand curb and came to a stop against a light pole. While Robert's car drifted to the left and ended up crashing into the front porch of one of the houses that line the street on that side.

The irony of it all is that the two men had no animosity toward each other. They were just unable to trust the other one to honor the promise they had made to the hellcat. They each felt that the other one was either going to try to get back at John or try to make him give up the money. Neither one wanted to take the chance and trust the other. Now both of them are dead, sad ain't it?

# 10

Cam went into the kitchen to check on John and to give Sephra a chance to clean up the living-room again. He found him still sitting on the kitchen floor, smiling. Cam walked over and helped him up and had him sit in a chair.

"How bad was it this time"? He asked.

"Three dead men one severely injured", answered Cam. "She actually let two of them go, that really surprised me. It looks like our girl is getting soft".

"I sure hope so", said John, "because I need her in my life for the rest of my life. So she needs to soften up a little.

Sephra entered the kitchen completely healed and wearing fresh clothes. There wasn't a mark on her. She headed straight for John and asked, "Are you alright"?

"Yes, I'm fine, and it looks like you are doing pretty well also", he joked.

Sephra looked over at Cam and asked, "Do you have any more of those steaks"?

"No", answered Cam, "but I have some pork chops, are you interested"?

"Sure, I'll give them a try", she said. "I seem to have worked up an appetite. Terrifying those men was refreshing, but now that I know what cooked meat tastes like I think I'll eat every chance I get". They all laughed at that and as Cam started cooking again, John and Sephra had the opportunity to talk some more on the subject of just how much he loved her. And again he brought up the idea of her giving him just two weeks to prove that he was worthy enough for her to spend the rest of her life with him. Since she couldn't die, all he was asking for was his lifetime. And sometime between five and six o'clock, he convinced her to give him the chance to try.

# THE LAST DAY

It was day fourteen; the last day John had begged Sephra to give him to win her over. John lived in Florida now after getting his affairs in order in North Carolina. He had given Cam $750 thousand, in one hundred dollar bills, for his help in solving his problems. Of course, Cam didn't want to take it, but then John and Sephra had talked him into taking it. John had cash in banks from North Carolina to Louisiana. He had handled his money like a good investment. He had his money working for him now; he lived off of the interest alone. He and Sephra had been inseparable since they'd left Cam's house. Sephra was still working on figuring out what was going on inside her own mind and body. She had started to look forward to John's attempts to win her heart. For the last few days, it had started getting interesting. She was beginning to enjoy the training sessions. John had promised her that tonight was going to be extra special.

Tonight John had set into motion the one thing that he hoped would win her for good. After eating out at a nice restaurant he took her back home. He started out in the Jacuzzi and then he brought her to the bedroom. He removed her towel and removed her bikini and laid her back on the bed. He placed a pillow beneath her head and asked if she was comfortable. She assured him that she was.

"Relax honey," he told her. "Let me do all the work, all I need you to do is stay relaxed. Do you need anything before we begin?"

"No, I'm good," she answered. Over the last two weeks, they had worked through the problem of John's premature ejaculation problem. When they first began touching each other, he would shudder and shoot his wad. He couldn't help it. She was the pentacle of perfection to John; he could look at her too long and lose his load. It took some work, but he'd finally managed to hold himself in check. He was in control of his body now. No amount of touching or kissing would make him lose it. Teaching her how to do things like kissing, and cuddling, were just as much fun to John as actually doing it. Kissing was the hardest thing to get around, but tonight he was going to show her what his love really felt like.

So he laid her back on the bed with her feet on the floor. He knelt down at the foot of the bed and took her right foot in his hand. He began using his lips and tongue to work his way around the inside ankle. He kissed and licked his way slowly up her leg. These legs were to him the most perfect legs on the planet. As he worked his way up her leg he began to hear her breathing start to increase. By mid-calf, her breathing was increasing and getting louder. When he reached just below her knee-cap, he moved around to the back of the knee in the bend, and when his tongue stroked the delicate skin there, she shuddered. Then another kiss and harder lick caused her to gasp and shudder in the throes of her first orgasm. As she quieted down from her very first orgasm, John moved on up her inner thigh, by the time he reached the triangle of delight, she had climaxed two more times. As he approached the prize he gently blew upon it, when he kissed it she shuddered again, and when he moved his tongue around the joy button her whole body quaked and she locked her legs around his back and arched up into a total body orgasm. She had her legs locked around his back and he felt that if she had another orgasm that she would break his back. As she climaxed, she rolled over onto her knees and stayed there for a few seconds before she quieted down and started breathing almost normally. Remaining on her knees, she began to rotate her hips slowly, moving her clit around and around his outstretched tongue until she gathered enough speed to cause another explosive orgasm. After she relaxed a little, he gently rolled her back over on her back and began moving up her torso. He received a satisfying shudder at her naval and continued up between her perfect breasts. He moved to her left nipple and felt her shudder again. He played there for a while and then moved to the right one. Being satisfied with the results he had gotten so far, he moved up to her neck. He kissed and licked her in all the right places as he got to her chin. He slowly moved over her chin and reached her mouth. He gave her a light kiss on the lips, and then he stayed and lightly probed with his tongue across her teeth until she parted them for him. When he inserted his tongue between her teeth and entered her mouth he also entered her for the first time with his rock-hard manhood, breaking her hymen in the process. She whimpered and gripped him harder to her breast. When he had finally fully entered her she went into another orgasm, this one was different from the others. She wrapped her arms and legs around him and held him tightly to her as she had orgasm after orgasm. John pulled his head back far enough to see her face and was surprised to see that tears were flowing freely from her eyes. Then he began to slowly move again, making each thrust penetrate deeper and deeper. And finally, when he couldn't hold back any longer he began increasing his strokes, causing her to flow with him. And after a little while, they both began to shudder as they climaxed one final time together. Then she released him, and pushed him up high enough to look into his eyes, and said, "I Love You!"

# CHAPTER 6

## 1

Humphrey Chalmers was enjoying the evening sun as it was descending toward the western horizon while lying on his back deck. His large tomcat, Billy, was leisurely lounging on his bare stomach as he usually did on every possible opportunity. He and his cats loved the moderate temperatures of the Florida panhandle. He had moved here from South Dakota to enjoy his retirement. So far he had no complaints about his neighborhood. It was nice and quiet and didn't have too many kids playing up and down the street. It was just him and his two cats living in the very spacious home he was able to purchase when he moved here. He considered this time as his, to do with as he pleased, and he used it mostly to just lounge around drinking his favorite drink, Pena-colada.

The last six months had been pure bliss. He had no neighbors on either side of him and he loved it. But yesterday he saw that someone had moved into the house on the right side of him. He was pleased to see that the couple didn't have any kids, and it didn't look like they had any pets either. He didn't have to worry about his cats being chased around by some new energetic dog.

As he lay there watching the sunset, he heard someone laughing and talking in the backyard next door. He raised his head and watched the young couple as they walked around the edge of their backyard. They were laughing and joking with each other as they made their way around the yard. Humphrey saw that the guy looked like your average young man, but his wife, (he assumed she was his wife), was a total knockout. He couldn't see what a woman that looked that beautiful would want to tie herself down to someone that looked that plain. It looked like they were getting along pretty well. They looked like your normal happy couple.

As they drew near his side of the yard, his tomcat, Billy, who was lying on his stomach jumped up and dug his claws deep into his stomach. He gave a loud hiss and jumped down and ran into the house through the cat door he had installed after he bought the house. The cat's loud hiss and Humphrey's loud shriek of pain drew the couple's attention.

"Hello," said John. "Are you alright?"

"Yes!" Humphrey said. "That stupid cat seems to have had some kind of fit. He got me with his claws on his way down. It hurt like a son-of-a-bitch. Oh. Pardon me ma'am for my foul mouth, I meant no disrespect."

"Think nothing of it," replied the beautiful woman. "I've heard a lot worse."

"Still, I hate that our introduction started out with my foul mouth." He said, as he got up and walked over to the fence to properly introduce himself. "I am Humphrey Chalmers, at your service."

"Pleased to meet you, Mr. Chalmers, My name is John and this is my lovely wife Sephra." said John Cramer.

"Lovely indeed," said Humphrey. "You are a very lucky man, John, to have captured such a lovely wife. I compliment you on your taste and your luck. It appears that you have caught yourself an angel."

"I am far from an angel, Mr. Chalmers, nowhere near it." said Sephra.

"Well, I count it a privilege to live next door to one so lovely." said Humphrey. "And please call me Hump, all of my friends do, and I truly hope that we can be friends."

"I'm sure we can be," said John. Sephra smiled and nodded. "I guess we will be talking to you later," said John. "We are trying to familiarize ourselves with our new property. This is a good looking piece of property, a big spacious house and a big yard. I think we are going to love it here."

"Great!' said Humphrey. "I've got to go see if I can't put something on these scratches caused by that darn cat. I don't know what got into that crazy cat. By the way, his name is Billy. The other one's name is Cleo, short for Cleopatra. She is around here somewhere. Do you have any pets?"

"No" Answered John. "No pets and I don't think I see any in the near future. But you never know."

Ok, see you later," said Humphrey as he made his way inside to doctor his wounds.

# 2

It's been three months since John and Sephra had that wonderful night when Sephra declared that she loved John. Since then they have been on a journey of learning each other and exploring what kind of relationship they were going to shoot for. They decided to try to live as normally as they could, just another young couple starting out on the adventure that is life together. So far, they have been having a pretty good time learning each other. Some nights John would lay awake in the wee hours of the morning thanking God for letting him encounter Sephra. He didn't know what kind of relationship Sephra had with God, but he knew that his faith was as strong as it has always been. He felt that no-one has ever been as happy as he is right now. Having Sephra in his life has changed his whole outlook on life. Every day was a new adventure for the two of them.

John planned on giving Sephra a whirlwind tour of the world. He wants her to experience the world in all of its gusto and beauty. Once they got their new house broken-in they would start traveling the world. He had it all planned out. First, they would explore Florida in all of its glory, and then the rest of the world. So far, Sephra seemed to be enjoying herself. She was slowly opening herself up to those strange feelings she's been having concerning John. As far as she knows, she may be feeling that thing John called love, but she had no way of knowing if that was what she was experiencing or not. All she knew was that whatever the feeling is it runs very deep. Just looking at John caused the feelings to stir up inside of her. She would want to touch him or kiss him every time. And of course, John was just eating it up. Just looking at John you could see just how happy he is. To John happiness has a name and that name is Sephra.

## 3

Humphrey was standing at his kitchen sink rinsing his dinner plate when he glanced up and saw someone standing at one of his neighbor's windows. When he saw the person standing there it made him mad as hell. Without thinking of the consequences he rushed out of his back door and started yelling at the man standing there.

"Hey you," he shouted, "get the hell away from that window, you pervert! We won't have this in our neighborhood!" As he shouted the stranger stood up from looking in the window and stared at Humphrey. As he stood up Humphrey caught his toe on the leg of his lounger and stumbled. He caught himself on the patio rail and looked up again at the stranger at the window. But he was no longer there. He jumped down from the patio and ran to the fence that separates the lots. And began calling out to John.

"Hey John!" He yelled. "Hey John, get out here, quick!"

John burst out of the back door and ran over to see what was wrong with his new neighbor. "What's wrong?" He asked.

"There was some guy looking in your window over there," said Humphrey. "I started yelling at him and he took off. I guess he was standing on something because when I called out to him he stood up and his head almost reached the edge of your roof. He had to bend over to look in the window. He is quick on his feet too, because I stumbled on the patio and when I looked back up he was gone."

"Did you get a good look at him?" asked John.

"No, it was too dark," said Humphrey, "but he was wearing something dark. It was almost like looking at someone's silhouette. You know, with the light shining behind them."

"I guess I'll be putting up some extra security lights tomorrow," said John. "And by the way, thanks for being so vigilant. We weren't in the back of the house anyway. But thanks."

"You are more than welcome," said Humphrey. "Maybe we can catch him if he ever comes back. I hope I scared him away for good."

"So do I," said John. "Thanks again."

John walked all the way around the house trying to see if he could see any evidence the peeping tom might have left. When he got back around the house, he saw Sephra standing at the window where the peeper was standing.

"Do you smell that?" She asked.

"Smell what?" asked John.

"That faint sulfur smell, it's right on the edge of detection." She said.

"No, I don't smell anything," said John. "Should we be worried?"

"I don't know," answered Sephra. "But I think we need to be careful for the next few days. It smells kind of like brimstone, you know, from hell."

"Oh no!" exclaimed John! "Wonder what do they want?"

"Nothing, I hope," said Sephra. "I've never been down this road before, so I don't know what to expect."

"Do you want to let's just leave town for a while?" Asked John?

"I don't believe that will do us any good." Said Sephra. "Do you remember how easily I found you every time I wanted to?"

"Yeah," said John weakly, "so they can find you just as easily. This sucks! Just when our lives are starting to blossom together something else has to join the party. But look, I've seen you in action, there is nothing in the world that can hold a candle to you. You are one tough chick!"

"Against mortals, I've never had to face off with a fellow demon." Said Sephra. "I imagine that the outcome will be a lot different than what we are used to. I don't know if I could win such a fight."

"I bet you could win," said John.

"I think we should try to avoid finding that out." Said Sephra.

They sat up quite late that night and the thought of lovemaking never crossed their minds. That was a first they usually couldn't keep their hands off one another. They each lay awake thinking about how fragile their future was beginning to look. John was thinking that he was just beginning to get to know Sephra well enough to anticipate what mood she was in at any given time of the day. While Sephra was thinking about losing John and all the new things she was learning to love about this beautiful world that we mortals normally take for granted.

# 4

John was up early the next day. He hopped out of bed and went into the bathroom to shave and shower. After he'd finished he walked into the bedroom with a towel wrapped around his waist. He stopped at the door to stare at Sephra because she was sitting up in bed with a faraway look in her eyes. He could tell that her mind was wandering far afield because her face was totally relaxed and looking more beautiful than he had ever seen her look before. He quietly crossed the room to get the clothes he was going to wear today. Before he was halfway across the room Sephra shook her head and looked up at John and smiled.

"Well, I asked around and no one knows anything about anyone assigned to check up on me," she said. "Maybe I was wrong about the smell of brimstone on the air last night."

"I sure hope so," said John. "I stayed awake a long time last night just thinking about ways to handle something like that. I came to the conclusion that we were screwed. I know that there is nothing I could do in a situation like that and that just pisses me off. I should be able to protect the woman I love, but I know all I would achieve is getting my ass handed to me on a silver platter."

"You are right," snickered Sephra. "If we ever do end up in a situation like that I want you to run, it doesn't matter which direction you chose to run just run and I will find you if I survive the encounter. Ok?"

"Sure," said John. "I'll run but I won't like it. No man likes to run from a fight. Even one that he knows he's gonna lose. It's just a guy thing."

After they got dressed and ate breakfast, (it was the only meal Sephra had learned to prepare perfectly), they went to the local Harbor Freight store. While they were there they purchased several security lights and an eight-channel security camera system. It came with four cameras and John bought two extra cameras to make sure he would be able to cover all the areas he thought would need to be watched. They spent the rest of the day installing the lights and the security system. After connecting the security system up to the internet he downloaded the app on both of their cell phones so they could instantly view any alerts that may come through. After they finished the installations they went out on the back patio to rest and relax a little while. As they reclined there in their loungers Humphrey called to them from the fence line.

"Good evening lovebirds," he said. "I see that you two have been busy." He said that because as he got near the fence a security light popped on illuminating that whole corner of the property. "It looks like you did a good job I can see all the way to the back corner of your lot." As he was talking both John and Sephra's phones rang at the same time. John glanced down at his phone and saw that he had an alert sent to him from his new security system telling him that something had triggered the camera at that corner of the house. The upper half of the screen was showing Humphrey standing at the fence talking. John was impressed, he -didn't know that his new system would do all of that.

After putting down his phone John asked Humphrey how he was doing this lovely evening. Humphrey said, "I'm a little worried about my cats, I haven't seen either one of them since before supper last night. I've gotten used to them sleeping at the foot of the bed every night. It felt weird last night without them there to keep me company."

No," answered John, as Sephra shook her head signifying that she hadn't seen them either. "Do you need some help looking for them? We would be glad to lend a hand."

"Nah," said Humphrey, "they are probably out chasing rats or something. This isn't the first time they have disappeared but they usually do it separately. There is always one around underfoot all the time. I just miss them they are kinda like my kids."

"I hope you find them soon," said Sephra.

"Thanks," said Humphrey. "Well, I guess I'll get back in here and start supper. Maybe that will bring them running. They are quite greedy," he laughed as he turned to go.

"Have a good night." Said John.

"You too." Said Humphrey.

After Humphrey had gone inside John turned to Sephra and said, "Do you remember how weird the cat acted last night when he saw us for the first time?"

"Yes," answered Sephra. "Sometimes cats have a bad reaction when a supernatural creature is around. But that usually doesn't happen unless it has had something bad happen to it in the presence of a demon. We usually leave cats and dogs alone. Actually, we don't usually interact with animals at all unless there's a special reason to do so."

"Do you think you could find his cats for him?" Asked John

"Sure, if you want me to," answered Sephra. She closed her eyes for a moment and then she broke into a big smile. "They are down in his basement crowded into the far corner as if they are afraid to move from that spot. It seems like they are trying to stay as far away from me as possible. Since I haven't interacted with either one of them, I don't know why they would react to me like this."

They got up and went inside to fix supper together. What they didn't know was that they were being watched, watched by a nearly 11'6" tall demon. A demon that was seething, it infuriated him to see the girl demon getting along with that human filth like it was a normal thing that always happens. It is not what any of the powered filth that summons him has ever permitted. Every time he gets summoned, (after he tries to break the controlling bond that links him to the one that called him), he gets ordered to do whatever he has been called for and then immediately sent back to hell to wait to be called again by another powered human. He would figure out what that girl demon did to allow her to remain on the mortal plain unmolested. If he tried to remain after he was ordered back to hell he would be tracked down and dragged back. The punishment for doing something like that was very severe. Even now he could feel the tug of hell pulling him back. He was determined to work out how to stay a little longer on the mortal plane after finishing what he was ordered to do. If she could figure it out, he was sure he could do the same. He took a step forward and just vanished.

# 5

Humphrey found his cats huddled together in one of the corners of his basement. After some bribing with some snacks he had gotten for them, they reluctantly left the corner and followed him back upstairs. After looking around the kitchen they seemed to visibly relax and they started winding around between his legs like nothing strange had just occurred. The cats weren't afraid of Sephra, but they could sense the malevolent evil that was radiating from the demon no-one had seen yet. They couldn't tell where it was coming from, but they knew that the best thing for them to do was to make themselves as scarce as possible. They had no desire to tangle with whatever was giving off that bad vibe. They would be alright as long as that thing didn't return.

Humphrey was just happy that he had found his babies. He truly did love them like they were his children. He didn't know what he would do if anything happened to them, As he prepared supper he kept glancing out the window to make sure the intruder didn't sneak back up on them. He didn't know the Cramers very well but he felt like they are really nice people. He hoped nothing happened to them because he felt like they could become close friends. As he was cooking one of Florida's violent thunderstorms popped without any warning. During one of the brilliant lightning flashes, Humphrey thought he saw someone standing at the same window looking in on the Cramers. As he was about to rush out in the storm to let John know that the peeper was back another sharp lightning flash showed him that no-one was there. With a sigh of relief, Humphrey finished cooking and sat down and enjoyed the terrific meal he had prepared sharing it with his best buds Billy and Cleo. He was enjoying the sound of the rain on the roof of his house. He loved the sound of rainfall but he didn't care for all of the lightning that almost always accompanies these pop-up storms. He was glad that they usually didn't last very long.

# 6

Sephra is sleeping fitfully she is having a dream like she has never had before. She is sitting at a table shared by six other demons. She doesn't know any of them personally but she feels like she should know one or two of them. They are not eating anything but are having a discussion about something that seems important. All eyes are on her at the moment while they wait for her to answer a question she doesn't remember being asked.

"What is it that you want to know?" she asked.

"How is it that you can stay on the mortal world without being chased down and dragged back," asked one of the demons?

"I was given permission to stay as long as I wished as long as I carried out my mandate," she said.

"And how have you not carried out your mandate?" asked one of the other demons?

"My target fell in love with me before I could kill him," answered Sephra. "And that seems to have negated my mandate. Don't ask me how something that stupid could have such a profound effect on my orders, but it has."

"Nonsense!" shouted the first one to start asking questions whose name is so long no human could pronounce it so we will call him Sourpuss because his face appears to be in a perpetual scowl.

"I can only tell you what I know about what happened and why," said Sephra.

Sourpuss jumped up from the table and pointed a crooked finger at Sephra and asked, "And how could he fall in love with you if you were doing your job the way we are supposed to do it? No human is going to fall in love with the demon that is tormenting him and scaring him to death. The only way that can happen is if you weren't doing your job by the book. Are you such a piss-poor demon that you can't even scare one human to death?"

"My methods have always been sufficient to the task at hand," said Sephra. "I have never failed to carry out my orders. This has caught me off-guard just as it has all of you. I have done everything I know how to do to change his mind, but he is very stubborn and thickheaded.

"Be that as it may, you will kill the mortal immediately so we can go on with our own agendas," said Sourpuss.

"I will not," said Sephra, "his life or death is mine to decide. He belongs to me as long as I want him to belong. When I decide to kill him it will be on my own timetable. My advice to you is to go on with your lives and leave me alone to deal with mine.

Sephra opened her eyes in bed lying beside a sleeping John. She was angry, very angry. The fact that her fellow demons thought that they could dictate to her how to handle her business, is completely ridiculous. They should know better than that. Josephine told her to handle John any way she chose, and that was what she intends to do. No-one was going to tell her how to perform her duties, not even Sourpuss even though he was thought to be one of the most powerful demons around these days. She wouldn't let that fact change her mind on the way she is handling John. She was enjoying the time she was spending with him. She was having fun. Every day with John was beginning to be more exciting than she would have believed.

# 7

John went out to start his day, (he had restarted his landscaping business once he knew that Florida was where he was going to spend his life with Sephra) and found that all four tires on his work truck were flat. The strange thing about it was that none of the tires were damaged but were simply deflated. Someone had taken the time to let the air out of each tire. They chose to leave the tires on the trailer connected to the truck alone.

"Now that is damned strange," said John. "Why would anybody around here want to play such a prank on me?" He couldn't recall having an altercation with anyone that should result in four deflated tires. As a matter of fact, he thought he was generating quite a fine list of future customers. He didn't think that the few kids that played farther down his street would have done such a thing. They all seem to be well brought up children they were always polite when he would drive by. They were all smiles and waves just as you would expect from early teenagers.

John walked over to his workshop and started his air compressor so he could fill the tires with air again. As his compressor cycled through he slowly walked around his truck to see if there was any more damage done to it. The only thing he found was a weird looking handprint on the left rear fender of the truck. The handprint solidified in his mind that it had to be a prank because the handprint was about twice the size of a normal hand. No-one had a hand that big unless the Hulk was real. After the compressor had pumped up he played out the air hose and began refilling his tires.

As he was finishing refilling his tires Sephra came out to see why he was still there. "What's going on?" Sephra asked.

"Someone let the air out of all the tires on my truck last night," answered John. "They didn't damage the tires they just let the air out of them."

"Why would someone do that to you?" Sephra asked. "I thought you were getting along with everyone pretty well."

"Come here and let me show you something," said John, as he walked back around the truck. As she joined him at the backend of the truck she was shocked to see the giant handprint someone had left there. She recognized the handprint immediately. She knew it had to be Sourpuss or one of his many minions.

"I think I know who did this thing to you," said Sephra.

"Who?" asked John?

"I think it was one of my kind that did this to your truck," answered Sephra. "They are jealous of the wonderful time I am having here on this mortal plain and want me to hurry up and finish you off so I can go back to hell with them. They see that I am happy and that infuriates them. I told them to mind their own business and leave me alone."

"So they are going to harass me until they wear you down? That ought to be fun." John said sarcastically.

"I'll handle this," said Sephra. "Don't worry about this happening again." She turned around and hurried into the house. Once she was inside the house and no-one could see her she vanished. Instantly she was standing in the domain of the demons. The landscape is hellish to look upon and there is an unease that overtakes you once you enter this plain. While not exactly in hell it runs a close second. Since these are the demons mortal-folk can summon it is important for them to be in a place that is accessible to mortals. When calling a demon a mortal can't reach into hell, that place can't be reached. So a special place had to be made that a human with power can reach.

She climbed onto a large boulder and called for Sourpuss using his real name. There was a sound of rushing wind and there he was standing in front of her with a big grin on his face.

"I figured I would see you soon," said Sourpuss. "How did you like the little gift I left for your mortal?"

"I don't like it at all," said Sephra. "Stunts like that are what give us a bad name. Our job is to do the bidding of mortals not try to terrify them when we feel like it. You just attacked a mortal without the demand coming from some other mortal. You know that is not permitted."

"Shacking up with the mortal you were called to kill is not permitted either," said Sourpuss. "It turns my stomach to watch you rutting with a filthy human. You were made for better things than that so kill the human and come on home. Since you spent all of your time in that mortal witch's head you don't know what you are missing by staying there with that mortal. There are planes of existence that you have never dreamed of right here so come on home and be with your family."

"Wait, what are you saying?' asked Sephra.

Realizing that he just might have said too much Sourpuss shook his head and said, "Nothing, I'm not saying anything. Forget about what I just said. I was just running off at the mouth. You just need to do what you were ordered to do so you can move on to other things. It's important not to stagnate in one place for too long."

"Leave John alone or there will be consequences," said Sephra. "I mean it. Stay out of our lives." Without waiting for an answer she vanished and reappeared in the living room of her new home. Why was Sourpuss going on and on about family? That conversation turned out to be really weird. Was there some connection between the two of them that she was unaware of? She spent the rest of the day trying to dig deep into her past trying to remember her past history.

# 8

It has been six weeks since the flattening of his truck tires. No-one has been skulking around the house anymore. Life was starting to feel relaxed and enjoyable once again. And now this thing is starting to happen that has him worried. It appears that Sephra's body is starting to reject normal food. This is the second time this week that she has had to jump up from the table and rush to the bathroom to throw up the food she had just eaten. John was afraid that her demon mentality was reasserting itself and if that was happening he didn't know if her desire to kill him might come back. If it does he will die willingly because he has experienced the closest thing to pure joy that anyone could ask for. When that time came he would face it like a man, a guilty man, because he did kill a lady named Josephine with his truck. So he is guilty of murder and he'll go without a fight. The part that he hated was how she would feel after she killed him because he believes that she really does love him now. He would do anything to keep her from having to go through that kind of pain.

Sephra came back in the room looking embarrassed about having to throw up. "I just don't know what is wrong with me," she said. "I was feeling fine and then the urge to throw up came on and I couldn't keep the food down. I'm sorry for messing up your breakfast again."

"Don't you worry about me you just make sure that everything is alright with you," John said. "How do you feel now? Are you alright? Do you want to try to eat something else to see if it will stay down?"

"No I think I'll wait a while before I eat anything else," she said.

John finished his breakfast and went out to start his day. He had an appointment scheduled for this morning and he didn't want to miss out on the opportunity to take care of the landscaping for a new industrial complex. If he got this place as a client he would have to buy a new truck and hire more employees or expand his present crew. Getting this contract could make or break a company and he knew that his crew could handle the workload so he wanted to be the first one to bid on it.

When John entered the lobby he noticed that he wasn't the first one to arrive. There was a burly looking gentleman sitting there reading one of the magazines that are always lying around in most lobbies. John nodded his head at the man and walked up to the receptionist's desk and asked if he could speak to the maintenance supervisor.

"That would be Mr. Walsh." said the receptionist. "He isn't in just yet but if you will take a seat I'm sure he will be in shortly." John thanked her and went to take a seat four seats down from the other man sitting there. As he was settling in to wait the man asked "I heard you ask for the maintenance supervisor, that's the guy I'm waiting on. Mind if I ask what you want to see him for?"

"Not at all," responded John. "I'm here to see if the company has a landscaping company hired to take care of the outdoor maintenance."

"You can go ahead and leave then if that's why you are here, I have that contract." said the man.

"Excuse me", asked the receptionist? "I know for a fact that we haven't hired any landscapers yet. You must be mistaken. I'm sure Mr. Walsh would like to talk to both of you."

Before either one of them could respond the lobby doors opened to admit a rotund gentleman that came waddling into the room. He duck-walked up to the desk and the receptionist told him that he had a couple of landscapers waiting to see him.

"Very well," said Mr. Walsh, "give me a few minutes to get set up and I will be right with you." He turned and walked to a door to his right. After he'd left the room the man turned to John and said, "Like I said I'm going to get this contract so you should just go ahead and leave because there is no way you will underbid my company. So why waste your time?"

"I think I'll wait," said John. "You never know I might get lucky."

"My company is already taking care of all the businesses up and down this street and we are going to get this one too. So leave."

"I think I'll just wait and talk to Mr. Walsh," said John. "Let's see if you can outbid me. I don't think you can but I'm willing to give it a shot. If you get the contract there will be no hard feelings at all. At least I'll know I gave it a shot."

"You are not hearing me," said the man. "I wasn't asking you to leave I am telling you to leave. I have been trying to be nice to you but you seem to be a little dense in the head. If you keep this up I may have to soften that head of yours up a little. You must be new around here and don't know the pecking order so let me educate you about the way things are around here. I have a special group of employees that handle all of my wet work and I don't mean mopping. You catch my drift?"

"Ah!" said John. "You are just another bully coming up out of the woodwork. I've had to deal with the likes of you all my life and I don't scare easily. My recommendation for you is to see if you can outbid me, if you don't, just go away and live another day."

"Are you threatening me?"

"Of course not, that is just a figure of speech."

"It had better be because I don't like to be threatened. I don't respond the way most people would I'll cut your head off and use it for chum the next time I go sharking."

"Wow! Sharking! I've heard that there are people that go out on the ocean to hunt sharks I always thought it was a joke." said John.

"It's no joke I promise you," said the man. "I advise you not to try me, now get the hell out of here. I won't tell you again."

"Mr. Walsh will see you now," said the receptionist looking at the man and nodding.

As he got up he looked at John and said, "Don't be here when I come out of this meeting." Then he turned and walked away.

John watched him walk away slowly shaking his head. People always thought they had the upper hand when confronting a stranger not having a clue of the danger they were putting themselves in. John knew that he should just get up and leave to prevent another bloodbath like the one in North Carolina, but he despised a bully. This guy doesn't even know his name and he is already threatening him. John decided to wait and see if he could get the contract.

"I wouldn't pay much attention to him, sir he just sounds like your typical street-level bully to me." said the receptionist.

John said, "I know they all seem the read from the same playbook."

"I know!" exclaimed the receptionist.

After about twenty minutes the man came out of the office and paused as he closed the door staring hard at John. He shook his head and walked on out of the lobby.

"He'll see you now, good luck," said the receptionist.

"Thanks," said John.

When John walked into the room he could tell something was wrong. Mr. Walsh's head looked like it was about to explode. John had no idea that someone's head could turn that red.

"If you think you are going to come in here and tell me how to do my job, you can just turn around and leave now!" shouted Mr. Walsh.

Holding both hands out in front of him, John said, "Whoa! I intend to do no such thing. I came here looking for a job not to lose one."

"Then have a seat," said Mr. Walsh. "What can I do for you?"

"My name is John Cramer, I am the CEO of Cramer Landscaping and I'm here to try to get the contract to maintain your outdoor area."

"I'm sure you can see that we are still finalizing the setup of our outdoor area and it will be another month before we are ready to start looking for a company to keep up that area," Mr. Walsh said. "Leave me your card and I will certainly call you when we are ready. I promise to give you the first opportunity to bid on it, alright?"

"Alright then," said John. "I'll be waiting to hear from you. If you don't mind, could you tell me what that other fellow did to make you so angry?"

"He came in here telling me how I had to sign a contract with his company because they could provide security and protection as well as taking care of our landscaping for some ridiculous sum of money per week," Mr. Walsh said. "Then he told me that I had no choice in the deal if I wanted my company to be successful in this community. Can you believe that there are people that still think that kind of intimidation will work in this modern age of security cameras all over the place? I'm surprised that anyone would try that these days."

"He is quite the character," said John, "he tried to force me to leave without talking to you by threatening to cut my head off to use to chum for sharks. I think he thought that he could scare me away but I don't scare easily. Thanks for the interview and the consideration."

"You are welcome, Mr. Cramer. I look forward to working with you," said Mr. Walsh.

As John walked by the front desk the receptionist gave him a thumbs-up. He waved bye to her as he exited the lobby and saw the man waiting for him. He was leaning against one of those heavy-duty pickup trucks. John saw that he was cleaning his fingernails with an oversized pocket knife. John tried to ignore him as he walked to his truck but he met him before he could get there.

"You're one of those hardheaded sons-of-a-bitches but I have a remedy for that." He said. "I'll be in touch with you in a little while because I guess I'm going to have to make an example of you. I didn't want this to happen but you are giving me no choice. My company is going to get this contract because you ain't gonna be around to interfere I promise you that you bastard."

John continued walking to his truck as the man threatened him. As he got in his truck he said, "Nice talking to you, have a great day." He started his truck and drove away. He hoped that the guy was just another gas-bag running off at the mouth. He knew that he didn't have anything to worry about because Sephra would make small work of him and his group of employees. He hoped they would be smart enough the move on after she gave them a warning to stay away. No-one needed to die over a bunch of grass.

While driving back home John kept checking his rearview mirror to see if he was being followed. As far as he could tell he wasn't being followed. He pulled into his driveway and drove on around to his utility shed to connect up with his trailer that has all of his mowers and weed-eaters and leaf-blowers loaded up for his next job. After connecting to the trailer he pulled beside the house and parked there. He climbed down from his truck and started walking toward the front porch. As he reached the corner of the porch he glanced out toward the street and saw the man from the industrial complex slowly driving by in front of his house. The guy is hanging out the window pretending to be shooting John with his hand like it is a gun. Instead of looking surprised John just nodded his head at the guy and walked on up the steps of the front porch and went on in the house like seeing the guy hadn't bothered him at all.

Once inside the house, John turned a looked out the window to see if the man was going to drive by again. Unsurprisingly he did drive by again. This time he drove by a little slower like he was trying to memorize the address. John came to the conclusion that the guy really was going to be a problem. While he was standing there Sephra came up behind him and put her arms around his waist and gave him a firm hug and asked, "What are you looking at?"

"Some jerk that I ran into this morning while trying to bid on a job," John said. "He tried to scare me into giving up on making a bid. I think he is just your everyday bully flexing his muscles."

"Do you want me to have a talk with him?' she asked.

"Nah, I don't think he is going to be too much of a problem." He answered.

"Ok." She said.

They joined hands and walked together into the kitchen where she was preparing lunch. John didn't like the idea that he had to turn to the woman he loved for protection when confronted by a bully. He always handled bullies on his own before he met her. Some battles went well and some didn't go so well but he would rather handle this guy on his own. John knows how to box some heads when he needs to. He doesn't like fighting at all if it can be avoided but he can hold his own most of the time. You'd be surprised at how many times John has had to deal with someone trying to muscle in on his landscaping contracts. Some people believe that if they want something you have all they have to do is threaten to do bodily harm to you. It must work sometimes because there is always some ass-hole trying to take something away from you. It happens so often to John that he has learned to expect it.

# CHAPTER 7

## 1

Chuck Filbert followed the stubborn man at a discreet distance so the man wouldn't get spooked. When the guy turned into a driveway Chuck pulled over to make sure he hadn't been made. He waited until he saw the man drive up beside the house towing a trailer. Chuck started coasting slowly up the street toward the house when he saw the man walking toward the front of the house. When he was sure the guy could see him he leaned out of the window and pretended to shoot him by pointing his finger at him. It surprised him when all he got from the guy was a nod of the head. He didn't even pause for a second he just kept walking around the front of his house and went inside. The man must have nerves of steel. That was not the response Chuck was expecting. He should have at least stopped in his tracks when he saw that Chuck knows where he lives. But he didn't and that really pissed Chuck off. The guy needs to be taught some respect and Chuck knows just the fellow that can teach him how to be respectful.

## 2

Chris Jones is sitting in his favorite bar nursing a shot of tequila in one hand and a salt shaker in the other one. He had been sitting here for quite a while just watching the patrons come in and leave. Chris is not a heavy thinker though it looked like he was there thinking about some huge issue in his life, but in reality, he was doing exactly what it looked like he was doing watching people come and go. Just as he finishes up his shot of tequila he hears the sound of a solid landing slap. He swivels around on his barstool to see what is going on. In a booth along the back wall of the bar are a woman and a man sitting across from each other. The woman is rubbing her left cheek and is looking at the man with murder in her eyes. In hush tones, he appears to be instructing her about the rules of the game. Although she has said nothing he quickly snaps out another slap that almost knocks her out of her seat.

Chris not being a heavy thinker doesn't know a whole lot but he does know that you don't hit a lady. Upon seeing the man slap the woman again he slides off his stool and walks over to the table and says, "Hey bub, maybe you oughta lay off the sauce because it looks like it's clouding your common sense."

"Maybe you oughta mind your own damn business," said the man as he slid out of the booth and stood up.

When the man stood up Chris took a step back because the man was about a foot taller than he was. When he stepped back the man said, "That's right bitch you are about to get your ass whipped." He snapped out a punch that landed in the middle of Chris' chest. The punch was solidly placed to do the most damage but it didn't even make Chris stagger. Chris looked up at the man and asked, "What did you do that for? I haven't done anything to you. I was just trying to give you some good advice. You shouldn't go around hitting folks like that, that is not nice at all."

The man looked over at the woman and said, "Look at what we have here Alice, a genuine blockhead. Who is too stupid to walk away when he is clearly outmatched. Now you sit right there and watch me school this fool." He drew back his left hand and made a fist. This time he was going to hit this idiot in the mouth.

Before he could finalize the punch Chris quickly punched the man in the solar-plexus knocking all the air out of his lungs and then with his left fist he punched the man in the mouth. The two blows were delivered so quickly that the man thought the punches had arrived at the same time. He was knocked back against the seat back and bounced back toward Chris just in time to receive the thundering upper-cut delivered by Chris's right fist. The blow was so powerful that it lifted the man off of his feet and slammed him into the back wall hard enough to knock the big clock on the wall askew. Consciousness was kind enough to leave the man before he hit the floor. His companion was sitting there screaming like Chris had turned into a bear or something.

The owner of the bar came over and placed his hand on Chris' shoulder and said, "You'd better get out of here Chris before she calls the cops on you. I'll take care of this for you."

Chris turned to the bar owner and said, "Ok Max, I appreciate that. You know I was trying to help the lady, right?"

"Yeah kid I know," said Max. "Get on out of here. The last thing you need is for some cop to come running in here trying to be a hero. Go home kid, I got this."

Chris was climbing into his truck when his phone rang, it was Chuck calling asking him to meet him at his house. Chris told him that he would be there within the next thirty minutes. He knew that he was about to get paid. He and Chuck had this on and off association that spanned several years. They weren't what you would call friends but Chuck knew he could depend on Chris to do anything he asked him to do. At 5'3" Chris wasn't a big man but he was wound tight with muscle. He looked like any ordinary black man until he took off his shirt. His upper body looked like it had been sculptured in granite. He was as powerful as he looked but he wasn't what you would call a bully. He viewed the occasional job he did for Chuck as him helping out an associate and nothing more. He had a pleasant-looking face that made him look friendly. When he smiled at you it didn't look like he would hurt a fly. But as the guy in the bar learned that if you cross paths with him you generally ended up hurt.

When he arrived at Chuck's house he saw Chuck sitting on his front porch drinking a beer. When Chris stepped up on the porch Chuck reached into a small cooler and took out another beer for Chris. Taking the beer Chris sat in the chair on the other side of the front door opened the beer and waited for Chuck to fill him in on what he wanted him to do.

Chuck didn't waste any time he turned to Chris and said, "I have a little something that needs to be taken care of." For the next fifteen minutes, Chuck filled Chris in on the problem he was having with the jackass. He told him where John lived and what kind of truck he drives.

He also told him that it wasn't a rush job because the contract wouldn't come up for another month or so.

Chuck said, "During that time I want you to put the fear of God in him. It looks like he thinks he is a tough guy. I want you to show him that he ain't all that. Soften him up so that the next time he sees me he'll take off running in the other direction. I want you to wipe that smug grin off of his face. Do anything you want with him short of killing him and I will do the rest, ok?"

"Sure," said Chris, "I'll watch him for a few days before I start in on him, you know, to learn his habits and routines. I'll have him ripe for whatever you want to do to him in maybe three weeks. Does that sound good enough for you?"

"Perfect!" said Chuck.

# 3

Over the last week and a half, John has been having some strange things happening to him. Someone was playing some pretty silly stunts on him involving his trailer that he loaded his equipment on. He always got his gas on the way home when he needed to top off his tanks and his gas cans. While working the next day he would need to put gas in a lawnmower or one of his other tools only to find out that his gas cans were empty. Even the gas can with the mixture for his chainsaws and weed-eaters. They would just be empty. Not damaged in any way, just empty. It was more of an inconvenience than anything else. Now John filled up first thing in the morning. He checked his security footage and found that it looked like kids doing the dirty work but they always wore hoodies and were well covered. You couldn't tell who they were. They knew exactly where to enter the yard to prevent the lights from popping on so he just got the infrared view and you can't identify anyone with infrared. John decided to sit up one night to see if he can catch the culprit in the act. He parked his truck right in front of one of his security cameras and waited up.

Crawling across the vacant lot beside John's house Chris is quietly approaching the fence when he spots someone else skulking across the same lot. He stops and lays as flat as he can so the person does not see him. Chris doesn't know who this guy is but he is without a doubt the tallest person he has ever seen. He figures the guy can't be as tall as he looks so it has to be the fact that he is lying on the ground that just gives him that impression. After the guy steps, (steps?), over the fence, Chris decides to creep on up to the fence so he can see what the big guy is planning on doing. To his surprise, the man goes up to one of the windows and starts looking into the window at something. He doesn't do anything but stare in the window. Chris is perplexed that the guy did all that sneaking around just to be a peeping tom. Chris remained lying flat on the ground and the tall guy stayed at the window until the lights went out in the room he was watching. The sound of a passing car caused Chris to glance at the street for a moment. When he looked back at the house the tall guy was gone.

Chris quickly surveyed the area around him trying to spot the tall guy leaving. He was nowhere to be found. Chris decided to backtrack so he could have time to figure out what he had just seen.

He realized that he was a short man but that guy had to be seven feet tall. He was sure that his eyes weren't playing tricks on him he knew what he saw. Now he had to handle this new guy so he can continue freaking John out. Emptying his gas cans had already caused him to change his routine. He was about ready to confront John for the first time. But first, the tall guy had to be chased away. His job was too important to let a peeping tom interfere in the process. After crawling across most of the empty back yard he got up and walked to where he had parked his truck. Just as he was reaching for the door handle someone pushed him from behind and pinned him to the side of his truck.

"Do whatever you want to the man but leave the woman alone," said a gruff voice next to his right ear. "Have I made myself clear?"

"Yes!" shouted Chris.

When he was released he spun around to confront his assailant only to find himself standing in the parking lot alone. He didn't understand how his assailant had disappeared so quickly. He hated for someone to manhandle him. Whoever this guy is he just opened himself up to a world of hurt.

## 4

Sourpuss is aware of the little man crawling around in the grass as he arrives to check up on Sephra and see how things are going since he flattened the tires. He goes up to the window and watches Sephra as she cleans up the dinner plates. It looks like the flat tires hadn't done anything to their relationship. She was smiling as she did the work even though she could do it all with just a wave of her hand. He knew he had to do something to break this stalemate so Sephra can wake up and start acting like the demon that she is. It is an embarrassment to see his daughter carrying on with a mortal the way she is doing now. He is not allowed to let her know that they are family because they lost that right in the fall during the first earth age. Demonic family bonds were broken when he and his fellow demons decided to follow the choir director Satan in his rebellion against the Allfather. And now he had to stand here watching her do this foul thing and not be able to let her know who he is to her. After she shut off the kitchen lights he stopped allowing the mortal to see him and watched him to see what he had in mind.

He watched him crawl away from the fence and eventually climb to his feet and walk back to his truck. As he was about to get into his truck, Sourpuss pushed his face into the driver's side window and held him there. That's when he told him to leave her alone. He wasn't trying to hurt the mortal but he did want him to believe that he was in danger if he bothered her. He could feel the fear and anger leaking from the mortal as he held him there. Nodding in satisfaction he vanished.

## 5

Sitting in the darkened room looking out the window at his trailer John missed the interaction between the demon and the man doing all those silly things to his utility trailer. Sephra came into the room and sat down on John's lap and kissed him lightly on the lips.

"See anything?" she asked.

"No, not yet." He answered.

"Are you sure you don't want me to watch the trailer while you get some sleep?"

"I'm good right now, but I could use a cup of coffee, do you mind?"

'I'll be right back," Sephra said.

John figured the vandal would return one of these nights so he could confront whoever he is and put a stop to all of the vandalism. Even though it's just gas it's still quite costly replacing it every day. He was determined to handle it himself instead of letting Sephra take care of it. He has no need for more money because the money he received every month from his rental properties would sustain them for the foreseeable future. He preferred to stay busy that is why he started his landscaping business back up. He'd been lucky enough to find a good reliable crew to man his mowers and trimmers and he was staying pretty busy down here in the sunshine state. He had learned early that the competition was pretty rough down here in Florida. You can find a landscaping business on just about every block in the suburbs. There are a few in the intercity also so you had to watch your back because there is always going to be one company or another trying to muscle in on your turf. So here he sat waiting to confront the latest stumbling block that someone had placed in his way.

# 6

Chris called Chuck the next morning to tell him about the new competition he had concerning the landscape guy. Chuck told him to take care of both of them and send him the bill. Chuck had no intention of letting someone else start taking care of the businesses on that block. He intended to be the only landscaper on that block for as long as he wanted to be. It doesn't matter to him if he puts someone out of business to keep his monopoly on that block he was determined to be the only extortionist milking the business owners on that block, period! It doesn't matter who these other people are they are going to find trying to horn in on his businesses is a mistake.

Chris felt that he had gathered enough info on John to cut short his campaign of vandalism and start with the threats. He thought that if he roughed John up a few times that he would get the message and move along. That usually worked with these new upstart companies. A little bullying usually goes a long way when you're trying to scare someone away. He drives slowly by John's house to see if he is at home. When he doesn't see his truck and trailer parked beside the house he quickly turns into the driveway and pulls up to the front porch. He climbs out of his truck and walks onto the front porch and rings the doorbell. When the door opens he almost shows a reaction because he has never seen a woman this pretty in his whole life. Seeing her makes him instantly hate John for being lucky enough to have a woman this beautiful. He clears his throat and says, "Good afternoon miss, is the man of the house at home?"

"No, he is not," she answered. "Can I help you with something?" she asks.

"Yes maybe you can," he answered. "Tell him that the job he bid on a few days ago has been awarded to another company so he doesn't need to go back there at all. Will you tell him that for me?"

"Yes," she said. "I will tell him."

Chris nods his head and turns to leave when the woman says, "I'll tell him but I don't think it will stop him from placing a bid anyway. He is stubborn like that."

Turning Chris asks, "What time do you expect him to be home this evening?"

"It varies," she said. "If you leave him your number I'll give it to him when he gets home."

Chris had no intention of leaving any type of evidence of him being here so he said, "I'll catch up with him later thanks for the help."

Sephra steps back and closes the door with a smile on her face. She could sense the emotions flowing off of the mortal on the front porch. She could feel the hatred flowing off of him for John even though he was trying to hide it from her. If she had not promised to let John handle these stupid mortals she would have put some fear in him. But a promise is a promise she would wait to see how John wanted to handle him. She could tell that the mortal wants to hurt John she just doesn't know why. Maybe John would know why when he gets home this evening. She returns to cleaning the house she has found that she really enjoys doing these small tasks around the house. Doing the work gives her time to do some thinking, she is able to reason things out pretty well while she is vacuuming or dusting it is quite enjoyable.

The vandalism had stopped after John stopped filling up in the afternoon so he decided to fill everything up again this evening to see if it would start back happening again. As he is filling up his gas cans he is approached by a short black man. Thinking that the man was going to walk by John nodded his head and kept filling up the gas can he was working on. To his surprise, the guy stopped right in front of him and just stood there looking at him.

"Can I help you?" asked John.

It took Chris a moment to respond because he couldn't see what the pretty woman saw in this plain-looking guy. Finally, he said, "Yeah, you can help me. I went to your house today to give you a warning."

"And what is that?" asked John.

"The contract on that new industrial complex has been won so you need to stay away from there. We don't want to see you anywhere near that sight. Do you understand?"

"No!" said John. "I was told to come back in a month and that is what I'm going to do. It looks like your boss is not used to having any competition well now he does. He'll just have to get used to it and underbid me."

When he finished talking Chris stepped up to him and grabbed him in the collar of his shirt and pushed him back against his trailer and got close up in his face and was about to speak when they both heard a voice yell from across the parking lot. "Hey, what are you doing there?"

They both looked over and saw a sheriff deputy getting out of his cruiser and start walking toward them. Chris quickly stepped back from John and quickly walks off. The officer walks over to John and asks, "Are you alright, buddy?"

"Yes officer thanks to you," answers John. "I think he might have been about to rob me. You just might have saved my life, thank you!"

"Think nothing of it," said the officer. "You need to watch yourself around some of these stores these thugs hang around looking for the opportunity to mess up someone's day."

"I will," said John. "Thanks again!"

The deputy walks off with a wave of his hand looking to see if the guy is still hanging around the store. He enters the store and asked the clerk if he saw what happened out at the gas pumps. The clerk told him, "No, I hadn't seen anything." By the time the officer had made his purchases and made it back to his cruiser John had finished up and left. He soon forgot the incident and carried on with his day.

# 7

When John got home he pulled his truck and trailer around the back of the house and parked in front of one of his security cameras and one of his security lights. He felt that no-one would be able to go near his truck without tripping one of his security features. After his encounter with the guy at the store, John felt like he knew who was bothering his equipment. John was tired of playing games with these people. He was ready to handle this and get on with his life.

As he walked around to the front of the house to check the mailbox Chris stepped out from the hedges with a gun in his hand and motioned for John to go inside the house instead. Surprised, John turned and walked up on the front porch and went on inside the house with Chris following close behind. As they entered the front room Sephra met John with a cold beer in her hand. When she saw who was with John she glanced at the gun he had in his hand and then looked back a John who gave a quick nod of his head indicating that he wanted her to do nothing.

Chris reached out and took the beer away from her and motioned for her and John to sit down on the sofa. After they were sitting down he sat on the loveseat directly across from them and popped open the beer. He took a sip and then he sat there staring at each one of them slowly. Then he said, "I just can't figure out what you saw in this shmuck that you were willing to spend the rest of your life with him. Explain that to me and I will get up and walk away from here right now."

"It won't make any difference now," said John. "You have brought a gun into our home and I can't let that pass. I'm going to have to punish you for doing that."

Chris let out a loud laugh and said, "I'm the one holding the gun and you are talking about punishing me? You have got to have a screw loose up there in that noggin of yours. I haven't decided what I am going to do with the two of you yet. Tell me what you told that cop at the store."

"What do you think I told him? I didn't even know who you were and I still don't. Who are you, and what do you want?" asked John.

"I want you to forget about that contract for that new industrial complex downtown," said Chris.

"You have got to be kidding me!" shouted John. "That place again?"

"Yes, that place again," said Chris. "My employer wants that place for his own reasons and I am supposed to make sure that it happens."

"And how are you supposed to do that?" asked John.

"I was going to threaten you and then beat the shit out of you but I changed my mind this afternoon at that gas station," Chris said.

John looked over at Sephra and said, "I'm going to try this one more time. If you wish to save your life you will get up and walk out of my house right now. I will forgive the gun just this once. But you will have to leave the gun here and get out right now. This is the last warning," said John.

Chris chuckled and said, "How stupid are you? I know that you see me holding this gun on you but you keep talking like you are in control of this situation. I've seen stupid before but mister you take the cake."

John shook his head and looked over at Sephra and said, "Okay, you can do your thing."

When Sephra stood up something inside of Chris caused his intestines to seize up and his instincts shouted, "Run!" He had learned a long time ago to listen to his instincts. So before Sephra could take one step toward him he was up and sprinting for the front door. John reached out and took Sephra's hand to keep her from going after him.

Chris burst through the front door and took two steps on the porch then he leaped from the porch without touching the steps and ran across the front yard and sprinted down the street as if he were running a 100-yard dash. He didn't stop running until he reached his truck. He only stopped running then because he slammed into the side of the truck at full speed. He bounced off the truck and landed on his ass about ten feet away. Shaking his head trying to clear it caused his head to spin. He sat there long enough to get his bearings and then he sprang back to his feet and rushed to his truck.

Once safely inside his truck, he took the time to wait for his head to clear enough to feel like driving was a good idea. While sitting there he played back the events that went on in that house. He couldn't figure out what was so scary about the woman. He had never felt as afraid of anyone in his life. He wasn't afraid of any man. He realized that there were men that he couldn't take hand-to-hand but he knew that they would know that he was in the game. He had no fear of losing a fight, that happens to everyone sooner or later. But that woman had put a fear deep down in his soul. The only option he had was to run and do it quickly. For some reason, he felt that his life *really* was in danger just like John said it was. Most people don't realize that there is a part of the human psyche that remains from the primitive time when fight or flight was a way of life. You knew when it was smart to fight or run. This time his kicked in and convinced his legs that this was an instance of run or die.

Remembering how beautiful the woman was made him question why he ran. If anything her beauty would make you want to run to her instead of away. He sat there replaying the conversation he'd had with John. He remembered the confidence John had shown even while he held the gun on him. It was as if John didn't fear being shot. He wasn't afraid of the gun at all.

Chris convinced himself that it must have been John's confidence that had spooked him into believing that his life was in danger, that is why he ran. That has to be the reason because that woman didn't look like she would hurt anyone. Maybe it was because of the threat he'd gotten the other night from the peeping tom. He had been told to leave her alone and might have had to hurt her when she got up. He didn't know what she intended to do but he might have had to hurt her to make her sit back down. Yes, that has got to be it, the threat the other night had reached deep down into his psyche and left an imprint. Left enough of an imprint to cause him to react the way he did when she stood up. He is not afraid of the woman, but he was paying heed to the threat that he had received concerning her safety.

Eventually feeling like he could safely drive his truck he slowly left the neighborhood wondering if he would ever have the nerve to return and do the job he was paid to do. He decided that he would confront John when he was away from home so he wouldn't have to chance hurting the woman.

# 8

John was watching the man sitting across from him holding a gun on him in his living room. He was watching the man's face after Sephra stood up. His face went through several different stages as John watched. First, there was confusion, then there was shock, then there was fear. Fear dominated his face as he jumped up and ran. By the time John and Sephra managed to get to the front door Chris was halfway down the block and was still picking them up and putting them down. John looked over at Sephra and asked, "What did you do?"

Sephra shook her head and said, "I did nothing. You saw me get up and I didn't have time to do anything. He just jumped up and ran. That is the normal reaction of a mortal when they first realize that they are facing a demon but I didn't let my demon half show this time. So I don't know what he was running from. He was smart to run but I didn't do anything to cause him to fear me. They watched the man run until he turned the corner a block away then they went back inside with both of them wondering what had spooked the man with the gun.

Thinking about the small person vandalizing his gas cans John realized that the person on the video could have been the short man that just ran from his home. So that was what the vandalism was all about. The little guy worked for the jerk at the industrial site. John hoped that the fright the man just got would dissuade him from continuing to aggravate him. He would hate to have to hurt him to make him stop. John knows that he has to keep getting new contracts because his work crew depended on him to keep them busy. Landscaping being a seasonal job made it very important that you make as much money as you can so you can make it through the lean months of the year. During the winter months in Florida, you only had to mow your lawn about half as often which cut back on the salary his employees received. He tried to keep them busy but it wasn't as easy during the winter months. He had a reliable group of people working for him and he refused to let them down when it came to keeping them busy. The men and women working for John knew they could rely on him to keep them busy the year-round.

# 9

Humphrey stared across the table at John and Sephra as they were finishing up their supper laughing at his latest funny comment. He could be quite charming when he put his mind to it. He had invited the Cramers over for dinner a week ago and they had agreed to come. After everyone was done with supper he invited them into his den for a few drinks before the evening ended. As Sephra sat down on the sofa both of Humphrey's cats jumped up on her lap. Startled, she almost blasted them out of existence but she managed to restrain herself. They all laughed at her reaction at being startled by them. John knew that she had almost hurt the cats and he was laughing in relief that she had managed to contain herself. She joined in with the laughter to cover what she had almost done.

Humphrey asked through his laughter if they had any more trouble with the people sneaking around their house?

"No, not really," answered John. "I'm thinking it was an isolated incident. It was probably one of the local kids about to pull a prank on the newcomers to the neighborhood. When you shouted at them you probably scared the living daylights out of them. They more than likely won't be back thanks to you."

Smiling Humphrey said, "Glad to be of service."

"Have you ever had any trouble like that since you have been living here?" asked Sephra?

"Not that I know of," he answered, "at least I don't think so. But I don't have such a beautiful wife like John has. They were probably trying to get a good look at you without you being aware of being watched. Forgive me John, but I believe Sephra is even more beautiful now than she was the last time I saw her."

"Thanks," said John. "I believe she gets more beautiful every time I look at her so I know what you mean. I feel so lucky to have found her when I did I can't imagine going through life without her." He looks over at Sephra and says, "Thank you for choosing me."

Unsure how to respond, Sephra lifted her wineglass and nodded to John. She never will understand the importance mortals put on looks. She had always looked like this. She didn't feel like she looked all that great but she had gotten used to the way mortals react to her when she walks into a room. They had no idea how dangerous she is. Lately, she had noticed that she has started having strange mood swings. One minute she is happy and the next she is sad for no reason. She had intended to talk to John about it but it had slipped her mind. She would try to remember to mention it tonight once they were back at home.

# 10

Sitting at home alone thinking about how he had reacted to the woman at that house where his latest victim lived. He had been trying to make himself go back and finish the job he was hired to do but he seemed unable to motivate himself enough to do it. He had promised Chuck that he would have John afraid of him in three weeks and now his time was running out. He had never failed to do a job once he was paid. Chuck had already paid for the service he had promised to deliver but this time there had been a hitch. The hitch was that strange beautiful woman that lived with the mark. There was something about her that scares the shit out of him and he doesn't know what it is.

Tomorrow he plans to follow John to his worksite and wait until his crew is busy working then he will get John away from them so he can confront him. He figures that he won't have to do much to rattle John's nerves to get him to forget about the industrial complex. Chris knows that John does not scare easily because the sight of a gun the other day didn't seem to frighten him at all. It will probably take an ass-whipping to convince him to forget about the site. From the looks of John, he didn't look all that tough. Chris thinks he can take him easily. A few well-placed blows to the body will show him that he is not the tough guy he apparently thinks he is. With his mind made up, Chris goes to bed early so he can get a good night's sleep so he will be in the best shape possible to go into battle with John. Not being a heavy thinker, he never considers the consequences of hurting John. He really should have taken the time to think this thing through.

Once John got his crew started on the first job of the day he went over to the industrial complex and met with Mr. Walsh so he could leave his bid for the landscaping of the site. Mr. Walsh was in a much better mood this morning and their meeting only lasted about fifteen minutes. After the meeting, John was confident that he would get the contract for the care of the place. As he was inserting his key into the ignition of his truck, someone climbed into the truck with him. Startled, John quickly looked over at the intruder and recognized him immediately. It was the guy that Sephra scared the shit out of the other day. And like before he had a gun in his hand.

"Do as you are told and you just might live through this," said Chris while holding the gun on John.

Recovering, John said, "Man, you need to get a life. And if you are here because of this job then you can just turn around and leave because I have already placed my bid and I doubt that your company can underbid me. You need to go tell your boss to forget about this site and move on. There are plenty of jobs out there needing a good landscaping crew all he has to do is go looking because I think this one is mine. The way Walsh talked the job is already mine. I don't think he liked the way your boss threatened him a while back. Your boss needs to learn some people skills you can't always bully someone into giving you what you want."

"Drive," said Chris, "go to that abandoned asphalt plant on Homestead Avenue where you went the other day, we need to have a little talk."

"I can talk fine sitting right here," said John. "If you think I am going someplace with you while you are pointing a gun at me you must think I'm stupid. You can say whatever it is you want me to know while we sit right here. And why in the world are you following me? You should be trying to find some other jobs for your boss.?

"You can do as I say and drive to where I told you to go or I can gut shoot you and sit here while you bleed out. You choose and choose wisely," said Chris.

John was looking into the man's eyes as he threatened him and realized that the man would do just as he said he would. So he started up the truck and headed for the suburbs. He knew where the abandoned asphalt plant was because it is one of the places he thought about buying to expand his business. He knew that the place has two large warehouses in the back of the lot that he would use as his garage and office so he could have a central location for his business that was away from his home.

As John drove he decided to try to talk the man out of whatever it is he was planning to do to him.

"You know that you don't have to do this," said John

"Yes I do," said Chris, "I've already been paid to do this job and I'm going to do it. This ass-whipping is inevitable so you may as well learn to live with it. If you hadn't gone back to that business and placed a bid you might have been able to get away with a warning. But you had to take your smartass back there even though I told you to stay away. This is your fault so take it like a man."

As John turned on Homestead Avenue he knew that if he thought hard enough about Sephra that she would be there in an instant but it had been a while since he had to defend himself and he felt that he needed the workout. John was the type that would never go looking for trouble but he never would shy away from a good fight either. So instead of being afraid of the upcoming fight, he was actually looking forward to it.

When they arrived at the plant John took a left turn into the driveway and drove up to the little pond and took a left and drove on another two hundred feet to the first warehouse and then he drove between the two warehouses and parked behind the first one.

"Now what?" asked John.

"Get out of the truck and give me the keys," said Chris.

John got out of the truck and tossed the keys on top of the cab of the truck and said, "The winner can climb up there and get them when this is over."

"You do think you are a bad-ass don't you?" asked Chris. "I oughta shoot your ass right now for that."

"Naw, you want to show me that you can kick my ass," said John. "You know that is what you want to do so let's get this party started. You talk too much!"

Chris headed for the front of the truck and John met him there. As they stood there facing each other Chris tossed his gun onto the hood of the truck. Taking advantage of John watching the gun as it landed on the hood with a thump Chris threw the first punch. He intended to knock John out with one punch but John was expecting the punch and turned enough to make the blow miss and land on his shoulder. Although it was a glancing blow it still knocked John on his ass. As John quickly jumped back up on his feet he thought that that was the hardest he has ever been hit. This little man has some power and it looked like he knew how to use it. It looked like this *was* going to be a workout.

Chris had the power but John had the skill so they appeared to be equally matched. They traded blows for the next five minutes without either gaining ownership of the fight. Neither one could manage to land a solid blow and it looked like they were dancing instead of fighting. The felling blow came when John skillfully blocked a powerful right cross and landed a straight jab into Chris's nose. John heard and felt the nose break and watched as Chris doubled over in pain and fell to the ground. John stepped in to land another blow when he realized that Chis was totally out of the game. He was in the fetal position cupping his bloody face and moaning like a baby.

Chris, on the other hand, was in more pain than he had ever felt in his life. He heard his nose break when John got by his right cross. He had never been hurt in a fight in his whole life. He was supposed to be the one standing looking down at John writhing on the ground in agony. Chris had no idea that a broken nose could hurt so bad. He was in so much pain that he was wondering if he could die from a broken nose.

"Are we done?" asked John. All Chris could do was nod his head. "Do you want to go to the hospital?" asked John. Again, Chris just nodded his head. John reached down and helped Chris get to his feet and slowly walked him around to the passenger's side of the truck. Then he went around to the other side of the truck and on his way, he picked up Chris's gun off the hood. Then he stood up on the driver's side door floorboard to get the keys off the top of the cab. John got a roll of paper towels from his toolbox and tossed it to Chris. With bloody hands, Chris rolled off a lot of sheets and began trying to clean up himself so he wouldn't look so bad when they arrived at the hospital.

"You need to tell your employer that he has lost that industrial complex and he needs to move on because I'm tired of dicking around with him," said John. "And if you ever come at me with a gun again I'm going to make you eat it. Are we clear?"

"I'm done," mumbled Chris. "Here on out, he is going to have to fight his own battles. You won't have to worry about me bothering you anymore. I'm going to give him his money back and tell him to not come to me anymore to do his dirty work." He said all of that while holding his head back trying to staunch the flow of blood from his broken nose with the paper towels.

At the emergency entrance, John asked Chris if he wanted him to go in with him. He shook his head no. John watched him as he staggered into the hospital. He didn't know if he would see him again but he felt that if he did that it would end a lot different than this time. John didn't know if he had just made an enemy or a friend, time will tell.

# CHAPTER 8

## 1

John and Sephra are enjoying eating supper when Sephra gives John a huge shock.

"I'm pregnant," said Sephra.

John, having just taken a big gulp of lemonade sprayed it across the table in front of him. He sat there starring at her like she had grown another head. When he could catch his breath he started firing off rapid questions at her, "Is that even possible? I never dreamed that we could make a baby together. Do you think it's going to be human? Is it a girl or a boy? How long have you known that you're carrying my baby? Is it going to be a normal pregnancy, the whole nine months, or is it going to be like Bella on Twylight?"

Sephra got up and walked over to put her arms around John because it looked like he was about to explode. "Calm down!" she shouted. "You're going to have a heart attack!" She gave him a big squeeze and gave him a little shake. "You are okay with this, aren't you?"

"Okay! I'm overjoyed," he said. "I'm going to be a dad! This is the greatest thing you have ever done for me! I love you so much. You are looking awfully sexy right now, I can hardly keep my hands off of you!" He slid his chair back from the table and picked her up and sat her in his lap. And started kissing her all over her face and down her neck.

All she could do was laugh and enjoy the rapt attention she was receiving from him. After he calmed down some she started trying to answer his questions, "Yes, it appears that we can have a child together.

And I don't see why it shouldn't be human. I don't know if it will be a girl or a boy. And finally, I don't know how long the pregnancy will last, we'll just have to wait and see."

John stood her up from his lap and took both of her hands and started dancing around the room with her. He was grinning so hard that it was almost impossible to make the music with his mouth to dance by. He couldn't think of another time in his life that he was this happy. It felt like he would float up to the ceiling. And that's when the doorbell rang. Still smiling, John went to answer the door. When he opened the door, he saw that it was Chuck and two huge men standing on his porch looking like they were ready for war.

# 2

Chuck was steaming mad. Chris had shown up to his house with a swollen up face and given him his money back. He said that he was unable to do what he wanted him to do and told him to not come to him anymore to threaten people. He said that he was out of the business of bullying folk. Then he just turned around and left without explaining why he was quitting or what happened to his face. Chuck had never had a black man quit on him before, they don't quit, you fire them! He almost jumped off the porch to grab him and tell him as much when he remembered why he always hired him. Chris was a tough cookie, Chuck did not doubt that Chris would beat him in his own front yard so he just stood there and watched him leave. He went back inside the house and went to his home office and took his address book out of his desk drawer. He sat down and started leafing through his little black book. He stopped on the page that had the Swartz brothers card pinned to it. They are twins and they are huge, plus they are expensive as hell but they get the job done.

Thom and Bob Swartz ran a local gym on the outskirts of town that catered to local athletes and folk trying to bulk up some muscle. Thom is 6'8", and Bob is 6'91/2" tall, and they are so broad-shouldered that it looks like they should have to turn sideways to walk through a door. When put together they almost weigh half a ton. There is no fat there, it is all muscle. They spent their younger years competing and winning Iron Man competitions. They participated in the ones that didn't require a beautifully sculptured body but brute strength of which they had in abundance. Now they just ran the gym. They have a lot of members at the gym and they could survive with just the income from that but they still sell drugs out of the back room. Plus they hire themselves out as bouncers and hired muscle for the local club scene. If you are smart you don't cross the Swartz brothers, they will hurt you!

At the moment, they are enjoying a drink with an old friend. It had been several years since they had seen Chuck and were surprised when he showed up at the gym. After a few minutes of talking about things from the past, Chuck got down to business.

"I have a little problem that I need you two to solve for me," said Chuck. The brothers didn't say a word they just sat there waiting for Chuck to carry on. "There is a new contractor in town that is causing me to lose money on my side of town. I have warned him several times to stay away from my side of town, but he is a smartass and he has a hard head. I'm going to need you fellas to soften that head up a little bit for me. You do still do these kinds of favors, don't you?"

"Of course," said Bob with a voice so deep that it sounded like it was coming from a barrel. "We are always here to help our friends in need. Who is he and where can we find him?"

"Actually," said Chuck with a smile, "I want to be with you when you approach him, I want to see the fear in his eyes when he realizes that he fucked with the wrong man."

"When?" asked Thom.

"How about now?" asked Chuck.

"Fine," said Bob. "Let's go."

On the way to John's house, Chuck filled the brothers in on what he thinks happened to Chris. He told them about how bad Chris's face was swollen up and how totally beaten he seemed to be. He didn't know what John had done to him but it was bad enough that it made him rethink his career choices. He told them that John didn't look all that tough but he seemed to have no fear. You could see that in his eyes. In each of their encounters, he had never responded quite right. He just seems cocky, like he is sure of himself and knows no fear.

As Chuck arrived at John's house he started thinking about all the money he makes from the other businesses in that seven-block area. This new complex would ensure that he got the maximum amount of money possible from any other area in the city. It would put him on top and he was not going to let this asshole keep that from happening.

"He has got a woman in there, use her if you have to," Chuck said. The brothers just nodded and got out of the truck. Together, they walked up on the porch and Chuck rang the doorbell. They could hear someone inside the house trying to sing or something. They weren't doing too good of a job of it. When the door opened they saw John standing there grinning.

When John saw who it was at his door his smile drained off of his face. "Oh, it's you," He said.

"Yes, it's me," Chuck said while pushing his way into the house. The brothers followed close behind him.

By the time John realized what was happening it was too late to keep them out of the house. He staggered back and shouted, "Hey! What the hell do you think you are doing? Get out of my house!" But it was too late, they formed a triangle around John to prevent him from getting away from them. Chuck grabbed John in the collar and tried to lift him off the floor but was unable to. When he couldn't lift him he shoved him over to Thom who instantly grabbed John by the collar and lifted him off the floor and held him there while Chuck talked.

"I told you to stay away from that new complex but you ignored me, then I sent someone to talk to you about it and I don't know what you did to him, but I would like to see you try to do it to these two gentlemen."

Hanging there, being held by two of the biggest hands he had ever seen John cleared his throat and said, "We had a conversation and came to a mutual decision to let it go. I'm going to give you folk the opportunity to walk out of here now but that's the only chance you are going to get."

"See," laughed Chuck. "Even now he thinks he has the upper hand. I'm beginning to think that maybe he *is* a little slow in the head.

As he was laughing and talking there was a blur and John was standing on his feet and Thom was nowhere to be found. One minute he was standing there holding John up off the floor and then he was gone. Chuck staggered back and did a double-take of John standing there brushing off the front of his shirt.

"Where did he go?" shouted Chuck at the same time that Bob said, "Huh?"

And then from what seemed to be a long way off, they could hear Thom begin to scream. It wasn't an ordinary scream, this was an agonizing scream of someone terrified and in mortal agony. It sounded like Thom was putting everything he had into that scream and it went on and on and then it just went away. The silence was deafening, Chuck and Bob looked at each other and didn't say a word.

"Run," John said in the quietness.

"What?" stammered Chuck as Bob grabbed John and asked, "Where is my brother?" Then he threw John at the sofa and ran out of the room looking for his brother. They heard him run out of the back of the house still calling for his brother.

"What? What did you do?" asked Chuck.

"I didn't do anything," said John getting up from the sofa where Bob had just thrown him and walking over to Chuck. "I've been standing right here with you. If you are smart you will run out that door right now and not come back here ever again. And believe me, I'm trying to save your life. Run!"

Taking his advice, Chuck broke for the front door only to run into the bulk that was Bob. Bob's face was a mask of fury and he grabbed Chuck and tossed him across the room into the far corner. He headed straight for John. When he reached him, he grabbed him by the neck and lifted him off of the floor, and screamed, "Where the hell is my brother? Tell me now or I will crush your scrawny neck!"

John grabbed his arm trying to keep from being hung in his living room. He tried to speak but Bob had him in a stranglehold and he couldn't breathe.

"Put him down!" shouted Sephra coming into the room covered in blood.

Bob did a double-take when he looked at her. When he realized that she was covered in his brother's blood he tossed John aside and dashed to where she was standing in the doorway. He intended to knock her back into the next room and rip her head off. When all of his bulk smacked into Sephra he folded up almost like an accordion and bounced back into the living room. After he stopped bouncing he reached up and grabbed his right shoulder because it was smashed, that whole upper side of his body was deformed from ramming into an immovable object. Through his screams, he yelled, "Where is my brother, bitch? What have you done to him?"

Sephra calmly answered him saying, "He is gone for good. If you don't want to join him I suggest that you leave now."

The apparent death of his brother and the agony of his crushed shoulder drove Bob beyond the breaking point. His mind simply snapped. One moment he was as sane as you or me, and the next, he was a raving lunatic. Screaming at the top of his voice, he jumped up and charged Sephra again and this time she let him shove her back into the next room. The instant they were out of sight of the others she teleported them both to hell which was the same place she took Thom to earlier. The instant they materialized there, they were beset by over a dozen demons. She stepped back out of the way and let the demons hold sway. She maintained her link to her house so that Chuck could hear as if from a great distance, the screams emitting from Bob. They were a terrible thing to hear. No one should ever have to hear those types of sounds coming from a grown man.

# 3

When the grinning John had opened the door it looked like he was having a good time right up until he saw them standing on his porch. As his smile drained away Bob thought that this was going to be an easy job. He and Thom enjoyed hurting people when they were sure that they wouldn't get into trouble over it. Doing favors for people like Chuck usually ended with the victim leaving town or finally giving in to Chuck's wishes. When Chuck forced his way into the man's house, Bob and Thom knew instinctively to surround the prey to keep him from running from the room. Forming a triangle effectively cut the man's ability to run from the room off. There was no way that he was going to get away from them now.

When Chuck pushed the man over to Thom, Bob started smiling. It was time to start having some fun. He stepped back to give his brother room to work when his brother vanished. One minute he was holding the man up in the air by the collar and the next he was just gone. There had been no warning, no scream, no noise he was just gone. The man was standing there brushing off the front of his shirt like he had just taken out the trash. It took a few seconds for all of that to sink in, and while they were standing there, Thom started screaming from somewhere in the back of the house.

"Run," John said in the quietness.

"What?" stammered Chuck as Bob grabbed John and asked, "Where is my brother?" Then he threw John at the sofa and ran out of the room looking for his brother. He checked every room he came upon as he ran through the back of the house. Not finding his brother, he dashed out the back door and jumped off the patio, and ran around the house. He was hoping that he could find out who was hurting his brother so he could kill him.

After running around the house twice he ran up onto the front porch and burst into the living room ramming into Chuck as he headed for John. He threw Chuck away from him like he didn't weigh anything at all. Chuck slammed into the corner and stayed there.

From Bob's perspective, everything had slowed way down. When he burst back into the house the only person he could see was John standing back in the middle of the room. He didn't even notice Chuck as he tossed him across the room. He was frantic to find out where his brother was and who was hurting him. He knew that John knew who was doing it and he was going to make him tell him or he would kill him right now. For the moment he was suffering from tunnel vision, all he could see was John and he intended to break him in half if he couldn't give him the answers he wanted to hear.

One-handed, he grabbed John by the throat and lifted him up from the floor, and started yelling for him to tell him where his brother was located.

In the fog of his mind, he realized that John couldn't answer him because he was choking him to death but he didn't care. Someone was hurting his brother, and he was going to make them stop. When the woman came into the room covered in blood and told him to put John down his anger instantly transferred to her. That bitch had hurt his brother and he was going to make her pay big time. So tossing John away again, he launched himself at the woman intending to pop that little head completely off her neck. When he reached her he was going to hit her like a linebacker and embrace her in a bear-hug but before he could wrap his arms around her he was confronted with the worse pain he had ever felt in his life. For some reason, intense pain had exploded from every part of his body, he knew without a doubt that he had broken his back. Then he bounced back into the other room grabbing his shoulder because he felt like he had dislocated it or something. All he knew for sure was that his shoulder hurt something terrible and it didn't feel right under his hand.

It was when the realization that she was the one that had hurt his brother and the agony coming from his ruined shoulder combined that his mind snapped. From that point, there was no coming back to any rational thought processes, the only thought in his head was KILL! That's where the strength to get back up and charge her came from. This time when he made contact with her he knocked her into the next room. Or that is where he thought they were. Until he realized that the men running up and attacking him weren't men at all. He didn't know what they were. As he watched, they started to rip him to shreds, and then they were eating the parts they were ripping off of him.

As I told you before, Bob was a mighty man. He and his brother used to joke about going down to hell and kicking the devil's ass and taking over hell. Now he realized that he couldn't overpower the smallest of these things that were beating and eating him. But he did try, he did the best he could with the one fist that he could still use but it was nowhere near good enough to repel even one. His screams went from fearful to desperate as they enjoyed their meal.

Hearing his pitiful cries cause both John and Chuck to feel sorry for whatever Bob was going through. No one should ever have to hear sounds like that coming from a grown man. Once again John told Chuck to run. And again he took him up on it. When he turned to run, he ran right into bloody Sephra and bounced back into the center of the room with John. Once there. He spun around to face John and dropped to his knees.

"PLEASE!" he begged. "I didn't know, I didn't know that you wanted that contract this much. Now that I know, I'm willing to negotiate and split the rest of those properties if you want a piece of those too. No, no, no, if, if, you want all seven blocks I will give them to you right now. No need to negotiate, they are yours if you want them. I swear to you on my mother's grave. Take them! Please! Just don't let her do to me what she did to them. We can work this out, I know we can! Believe me, please! I promise to never bother you or her ever again, you can trust me! I promise!" Now he was crying.

John looked up from the man kneeling in front of him and looked at Sephra and asked, "Can we let him go?"

"That is your decision," she answered. "If you let him go he is going to have to keep his word to you because I won't let him hurt you. Can you keep your word mortal?"

Still on his knees, Chuck spun around somehow to face Sephra, and said, "I will keep my word, ask anybody and they will tell you that I am a man of my word, believe me! You won't have to ever worry about me again. Just let me live, please!"

Looking to John, Sephra nodded her head and motioned for Chuck to get up. As he got to his feet, he turned to John and said, "Thank you! Do you want me to turn those other contracts over to you now? I was serious, you can have them all!"

"No," said John. "You can keep them but you are going to have to renegotiate those contracts into fair bids. No more extortion, stop robbing those businesses. If you promise to give them security do it right and stop hiring people to hurt honest folk, if you can do that then you can go."

"I can do that. First thing Monday morning you have my word," he promised.

John motioned for him to go and he ran from the room hoping that John was a man of *his* word. When he got in his truck and drove away, he didn't relax until he was almost home. The first thing he did when he got home was to pour himself a stiff drink then he went to his office and began drawing up the new contracts. He intends to keep his part of the bargain. He wonders if he will ever see those brothers again, he doubted it because he had never heard anyone scream in pain and fear like that before. He knew that if they did survive that he would be their next target. Never being beaten in anything they ever tried to do would probably make them sore losers and they could probably hold a grudge. He didn't doubt that if they ever came for him that they would kill him just for getting them involved in this mess. Now he thought he understood what made Chris walk away from this business. He wondered what Chris had to promise to get away from the two of them?

When Sephra returned to the living room she found John sitting on the loveseat with his legs folded underneath him. He had a worried look on his face when he looked up at her as she approached him.

Then he asked, "Is the baby alright? They didn't do anything that might have hurt it, did they?"

"No," she answered. "I didn't do anything to them. They always talked about going down to hell and taking it away from the devil, I just gave them the chance to give it a try. All I did was take them there. I don't understand why it is so easy for people like the man you let go to talk people into doing bad things for them. They came here willingly to hurt you for him for money. I don't understand a lot of the things you mortals do."

"So, you didn't kill them before you took them to hell?" he asked. "Wow, how does that work?"

"Taking them to hell in their mortal bodies makes it possible for the demons to wreak havoc on their physical bodies and torment their souls at the same time," she said. "They are going to live for eternity and know a type of suffering that very few mortals have ever experienced. The Allfather did the same to a few mortals in the distant past, only he took them to live forever with Him in Heaven. Their experiences were a lot different for them than it was for these two. When they think that their torment is finally over, they will find that they have been put back together again and the torment will start all over again. And that is for eternity."

Hearing her explain it so clearly reminded him of the conversation he'd had with Cam a few months back. The fact that he had willingly given himself to a demon because he had fallen in love was consigning himself to hell for eternity. A shiver ran down his spine as he contemplated his fate. Then he looked into the eyes of his true love and all the doubt went away. He had made his bed and he was willing to lay in it. He held out his hand and she took it and sat down beside him, she was aware of what he was thinking about and the thought came to her that love conquers all.

They sat there immersed in their separate thoughts believing that this *uncharted territory* they were traveling would somehow have a happy ending. This strange love they both were experiencing was changing the fabric of the wall between mortals and supernatural beings. They didn't know that it was happening but they knew that they loved each other more than it should be possible. They each were willing to lay down their life for the other one without a moment's hesitation. That is *real* love!

# <u>THE END</u>

Printed in the United States
by Baker & Taylor Publisher Services

Printed in the United States
by Baker & Taylor Publisher Services